SACRIFICIAL CHILD

EDMANTHA HALL

SAGEBRUSH PUBLISHING

CANTON, TEXAS

Edmantha Hall/Sagebrush Publishing
Printed in the United States of America
edmanthahallbooks.com

Publisher's Note: This is a work of fiction. Names, characters, places, and incidents are a product of the author's imagination. Locales and public names are sometimes used for atmospheric purposes. Any resemblance to actual people, living or dead, or to businesses, companies, events, institutions, or locales is completely coincidental.

Sacrificial Child/ Edmantha Hall. -- 1st ed.

ISBN 978-1546752080 Print Edition

Other works by Edmantha Hall

The Human Megmador

Destiny

I am dedicating this book to my loving sister, Melissa Hall: 03/02/1942-09/15/2013,
And to my wonderful brother, Edmantha Hall: 03/13/1948-4/22/2014
who's pen name I used for my book.

ACKNOWLEDGMENTS

Thanks to the Rocky Mountain Fiction Writers at Southwest Plaza in Littleton, Colorado, who encouraged me to write, AND to my editor.

CHAPTER 1

CHILDHOOD ABDUCTION

Linda Fluger shared a two-bedroom mobile home with her parents in an incorporated community near Tallahassee, Florida. Their place stood on two acres at the end of a narrow dirt road with numerous potholes.

Her father, Adler, had emigrated from Germany during his mid-twenties. Her mother, Helena, was Italian American—with no relatives.

On a Friday morning, Linda sat across the kitchen table from her mother.

"If the weather turns nice tomorrow, I promised Ellen I'd bike to the lake with her," Linda said. "I got another A-plus in math, Mother. A perfect paper."

"That's good, dear," her mother replied. She sipped her coffee and read the newspaper.

"I want to go to college," Linda said proudly.

"We've had this conversation already. We can't afford to pay your way through college."

"What do you expect me to do for the rest of my life? My teachers said that if I keep my grades up, I might qualify for a scholarship. Then you and Daddy won't have to pay a thing."

"You can get a job at the grocery store where your father works, and we always need someone to work evenings at the diner. We don't want you all alone in some big city."

"You used to live in New York City. Why don't you ever talk about it?"

"There's nothing to talk about. You don't want to be late for school."

"I'm going to college, Mother. If you and Daddy won't help me, I'll do it alone."

Her mother didn't respond, just kept her nose in the newspaper.

Linda hurried through her breakfast and drained the last of her milk. She placed her lunch into her book bag, pulled on a sweater, and stuffed a clear plastic rain cap into her pocket. After dashing out the back door into a slight drizzle, she entered a storage shed near the back of their home. Stopping just inside, she looked up to see a bearded man as tall as a tree. Her father rarely had company—and no one like the stranger she saw. He had long, brown, greasy hair and a beard lined with specks of gray.

"Linda, this Mr. Gibson," her father said in broken English.

An odor of raw sewage and kerosene mixed with

tobacco emanated from Mr. Gibson. The stranger wore a green work uniform, like a mechanic. Grease stained his scuffed brown boots.

Linda glanced up at him again, her nose turned up in disgust.

"Where manners?" her father scolded.

"Good morning, Mr. Gibson." Then she ran back into the rain, jerked open the passenger door of her father's Opel, and jumped inside.

Before she closed the door, her father beckoned her with his hand. "My friend give you ride to school, Linda."

During bad weather, her father usually drove her the short distance to the bus stop.

She shivered. "I don't mind walking, Daddy. I'll get my umbrella."

The mountain of a man took giant strides to an old, rusty Ford truck with numerous dents and scrapes along the body and opened the passenger door.

Linda stepped out of her father's car, clutching her bag in her arms, her back as stiff as a board.

"Go, Linda," her father said. "You get drenched."

Mr. Gibson still held the door open, as if the drizzle didn't bother him.

Linda rushed to the vehicle, threw her bag onto the seat, hopped up on the running board, and climbed in.

The man slammed her door shut, walked around to the driver's side, lowered his head, and swung into the seat. When he started the engine the vehicle shook, belching black smoke from the exhaust pipe. He backed the truck up, leaving muddy tire ruts on the sparkly brown lawn, and they drove off. Linda glanced back, but her father had disappeared.

Linda saw her closest neighbor, Ellen, as she rushed toward the bus stop under a wobbling umbrella. Although Ellen was almost two years older than Linda, the two girls had been close friends since grade school.

Linda sat straight up in her seat. "There's my friend. Can we give her a ride?"

The man kept his eyes on the road. "Nope."

Linda waved at Ellen as they drove past. "Why not?"

He didn't respond.

Each time the truck hit a pothole, the stranger ducked his head to prevent it from hitting the top of the cab.

When his gray eyes weren't on the road, he looked over her body from head to foot, like the boys at school who drooled over pretty girls. She'd heard about child abductions—most of the victims never returned home. She pulled her skirt down as far as she could and laid her book bag in her lap. *Why did Daddy ask this man to take me to school?*

Each time his eyes darted from the road to her legs, her muscles tightened.

"You're a pretty little girl. Bet you have lots of boyfriends," he said.

Linda's hands tugged harder at the hem of her skirt. Her mother always referred to her as the ugly duckling.

"No, I don't," she said. When she snuck a wary glance at him, his gray eyes met hers. Jerking her head, she stared straight ahead again.

They passed children huddled under the bus shelter, trying to stay dry. The man hit his brakes at the stop sign at the end of the road, waited for a car to pass, and then made a left turn onto a two-lane blacktop road.

His eyes narrowed in on her bare legs again. "I like pretty girls."

"School's that way," she said, pointing. "You're going the wrong way."

"Why don't we skip school today? Play hooky? Have you ever done that?" he asked.

"No," Linda snapped. "I want to go to school. I've never missed a day."

He smirked. "This is a hooky day. A fun day."

"No, it's not. You take me to school like Daddy said." she demanded.

He reached out and stroked her hair. "I like blondes too."

"Don't touch my hair, you jerk."

Linda's fear grew the farther the stranger drove. Her mouth became dry as she surveyed the less traveled, lone country road. When he stopped at the next intersection, she frantically groped for the door handle to flee. There wasn't one, or one for the window. She pounded on the passenger window. "Let me out of here."

The raindrops grew larger, pounding hard against the

windshield. Her breathing grew ragged as the windshield wipers continued to click back and forth.

As her adrenaline peaked, she squirmed in her seat and found the courage to yell, "Stop this truck. Let me out."

The man threw back his head and laughed.

Ellen's mother's boyfriend had been sentenced to thirty years in prison for raping Ellen and attempting to murder her last year. The scar where he'd slit her throat would remind Ellen of her ordeal forever. She'd described all the graphic details of her rape to Linda.

The horror of the old, stinky man touching her caused sheer terror to ripple throughout Linda's body. Pressing her back against the passenger door for leverage, she bashed his head with her book bag. When that didn't work, she clawed at his tree trunk of a neck. He held her at bay with a choking grip around her neck.

"I have ways to handle a wildcat like you, little girl," he said.

Her fists pounded air until she became exhausted. Gasping for breath, she clawed at his arm, but his sleeves were so thick that she only broke her fingernails. Images of him raping her flashed through her mind like an unfolding nightmare.

Shifting her eyes around frantically, she tried to find any means of fighting back. Then, suddenly, she grabbed the steering wheel and jerked it. The truck skidded into the oncoming traffic lane. Through the rain, and at a distance, a lone car stopped. The passengers gawked as the man got the truck back under control. Linda urgently flailed her arms and screamed at the two people in the oncoming vehicle. They stared in uncertainty as they began to creep past.

The man loosened his grip on her neck, and she gasped for air.

About a mile farther, the brakes hissed as the truck abruptly decelerated, throwing her forward and into the dash. The gushing rain limited visibility, but she heard the sound of rocks crunching under the tires as the stranger made a right turn onto a gravel road that curved into the forest. He navigated through the wooded area, parked in front of a chained gate at the end of the desolate road, and killed the engine. A weathered sign read: "NO TRESPASSING."

The man stuffed the keys into the pocket of his pants and stepped out of the vehicle—leaving his door open, perhaps to tempt her to flee. Linda slowly regained her strength, her heart thumping in her chest. She looked around the area. There was not a car or person in sight. The idea of being alone in a secluded area with a stranger stirred her worst imagination. Her lips trembled, tears spilled from her eyes, and she shook uncontrollably. Dashing across the seat, she scrambled for the driver's door, but before she reached it, a powerful paw grabbed her by the arm and yanked her out. The left side of her head hit the doorframe with a thud, and Linda thought the blow had cracked her skull. Her world spun, and her ears rang.

"Stop," she screamed, chest heaving. "Don't touch me." she continued yelling at the top of her lungs. She threw punches at his face with all the strength she could muster. Fear bombarded her like the pouring rain. "Daddy knows I'm with you."

She'd never thought such a thing could happen to her. She pulled the man's hair, but he didn't let go. She shrieked as he forced her to the ground. Digging her fingernails into his cheeks like a wildcat, she caused him to lose his balance. The man tumbled and rolled on wet grass as needlepoint bullets of rain bombarded them. Before Linda could stand, giant hands pinned her shoulders to the ground, and savage eyes stared down at her. She grabbed a fistful of his beard and yanked.

"Ouch," he yelled. "You little …" He released her.

"You'd better leave me alone. Help." Linda bolted, but he caught up with her, grabbed the collar of her sweater, and tackled her down again. Her bottom lip split when her face hit the ground. Tasting blood, she turned, jabbed her fingers into his eyes, and staggered to her feet.

He clutched a handful of her hair, turned her around, and slapped her face.

She tried to catch her balance, but she hit the ground again.

"Please, let me go," she cried.

The monster pinned her down, using a powerful knee

against her back. His weight dug into her spine until it bowed. He tied her hands together and taped her mouth shut to stop her screaming. He then bound her ankles and connected the rope to the one that secured her hands, causing her knees to curl in front, which forced her into a fetal position. She gasped for breath, and her stomach churned. He covered her nose with a rag doused with a chemical that burned her throat and made her eyes water. Dizziness dominated her head as she struggled to free herself from the ropes that dug into her flesh.

***

Darkness turned to light as the blurry figure of Linda's abductor came into focus.

The storm had ended, and dim sunlight filtered through narrow cracks in windowless, weathered board walls as the day waned. Birds chirped and the wind rustled outside. Overhead, rusty tin-covered two-four-wide rafters. The odor of old urine mixed with smoke from a wood-burning stove filled the room.

The soreness of Linda's breasts and the burning pain in her groin alerted her to signs of rape. The enormity of the situation seized her. She clenched her fists and whimpered.

Suddenly, a big, puffy face with a tobacco-stained tongue, caged in missing teeth, came into view. He peered down at her with a wide grin. One eye narrowed while the other stood wide open. He had two moles near his nose, and his eyebrows grew together. The sight of him made Linda's stomach roll. He stood nude and hairy, like a silverback she'd seen in the zoo. Other than in magazine pictures, Linda had never seen a man's genitals. Like a bull, two large balls dangled behind his penis. One hand clutched a huge, shiny knife that glinted silver in the dim light. The other hand held a bottle of booze. Throwing back his massive head, he took a swig, burped, and caressed her body with the blade of his knife.

Linda lay naked on dirty linens in a squalid one-room shack. She shivered from the cool air, refusing to think about her future with the monster who was holding her captive. She realized she had wet herself.

Linda shook her head and twisted her body, but the constraints didn't budge. As she squirmed on the lumpy mattress, the bedsprings squeaked in agony. Her heart pounded faster than she'd ever imagined it could. She closed her eyes. She had never felt so helpless.

When she opened her eyes again, her abductor was still there. It wasn't a dream, and he wasn't going away. Daddy would come for her—find her, protect her, comfort her, and make everything better.

"See me?" he uttered in a deep, hollow voice. "I'm your master." He pointed to her. "You're my slave. You'll only refer to me as Master. We're going to have so much fun, little girl—just you and me." His words came without a tremor or a change in his demeanor.

She winced.

Master took another gulp from his bottle, coughed, and cleared his throat. He sat on the bed next to Linda. When he tried to kiss her, she turned her face away. His breath threatened to make her heave.

"Oh, you're not going nowhere, little girl." He smiled as she continued to struggle. "You'll do exactly what I say. If you're nice to me, I just might let you go. Oh, don't stare at me with those watery peepers. Scared, are you?"

Linda nodded in horror.

He moved to the wood-burning stove—the exhaust pipe extended through the ceiling. He removed a coffee pot and sat it on the floor. Using a screwdriver, he opened the round port on top of the stove, and—one by one—he dropped her shoes and clothes into the fire. He tossed back his enormous head, chuckling. "You won't need those."

Linda inhaled a gust of pungent smoke from the open port.

Daddy is looking for me.

She slowly scanned the room. A two-by-four barricaded the only door. A flickering oil lamp and a plate of food sat on a homemade table, and an old, tattered sofa was wedged against it along the opposite wall. The place had no kitchen—just shelves with a few plates, glasses, and silverware. An uneven row of old pots and pans hung on the wall behind the stove, and a woodpile was stacked in the far corner.

Her terrified eyes darted back and forth. She glanced up at the ropes that secured her hands to a rusty, antique metal bedpost. He had hogtied her to the head of the bed, restricting her movement. Mounted above the bed was the dust-covered head of a deer with wide antlers. Would she end up like that—the man's trophy? Linda tried to force the tape from her mouth with her tongue, but it was unyielding. She frantically took deep, quick breaths, but she couldn't get enough air.

Holding a plate in one hand and the knife in the other, Master again approached her and set the plate on the bed. He then ripped the tape from her mouth. The huge knife slit the rope like butter, freeing her from the bedpost, but he kept her hands bound in front of her.

Linda sat up, whimpering, desperately sucking in air. "Daddy," she cried.

"Here. Eat this," her captor said, shoving a spoonful of mash potatoes into her mouth.

She spat the food into his face and screamed until he stuffed a dishtowel into her mouth. She shook her head like a mad dog, forcing the towel out with her tongue.

Wiping his face on the sheet, the man quickly glanced around the shack, then rushed to the door, removed the barricade, and ran outside, naked. Linda's screams echoed out the open door, loud and shrill.

Carrying a roll of duct tape, Master ran back inside, peeled off a section, and taped her mouth, again silencing her. He peeked outside prior to replacing the barricade.

A backhanded slap knocked Linda across the bed, burning her cheek like a flame. "Keep your mouth shut, or you'll be sorry." He grabbed two fistfuls of her hair, jerking her face toward his putrid breath. "Calling for Daddy, huh? Isn't that cute? Your daddy gave you to me, little girl. He said, 'Take her out and kill her. We need the insurance money.' He told me where to leave your body. Can you imagine those dirty rats, offering me only five thousand dollars? I insisted on twenty, and they agreed." He paused, as if waiting for his words to sink in. "They have a hundred-thousand-dollar life insurance policy on you."

The words stung and raced around in Linda's mind. Her parents had never shown any loving emotions toward her, never praised her for performing well in school, and never discussed her future education. They'd provided her with the basics—food and shelter, nothing beyond that. And Daddy had never asked her to ride with a stranger in the past. Was what the man said true? Had her parents asked him to rape and kill her?

She was alone in the world. No one cared for her. She hated her parents, because they hated her. She wanted them to pay for her suffering, the pain and agony she was enduring.

The man controlled her destiny, and that thought drained her energy. She shook her head and wept. Her life was ending soon. She bit her lower lip and stared at the floor as if it would provide answers, resolutions.

Master dropped onto the bed and sipped booze from his bottle.

Linda looked into the distance, her hopes fading by the second. But then she had a realization. She could identify the man and reveal her parents' involvement in her kidnapping. Self-preservation, the will to live at any cost, kicked in. The heat from the stove beckoned her like a bright light toward the future—her future.

She stared past Master, concentrating on the glow near the center of the room. In front of the wood-burning stove, her parents appeared. They didn't say a word. Both flashed devious smiles.

A woman with white hair and lines of wisdom on her face stood opposite her parents, a blue beam glowing behind her head.

"Linda, darling," the woman said softly. "My name is Blossom, I'm the grandmother you shall never have. It's up to you to survive this ordeal. I know he's larger and stronger than you, but he has weaknesses. Concentrate on what you've seen on TV and use it to your advantage. Get the knife and attack the most vulnerable parts of his body."

With eyes locked on the woman, Linda sat straight up, rigid. "Yes, Blossom," she whispered.

"Be courageous." The woman jerked her head in the direction of her parents, who no longer smiled. "You don't want them to win, do you? You have the will to survive." She pointed to Master. Her lips curled back in a snarl. "Kill him."

Linda nodded. Suddenly, her future brightened. A small drop of anticipation sparked in her heart.

The man turned, following Linda's gaze. "Hey," he said. "Who're you staring at? Your daddy?"

Linda never took her eyes off Blossom. "My friend."

"Don't you go weird on me, kid. There ain't nobody here but you and me. Now I know why your parents wanted you gone. You're a nutcase."

"You're going to die," Linda yelled. "Blossom told me so."

Master leaped to his feet and threatened her with a backhanded swing that stopped in midair. "Talk to your imaginary friend again, and I'll kill you both." He grabbed her shoulders and shook her so hard her head snapped back and forth. His dragon breath hit her nostrils like the stench from a rotting animal. "Your parents don't want you. What part of that don't you understand?"

Ellen had said that men's genitals were sensitive, and Linda wanted to know how sensitive. Rolling onto her side, she kneed Master in the groin. He yelled out in pain, landing on the floor. When he regained his composure, he beat her with a bamboo fishing pole, leaving her entire body covered with burning welts.

"Try that again," he warned, "and I'll cut off all of your toes. Understand?"

In throbbing pain, she stifled a sob and then nodded.

***

The next morning, Master untied Linda's hands.

"Scream and the beating you got last night will be nothing compared to what I'll do to you." Leading her to the table, he forced her to sit in front of a plate of food.

She ate her breakfast, then guzzled down a warm bottle of strawberry soda. Whatever he'd used to put her to sleep had left her thirsty. She drank two more bottles of soda.

After wolfing down her food, she said, "I need to use the bathroom."

He sat across the table and slurped his coffee. Food littered his beard.

He glared at her. "I need to use the bathroom ... what?"

She glanced at the floor. "I need to use the bathroom, Master."

He jerked his head toward a five-gallon plastic bucket. "Over there."

She sniffed. "I need to do number two, Master."

He retrieved a roll of toilet paper from a box next to the wall and slammed it onto the table. Again, he motioned her to the far corner of the room.

She did her best to hide behind the woodpile. Although he didn't watch her, she had a hard time going. She cleaned herself and stood.

"Put the lid on it," he said.

After the beating Linda had received the night before, she was careful to obey Master. And because of that, he gave her more freedom. She wanted to live another day, another hour, or even a few more seconds. He controlled the only weapon in the room, and he kept it well out of her reach. She would wait for a chance to get his knife. If she didn't succeed, what did she have to lose?

Between country music songs from a portable radio, she heard nothing about her disappearance. Was it because her parents had never filed a missing person's report with the local authorities? Although she didn't want to believe it, she realized Master spoke the truth. Her parents wanted her dead.

A helicopter whirled overhead. Perhaps it was a search party looking for her. "Where are we?" she asked.

He smirked. "Little girl, don't worry about where you are. A better question would be, where you are going."

***

After nine days in captivity, with the help of Blossom, Linda had tricked Master into believing her spirit was broken—that he had completely gained her obedience with threats and intimidation. He'd fallen asleep in bed with the knife in his hand, palm up. Linda quietly moved from the sofa and approached him, her heart pounding in her chest and her body shaking uncontrollably. He lay on his back, snoring with his mouth open, drooling saliva into his beard. As she stepped closer, she kicked over an empty booze bottle, and it rolled under the bed. Panic crushed her insides like a giant hand. She held her breath. If he woke up and found her holding his knife, he'd kill her.

Master didn't stir.

The air had turned from cool to a sultry heat. Sunrays filtered through holes in the wall. Sweat dripped down Linda's face, and her palms were wet. Clasping both hands together, she managed to steady them. Carefully, she moved one of his fingers from the knife, then another.

He flinched, curling his fingers back around the handle.

Linda tried again. Slowly, she opened all of his fingers and retrieved the knife. Holding the weapon he'd threatened her with gave her a renewed sense of hope, of power. The weight of the knife made her heart pound even faster. Was she strong enough to kill him?

"Do it now," Blossom urged. "It will bring him to submission."

The shiny knife wasn't so frightful anymore. She hesitated, but only for a moment. Gripping the knife with both hands, she raised it over her head and held it there, her hands shaking out of control.

Linda lowered her arms. She couldn't do it, so she decided to flee.

Master's red eyes fluttered open, and his meaty hand grabbed her thigh.

Blossom didn't need to tell her where to attack. She plunged the knife down with all her strength and stabbed him in his groin.

Jerking up into a sitting position, he screamed, rolled over, and landed on the floor in a fetal position, grasping his bloody genitals. As he cried out in pain, Linda jumped back, gripping the knife's handle with both hands, and watched him squirm and thrash about on the floor like a dog run over by a large vehicle.

"Attack his neck," Blossom urged. "You can't let him get up. He'll kill you."

The room moved about like a whirlpool as she gripped the weapon high above her head, her hands still shaking. She concentrated on his thick tree trunk of a neck. With an exasperated grunt, she thrust the knife into it with all her might. The blade entered the side about six inches below his ear. A guttural gurgling sound escaped from his mouth as warm blood pulsed from his wound, sprayed her body, and drained the life from the monster who no longer controlled her. She yanked the knife free and jumped back.

He thrashed about on the floor, frail and helpless, his face in shock. Struggling like a fly in a spider's web, he gripped his wound with a bloody palm, let out a painful bellow, and feebly swatted at her.

Linda maneuvered behind him and powered the blade into the opposite side of his neck, again and again. The knife penetrated his flesh, making a swishing sound like a watermelon splitting open. The handle had become slick with blood, and it slipped a few times, cutting the web between her thumb and index finger. Exhausted, she stopped to catch her breath. Then, after she had rested for a brief moment, she mutilated his body again, making sure he wouldn't get up and chase her, like victims she'd seen on TV.

She continued stabbing him long after he'd stopped moving. Several times, she drove the weapon into his stomach, up to its hilt, with the little bit of strength she had left, grunting with every thrust. She stood back and studied his mangled form, then her own hands, covered in blood. Blood pooled on the floor—wild patterns sprayed the bed—and some dripped from her open mouth and chin and matted her hair. Trembling uncontrollably, she clenched the knife in both hands. Her fingers wouldn't let go. Tearing her eyes from the scene, she dashed to the door—toward freedom.

Linda removed the two-by-four barricade separating her from the world and dashed outside into the midday sun. Still gripping the knife, barefoot, naked, and covered in blood, she followed the only dirt road out, running as if death were at her heels.

When she reached a well-traveled dirt road, two men in a maintenance truck stopped, but she ran away, screaming.

"Don't touch me. Leave me alone," she yelled.

The truck drove around and stopped in front of her, blocking her path. Both occupants leaped from the vehicle with their hands extended defensively.

"Drop the knife," the driver said.

The passenger jumped back as she stabbed the air in front of him. "I'll kill you, like I did that man who raped me," she screamed.

The driver threw a tarp over her head, blinding her. They wrestled the knife from her grip and forced her into the truck between them. With fingers digging at the tarp, Linda ripped it from her head, dug her teeth and nails into the passenger's upper arm, and leaped from the moving vehicle. The men caught her again. This time, they wrapped her so tightly she couldn't move.

"Blossom, help me," Linda pleaded. Her friend didn't appear.

The shorter man in the passenger seat held her in his lap as he studied the wounds on his arm. "We're taking you to a doctor. We're not going to hurt you."

Linda wailed as the truck meandered through the thick forest, pleading with the men to let her go. Now two lunatics held her captive rather than one.

But then relief—the sight of traffic, homes, and businesses. When the driver killed the engine in the parking lot of a rural clinic, she wanted to jump from the truck and run inside.

The driver walked around to the passenger's side, opened the door, and carried her into the office, while the other man held open the front door.

A nurse rushed to their rescue. "How badly is she hurt?"

"We don't know," the man said. "All we can see is blood. She's naked. Claimed a man raped her."

The woman swiftly led the way into an open examination room. The man carried Linda inside and placed her on the table.

"I can take it from here," the nurse said. "Where did you find her?"

"In the swamp near Possum Trot."

"Call the sheriff. He'll want to talk with you two," the nurse said. "Wait outside."

The men left the room, closing the door behind them.

The nurse removed the tarp and examined Linda's body. "You hurt anywhere else other than your hands?"

"My head." Linda sniffed and touched the left side of her head. "And down there."

Using cotton balls and a solution she retrieved from the cabinets, the nurse started sponging the blood from Linda's hands. "I'm sure you'll need stitches. What's your name, honey?"

When Linda glanced down, she saw that she was wearing a gown but didn't remember putting one on. She sobbed, "He raped me, said Daddy told him to kill me for my insurance money."

"Sweetie, he just said that to make you believe your parents don't love you, weren't looking for you," the nurse explained.

"Daddy told me to ride to school with him, but he didn't take me to school. He took … me." She went into a crying frenzy.

The nurse placed an arm around Linda's shoulder.

"The doctor will be with you shortly. I know you've had a traumatic experience, but you're safe now."

A male doctor entered. "Hello, young lady." He checked her hands, shone a pencil-sized light into her eyes, and checked her scalp. "How did you hurt your head? There's quite a lump there."

"When that man pulled me out of his truck, my head hit the side of the door," she said with a sniff.

"The sheriff's on his way," the doctor said to the nurse. "We'll need a rape kit. Schedule an appointment with a neurologist. Is all of this blood hers?"

"No," the nurse said. "She has cuts on her hands, but I believe most of the blood belongs to someone else."

Linda protested, withdrawing her hand. "Ouch. That hurts."

"Sorry. I need to clean your hands before the doctor can stitch them up."

The doctor said, "Get some epinephrine. I'll give her a local."

Linda didn't object when the doctor examined her cuts, but she wouldn't let him check her ... down there.

"Call Dr. Edwards here for a vaginal exam," the doctor said.

When the nurse opened the door, a police officer was standing outside. "Can I come in?"

"Yes," the doctor said. "She keeps saying her father paid a man to rape and kill her. Hope you can get more out of her."

The officer held a pen and a small spiral notepad in his hands. He introduced himself as the sheriff. "What's your name?"

She hugged herself and wept. "Linda Fluger."

"How old are you, Linda?"

"Thirteen."

He opened his notepad, ready to take down information. "I need your folks' names and address."

Linda held her palms upward in her lap. "I don't want to talk about them."

The sheriff's voice was gentle, yet firm. "I'll need this information so I can catch the man who hurt you."

Linda kicked her feet. "Oh, he's not going anywhere. I killed him—twice."

"I still need the information."

"Helena and Adler Fluger. Route 2, Box 27, Logan."

The officer glanced at the doctor. "Logan? Where's that?"

Linda sniffed and dabbed at her eyes. "We live in the countryside. Logan is the closest town."

The sheriff's radio blasted. "There's only one shack down the road where the oil workers saw the girl running from," a voice said. "The man is DOA, multiple stab wounds. What carnage."

The sheriff said, "Get the county investigator down there." He turned his attention back to Linda. "Which state is Logan in?"

"Here, in Florida," Linda said.

"You're in the state of Louisiana, not Florida. Do you have relatives we can contact other than your parents?" the sheriff asked.

"No, none." Tears rolled down Linda's cheeks and dripped from under her chin.

Static blasted from the sheriff's radio. "Linda, do you know how the man got you into the swamp?" he asked.

"No. He covered my nose and mouth with something that put me to sleep. This is the first time I've been out of Florida—with that man."

"Do you know the man's name?" the police officer asked.

"Daddy told me, but I forgot. He made me call him Master," Linda said.

"You're safe now. The doctor is going to take good care of you," the sheriff promised. He turned to the doctor. "I'll check this out and get back to you later."

The nurse returned with a tray containing hypodermic needles and other things Linda had never seen before.

"My friend, Blossom, is speaking to me. Do you mind if I talk to her?" Linda asked.

"You may talk to Blossom anytime you wish," the doctor said, concentrating on her hands. "I'm going to stitch up your cuts. Don't look."

"Blossom said I won't feel a thing." Somehow, the blood didn't gross Linda out as it would have a few days ago.

The doctor injected clear liquid into Linda's right hand.

"Thank you, Blossom," Linda said. "You've helped me so much. I don't know what I would've done without you."

"Where is Blossom?" the doctor asked.

"Standing next to you. Can't you see her?" Linda asked.

"Yes," the doctor responded. "I'm glad you had a friend to help you."

Linda flinched. "Master forbade me to talk to you, Blossom. He said that you aren't real and I'm crazy."

The doctor said, "What about a psychological exam? Is that okay with you?"

"Will it hurt?" Linda asked.

"Not one bit," he said. "A doctor will give you a written test and ask a few questions, that's all."

After the male doctor stitched her hands, a female doctor, Kay Edwards, came to Linda's rescue. The woman was young and kind, like a big sister. Linda allowed Kay to complete a vaginal examination. Afterward, Kay led Linda to a chair in an office where the sheriff and the male doctor waited.

"We can handle it from here," the male doctor said.

When Kay started toward the door, Linda screamed, "Don't leave me, Kay."

Kay moved next to Linda and took a seat.

Linda hugged her, and she hugged back.

"Your diagnoses, Doctors?" the sheriff asked.

Kay answered, "Linda has been brutally and repeatedly raped. Marks on her back indicate a recent flogging. She's still in a state of shock."

"I concur with that," the male doctor said.

"Surely you're not charging her with anything, Sheriff," Kay said.

The sheriff collected information from Linda, stuffed his notepad into his pocket, and stood. "A background investigation revealed that the attacker, Mike Gibson, was a known pedophile. He got early release on a thirteen-year sentence for raping another teenage girl nine years ago. Consider this case closed. Self-defense."

Kay rode with Linda to a special hospital in New Orleans. After a bath, Linda received a hospital gown, and a nurse led her into a room that she would share with another teenage girl. Linda had no choice but to say goodbye to her new friend. Kay promised, however, to phone the next day and visit her on the weekends. The medication the nurse gave Linda caused her to instantly sleep.

CHAPTER 2

SABBATICAL

D r. Linda Harrison approached the crosswalk that separated the north and south wings of the University of Munich Hospital. She draped her heavy wool coat over her left arm, and her purse hung from her right shoulder. A gust of cold wind smacked her head on as she opened the door leading to the north wing, and the force almost knocked her off her feet. She struggled through the door, and it banged shut behind her, almost closing on her hand.

From the glass skywalk on the third floor, Linda could see that three lanes of rush-hour traffic crept in both directions. Other than muffled beeping horns and rumbling engines, the only sounds she heard echoed from the harmonic tapping of her pumps on light gray tile and the hum from electric heaters overhead.

She had spent the last two months teaching advanced medical students. Now she looked forward to a visit with her first cancer patient in Germany. When she entered the north wing, busy chatter occurred between two approaching nurses. Wobbly wheels from breakfast carts rattled, and the aroma of food permeated the air.

A lone male, about forty years old, occupied the nurses' station. He stood at her height, five feet six. He had a fair complexion.

"Good morning, Nurse Hoffmann," Linda said in German. "I'm here to see Dr. Czesak's patient in room 402."

"Mrs. Fluger," he said.

The hairs on the back of her neck stood up, and she held her breath for a moment. "Fluger."

The nurse dropped into a chair behind his computer and hit a few keys. "She's in bed A. The one near the door. I believe her husband is with her."

"Do you have a locker for me?" she asked.

His face remained serious as he shoved a key across the desk. "Number fourteen. Store your things in it. Do you have your badge yet?"

Linda smiled, retrieved an electronic photo card from her pocket, and slipped the lanyard around her neck.

The nurse pulled a laptop from the shelf behind him. "Do you have your user ID and password?"

"Yes," she said.

In the doctors' lounge, Linda stowed her coat and purse in her locker, pulled out a new white jacket, and slipped it on over her suit.

Two doctors standing near the window were engaged in conversation and having coffee. The one who approached Linda was about her age.

"Hello," he said. "I'm Dr. Eber Bauer. Coffee?"

"Dr. Harrison." She shook his hand. "Black."

Dr. Bauer poured coffee into a Styrofoam cup and passed it to Linda. The man stood a couple of inches taller than her, with a generous amount of light, wavy hair. He had a pleasant, soft face and rich, coffee-brown eyes.

"Call me Eber. Are you new here?" he asked in a charming voice.

"Linda. Yes. From the States, New York City. I'm on sabbatical here for six months. I take it that you're on the staff?"

"No," he said. "I perform surgery here quite often, but my clinic is nearby. I'm a cardiologist. You speak excellent German."

"I had a German father. He taught me."

"Do you live with your family back in America?"

"No. I live alone, but I have a friend staying at my apartment while I'm away."

"What do you do here?" he asked.

"I teach classes. This is my first morning seeing a patient. I'm performing surgery tomorrow morning under Dr. Czesak."

He nodded. "Head of the Oncology Department. We play football on opposing teams."

"Dr. Czesak is a huge man ..."

"That's why his team usually wins."

Linda glanced at her watch. "I have to go, Dr. Bauer. I'll see you around."

"We're having a gathering Friday, if you'd like to come. A few of us meet at the pub down the street after work. I'd like to walk you there, if you don't mind."

"I'd love to come." She smiled at him. "I'll see you Friday after work. Goodbye."

Rather than wait for the attending physician, Linda entered the solitude of room 402, expecting to converse with a local patient in the almost flawless German she'd learned from her father.

The bathroom stood on the right of Mrs. Fluger's bed, and a whiff of Lysol came from it, lingering so strongly in the room that Linda sneezed.

A white privacy curtain concealed the other occupant. Early morning sunlight beamed through the window opposite the beds and brightened the small room. An ornate basket of flowers sat on a mahogany nightstand at Mrs. Fluger's bedside. Next to the bed sat a tray with a clear pitcher of ice water and an empty glass.

The patient sat upright in bed, her back resting against two fluffy pillows, her eyes etched with crow's feet. Her short brown hair, gray at the roots, needed grooming.

A casually dressed man with a receding hairline sat by the woman's bedside, slumped in his chair. He gently held her left hand in both of his. The veins in the thin man's hands and neck resembled a roadmap, and his cheeks had deep crevices.

With the exception of an occasional strangulated cough from behind the curtain, the place was quiet.

"Guten Morgen. I'm Dr. Harrison," Linda said in German, glancing at the couple before her. "I'll be assisting Dr. Czesak with your surgery."

"Guten Morgen," they replied.

Linda placed her laptop on the waist-high workstation next to the window and powered it on. Multiple icons popped up on the screen. As Linda opened the hospital records, the old man croaked at her back, "Dr. Czesak said you're the most prominent oncologist in America."

"I can't agree with him, but I always do my best. Mrs. Fluger, what's your first name?"

"My name is Hel … Helena." The woman spoke with an American accent.

Linda's fingers froze on the keyboard. She slowly turned, eyed the couple behind her, and then looked at the computer again. The letter "F" had run several lines across the screen. Her heart fluttered, and an icy chill penetrated her rigid body. The couple's piercing eyes extracted life from her like a foreign entity, draining her energy. She couldn't utter a word as she drifted back in time. Her childhood flashed before her eyes. Twenty-two years had passed, but she knew with certainty that they were her parents. They represented ghosts from her past, a nightmare that had robbed her of her childhood and would continue to haunt her for an eternity. No matter how hard Linda had tried, she couldn't bury her past.

It constantly ran through her mind like the blood that flowed through her veins.

Her parents were in their mid-sixties but looked ten years older.

"There you are, Dr. Harrison," Dr. Czesak said. He was tall and bulky, and always in good humor—very personable. He looked more like an athlete than a surgeon.

Linda forced her eyes from the couple, excused herself, and fled the room as if it were ablaze. She rushed down the hallway, entered the ladies' room, and dropped into a lounge chair. No matter how hard she tried to stop the motion, her knees bounced up and down as her heels involuntarily clicked on the floor. She dabbed sweat from her trembling upper lip. For the first time in years, she had the urge to talk to her old psychiatrist. Tears flowed down her cheeks as pressure boiled inside of her, ready to explode like a hydrogen bomb.

Rising to her feet, legs as heavy as logs, Linda struggled to the sink, gripped it with both hands, leaned over, and threw up. Then, after a few moments frozen in place, she rinsed her mouth several times, patted her face with a paper towel, and studied herself in the mirror. Of course, they didn't recognize her. She'd been a teenager the last time they saw her, and she'd changed drastically since then. She'd had rhinoplasty surgery to reshape her nose, her square chin was now round, her light hair was darker, and her yellow, crooked teeth were now white and perfect. But even if she did resemble her former self, her parents would likely think little of it. They probably assumed she was living out the rest of her life in a mental institution—because she knew they'd paid a man to kill her.

Taking a deep breath, Linda smoothed the creases from her jacket, combed fingers through her hair, and curled her lips up into a faint smile. Minutes later, she reentered her patient's room, strong and vigorous.

Czesak's blue eyes narrowed in on hers like a beacon. "What's the matter? You looked like you saw a ghost."

"I had to use the ladies' room," she said, meeting his concerned gaze. "I think something I ate disagreed with me. Mr. and Mrs. Fluger, I'm sorry for my abrupt departure."

Czesak lowered his head to her level and gazed into her eyes. "Have—have you been crying?"

"I choked on my saliva. Went into a coughing frenzy. I'm fine—really." Linda cleared her throat and tried to remain calm. She hit keys on her laptop. "I'd like to study Mrs. Fluger's medical history."

Dr. Czesak smiled. "Mr. and Mrs. Fluger, you've met Dr. Harrison from New York City." He chuckled. "She's the only ambidextrous surgeon I've ever met."

Linda nodded but avoided eye contact with the couple.

Czesak patted Mrs. Fluger's hand. "Dr. Harrison is here on medical sabbatical. She'll be performing your surgery, young lady. I'll be there to assist."

"We appreciate her service," Mr. Fluger said.

Studying the computer screen, Linda discovered her mother's failing health: diabetes, kidneys operating at sixty percent, high blood pressure, and now ovarian cancer. Medical records also revealed that Mrs. Fluger had a prolapsed uterus, which had prohibited childbearing. Linda's eyes focused on the screen, her mind lost in a cloud of confusion. How had Helena Fluger given birth to her then? If Helena Fluger wasn't her biological mother, who was? Had they adopted or kidnapped her?

Linda closed her eyes and let out a deep breath, allowing the good news to sink in. She despised the couple for the misery they'd put her through, but it felt great knowing that her real parents weren't responsible for destroying her childhood. Mrs. Fluger wasn't Linda's biological mother. The woman was a patient, and Linda would treat her accordingly—do her best as a surgeon to mitigate the damage caused by the cancer and help the woman recover.

***

When Linda and Dr. Czesak entered the operating room dressed in surgical greens, the operation team had everything prepped.

The anesthesiologist sat at Mrs. Fluger's head, explaining his procedure.

After the patient was under, Linda's job began. Her hands were calm when she made an incision below the navel from hip to hip. Her scalpel slid through flesh like gelatin. The reproductive organs she was about to remove hadn't given her life—another woman's had. Who was Linda Fluger—Linda Harrison?

"Suction," she said to the nurse.

The surgical nurse vacuumed away the blood as quickly as it appeared. Linda removed one malignant ovary, then the other. She removed the uterus, fallopian tubes, and surrounding cancerous tissue while Dr. Czesak hovered over her shoulders.

"Looks like you got all the cancerous tissue," he said. "I'll prescribe radiation treatment."

As Linda washed up, her mind drifted back to Helena and Adler Fluger. She'd copied their address and phone number from Helena's hospital records. *Who are my real parents?*

***

Nightmares from Linda's past surged throughout the night like a raging storm. In the morning, she canceled her four-day tour of the countryside and took the first available flight back to New York City. She fidgeted in her seat, finding comfort only in alcohol. No matter how much she resisted, the dark apparition from her previous life kept blasting back.

"I'll have another Bloody Mary," Linda said to the flight attendant as she raised her empty cup into the air.

Tears rolled down her cheeks as childhood memories flowed through her mind like dust in a windstorm.

The young flight attendant asked, "Ma'am, are you all right? You haven't eaten anything."

Linda wiped her eyes with a tissue. "I'm fine. Thanks for asking."

CHAPTER 3

RETURNING TO NEW YORK CITY

D r. Linda Harrison arrived at LaGuardia Airport on an overnight flight from Germany and took a slow-moving taxi through six inches of dirty snow. She removed her gloves and brushed back the hair from her forehead. Stoplights gently swayed in the wind, and their faint reflections flickered inside the cab as it drove through the city. The driver's accent was Jamaican. Refusing to converse with him during her trip home, Linda listened to annoying rap music along with the sound of the rumbling engines of other motorists. Absently, she watched as the world moved past her window. Green street signs with white writing were just blurs. Before long, the distant silhouette of the city came into view ahead, buildings speckled with dim lights. Linda clutched her scarf in both hands as the wipers clicked back and forth, clearing blankets of snow from the windshield.

Although tragic things had happened to her, she was

like a cat, always landing on her feet. Still, her energy was depleted, and the medicine she'd taken for her headache hadn't stopped her head from pounding like a drum. She couldn't wait to take something stronger, jump into her own bed, and sleep all day. She closed her eyes for a moment. Anticipation squeezed her heart as her mind spun ahead. Today, she would sleep. Tomorrow, she would start searching for her real parents.

***

Linda snapped out of her reverie when the driver parked under the canopy of her apartment building and popped open the trunk. The door attendant rushed outside and piled her luggage onto a cart.

She paid the driver and stepped out into the frigid air, a sharp contrast to the mild climate she'd left in Germany. As Linda trailed the attendant through two sets of sliding glass double doors, a rush of arctic air blew in behind her.

From the coffee shop, the aroma of a Colombian blend hit her nose. Residents were perched on sofas and lounge chairs, reading the morning newspapers. Some stood in line for their morning caffeine fix. A few tenants stared out of plate glass windows and chatted about the early November snowstorm. Linda recognized faces but didn't know their names.

Bob, the security guard, conversed with a resident about an illegal sublet from his station on the right side of the door. Linda avoided him whenever possible. He looked about thirty and wore his thick, raven hair like an old gangster—slicked back with gel. He stood an inch shorter than she was, about five feet five. His long sideburns and bushy mustache reminded her of a chef. A worn leather jacket covered his security uniform. Bob was Italian and wanted to become a mobster. In fact, he'd bragged about trying his luck with a few known affiliates. Before the elevator doors closed, he waved at her. She waved back.

Linda stepped off on the seventh floor, with the attendant pushing his cart behind her. At the door, she tipped him a twenty.

"Want me to take these inside?" he asked.

"That won't be necessary. I can manage from here," Linda said.

He stacked her bags on the side of her door, thanked her, and headed back down the hallway as the rumbling wheels echoed in the distance.

Gripping the handle of a bag with one hand, Linda turned keys in two locks and shouldered the door open. When she entered her two-bedroom apartment, she immediately noticed that the burglar alarm system was off, and the unmistakable stench of decaying flesh overwhelmed her, bringing back memories of medical school. The thermostat was at the max, and the desert heat hit her like a wave. The blackout curtains made the place darker than deep space. She flipped on the light switch with a trembling hand. Her eyes bulged, and her lids fluttered rapidly, when she saw the overturned furniture and appliances pulled from the walls. A dark figure lay on the floor in front of the guest bedroom at the end of the hall. Her hand went to her throat. Next, she turned on the hall light, exposing huge, bare feet. Her stomach knotted in apprehension. She shivered and whispered, "Beaulin?"

Linda peeked back into the empty hallway and pushed her door wide open, just in case she had to make a quick exit. "Beaulin, is that you?"

Holding her scarf firmly over her mouth and nose, she slowly approached the figure. The odor of decomposing flesh intensified. His dislocated nose and the wounds on his bloated face resembled a tortured prisoner of war, but she identified Beaulin by the tattoos on his arms and neck. He lay naked, with a puddle of black goo surrounding his head and upper torso. His genitals were missing, and his throat was cut to the spine, leaving his larynx open like a severed hose. His hands were behind his back, probably tied, and duct tape covered his mouth. Her stomach lurched, and her heart pounded so hard she thought it would explode.

As a doctor, she'd witnessed death, but she'd rarely seen murder victims. Besides, Beaulin wasn't a patient, but a friend.

Backing away from the gruesome scene, she rushed into the outer hallway and looked in both directions. Two giggling teenage girls entered an apartment three doors from hers. Her world swirled as she gasped for fresh air. Her entire body trembled, her stomach boiled, and her legs went limp. Bile rushed out of her throat, and the Bloody Marys she'd consumed on the plane erupted, leaving a red stain on the gray carpet and a foul taste in her mouth. She tried her cell phone—dead battery. With unsteady hands, she closed the door, left her luggage outside, and headed back down to the main floor.

When the elevator halted, she stepped into the lobby, shuffled to the security counter, and grabbed the edges with both hands. Bob's head jerked up from his computer screen. "Welcome home, doll. Cold out there, huh?" He leaned over, gazing directly into her eyes. "Your face is pale. You sick?"

The calmness in her voice surprised her. "I need to use your phone."

He leaned further over his desk. "Is the building on fire, honey, or did someone steal your cell phone?"

When Linda reached over his counter, Bob blocked her hand. "No can do. Building rules. You can't use this phone except for an emergency."

"This is an emergency," Linda insisted, clawing at Bob's dragon-tattooed hand. "It's Beaulin."

"Oh, the big candied cherry." He chuckled. "What happened? Did he slip on his high heels?"

"He's dead. Murdered," Linda blurted out.

Bob's jaw dropped, and his fingers loosened around the phone. "Are you sure? He could be asleep."

"I know a dead body when I see one," she said.

Still gripping the edge of the counter, Linda struggled to maintain her equilibrium. "I need to sit."

Bob appeared at her side, placed his arms around her waist, and led her into the vacant security manager's office behind his workstation.

Linda waited for the cops to arrive while Bob paced around the lobby. The color had drained from his face, and he stuttered a few words. He didn't seem to know what to do with his hands, so he kept shoving them in and out of his pockets. Five minutes later, two uniformed cops showed up and began questioning Linda about her relationship with Beaulin and her whereabouts during the past few weeks. Bob escorted them upstairs, while Linda remained seated.

***

Linda sat behind the chief of security's desk and stared out into the early dawn, watching commuters struggle their way to work—some in cars, others on foot. Tears rolled down her cheeks as silently as the snow that melted on the window. She sniffed and wiped her nose on the scarf hanging around her neck. Linda wasn't superstitious, but she'd had a run of bad luck with friends in the past. Beaulin was the closest friend she'd had in a long time. He had been vibrant, full of energy.

After she waited for over an hour, she watched a man

and a woman approached the office from the other side of the glass wall. The man opened the door and entered, carrying a manila envelope Linda recognized. He flashed a badge. "Dr. Harrison, I'm Detective Coombs. This is my partner, LaFee." His green eyes were warm, his voice soothing. He stood tall and was muscular, as if he'd spent lots of time in a gym. He had a soft, pleasant face and bright red hair. Detective Coombs picked up a box of Kleenex from the top of the file cabinet, dropped it onto the desk in front of Linda, and landed in the chair closest to hers.

The woman, LaFee, closed the door behind her.

Coombs placed an envelope on the desk. "Are you all right?"

Linda wiped her face and blew her nose. "No. I'm not."

LaFee took the other chair in front of Linda. "Must be quite a shock to come home to. We positively identified the body as Mr. Beaulin Bartell."

"How did you identify him so fast?" Linda asked.

LaFee scooted her chair forward. "We have access to the most sophisticated crime database in the world. CSU rolled his fingerprints, entered them into CODIS, and got a hit."

Coombs pulled a notepad from his pocket, flipped it open, and checked his notes. "Dr. Harrison, you told the officers that Mr. Bartell was just visiting. Was he a boy-friend or a relative?"

Linda sniffed. "Friend. Strictly platonic. He

works—worked—in nightclubs as a crossdresser and co-median. Traveled a lot. Whenever he visited New York, he stayed with me."

"Did he ever bring friends over?" Coombs asked.

Linda's heart ached as she thought about the pain Beaulin must have endured. "No."

LaFee held a small pad in one hand and a pen in an-other. "Where did he work?"

Linda swallowed hard and dabbed at her eyes again. "Various places. I have his agent's card. He should know."

Coombs scribbled notes and flipped a page on his pad. "Did he mention problems with anyone?"

Linda said, "He was gay. I'm sure he had problems with lots of people."

"Threats from anyone in particular?" LaFee asked.

Linda's headache intensified. "If so, he never told me."

Coombs reached across the desk and touched her shoulder. "Just a few more questions and we'll let you go."

LaFee crossed her legs, took a deep breath, scowled at her partner, and folded her arms. Her tone sharpened. "Coombs, let's move on—if you don't mind."

"Mr. Bartell's wallet contained more than five hundred dollars, so robbery wasn't a motive," he said. "Is anything missing from your place?"

Did they expect her to completed an inventory after finding a body in her apartment? "I don't know. I didn't check."

"Seems they were searching for something specific, a

large object," LaFee said. "They didn't take the TV or the computer. Do you have a safe?"

"No. Why do you think they were targeting something?" Linda asked.

LaFee coughed. "The place wasn't in that much disarray. Drawers were pulled open but not dumped."

Linda shivered, but sweated, under her coat. "Well, it's quite a mess to me."

"Mr. Bartell was tortured," Coombs said. "Someone turned up the heat to speed up decomposition, probably to throw off his time of death."

As she stared out the window, Linda's mind drifted like falling snowflakes. "I noticed."

Coombs asked, "You sure he didn't mention anyone threatening him?"

Linda stood, removed her coat, and draped it across her lap. She'd never forget the first time she'd met Beaulin. She'd probably saved his life. "No, he never discussed his private life with me. What do you think they were looking for?"

LaFee's voice raised an octave, and she shot Linda a smoldering glance. "You tell us."

The woman's behavior gnawed at Linda's guts. "If he brought someone here, it was after I'd left." She trembled. "Do you think they'll be back?"

LaFee checked out Linda's body as a man would. "If they think you know something, it's possible. It's also possible they found what they were after, or maybe they're convinced it's not here."

Linda blew her nose. "Why didn't he just give them what they wanted?"

Coombs leaned across the table, again rested a hand on her shoulder, and gently patted her back. "Maybe he did."

Linda usually flinched or tensed up when men touched her, but Coombs was different. His touch soothed her, maybe because of the trauma in her life.

He slid the manila envelope across the desk. It was Beaulin's last will and testament, addressed to Dr. Linda Harrison. It read: "OPEN ONLY IN CASE OF MY DEATH." Linda opened the package, but before she could remove its contents, Coombs retrieved it.

For the first time, Linda noticed how empty the office was. Only a computer, a coffee cup, and a folder sat on the L-shaped desktop. A two-drawer file cabinet stood to the left. Tacked on the opposite wall were stick-figure crayon drawings of a man, woman, child, and cat.

LaFee twisted in her chair as if she had a bad rash on her butt. "We need to contact his relatives."

Linda fished her wallet from her purse, retrieved Beaulin's agent's business card, and passed it to Coombs.

He accepted the card, studied it, and shoved it into his breast pocket. "We'll finish this interview later. You get some rest. Stay with a friend or get a hotel room. We'll get back in touch with you."

Linda wanted Coombs to stay and comfort her, but his partner intervened.

LaFee rose to her feet and jerked her head toward the

door. "Let's go, Coombs. Dr. Harrison, we'll contact you concerning a more thorough interview."

As Coombs headed for the door, Linda stood. "Detective Coombs."

He turned. "Yes, Doctor."

She wanted to bury her face in his chest. "Give me a few days."

As the two detectives left the office, Linda thought about Dr. Eber Bauer. She also felt comfortable with him, but he was in Germany.

***

Two days after discovering Beaulin's body, Linda entered the local police precinct. Four dozen chairs lined the left side of the room, and the seating area had almost reached its capacity. Straight ahead, a glass wall separated the room from a larger secured waiting area. A police officer manned the front desk on the right. A closed door stood on either side of him.

The last time she'd entered a police department, as she recalled, the authorities had detained her for six years for beating her foster brother to death during an attempted sexual assault.

The officer sifted through papers on his desk. His head snapped up when she approached. "May I help you, ma'am?"

"I have an appointment with Detectives Coombs and LaFee."

"I need to see a government-issued photo ID please."

A nervous hand dug into her purse, pulled out her wallet, and placed her driver's license on his desk.

He typed information into his computer, returned her license, gave her a visitor's badge, and asked her to take a seat.

She removed her coat and sat between a woman with a dirty toddler and another who looked like a soccer mom. Her mind spun, now dwelling on the past. Who was she? Who were her real parents? What was her surname? Did she have siblings, other relatives? Alone in the world, she wanted a family, a sense of belonging. The empty void in her life had turned into an ache—she had no relatives, and now Beaulin was gone.

A female officer brought her back to reality, yelling out, "Dr. Linda Harrison."

Linda forced her traumatic past and loneliness back into the dark abyss of her memory banks. She jumped to her feet. "I'm Dr. Harrison."

"Follow me," the woman said.

The officer scanned her badge on the electronic door lock and led Linda through the secured waiting area. She explained that the elevator on that side of the building was out of order and apologized for having to take an alternate route.

A handcuffed drunk berated two police officers, because they had arrested him for urinating in public. The hard-faced homeless man struggled with the officers. "I had to go. At least I hid behind a dumpster."

An elderly woman, wearing dowdy clothes and using a walker yelled, "What?" She leaned her left ear in closer to the officer.

The policeman shouted, "We're booking you for shoplifting. Do you understand your rights?"

Linda followed the officer through another door, leaving the chaos behind her. The escort led her into an interview room on the fourth floor.

"Have a seat. The detectives will be with you shortly." The officer left, closing the door behind her.

Standing in front of the chair near the back wall, Linda removed her coat and placed it across the back of the chair. The room looked nothing like the ones she'd seen on television. It had the appearance of a six-by-six jail cell. A reinforced vertical iron bar attached to the wall on the right side of the table brought back the time she'd spent in jail. Glancing up, she saw a camera mounted above the door. The table stood bare—no newspapers or magazines.

They were watching her. She twisted and shifted in the chair for twenty minutes before the door opened.

LaFee entered the room first, her badge hanging from a lanyard around her neck, her face stern. An African American detective followed her inside and closed the door behind him.

LaFee carried a paper cup of coffee in one hand and a notepad in the other. "Dr. Harrison, this is Detective

Jansen." She managed something between a grimace and a fake smile. "Would you like something to drink?"

Linda glanced at the two. "No thanks," she said.

Jansen stood over six feet tall, was about thirty-five, and had a slender build. He wore his badge on his belt. After selecting the chair on the left side of the table, he turned it backward, straddled it, and teetered. "Sorry for keeping you waiting, Doctor."

LaFee took the chair on the opposite side, leaving Linda in clear view of the camera. She wondered why only one detective took notes, especially since the room had surveillance. Earlier, she had been too distraught to notice the woman's physical appearance. Now she saw that LaFee was at least six feet tall, with blonde highlights in her short brown hair. She dropped her pad onto the table but held on to her cup.

Linda studied her eyes. "Where's Detective Coombs?"

LaFee took a sip of coffee, glanced at her notepad, and cleared her throat. "Coombs has been reassigned to another case. You'll be dealing with us from now on."

Linda tensed. "From now on?"

LaFee's stone-cold stare made her even more uncomfortable.

"Until we solve this case." LaFee took a deep breath and plunged in. "We know you're busy, so let's get right to the point. Dr. Harrison, you have quite an interesting past. You killed a man at age thirteen, claimed self-defense, and spent time in a mental hospital. A year later, you beat your foster brother to death and remained in juvenile detention until the age of eighteen. My, don't we have a temper?"

Linda's pulse jumped. Sitting straight up in her chair, she almost came to her feet. "The man abducted, raped, and tortured me. Said my parents hired him to kill me. The boy in foster care touched me inappropriately, and my intention wasn't to kill him. The judicial system sealed those records. What does my childhood have to do with this case?"

Jansen smirked, his voice menacing. "We'll ask the questions, Doctor."

A wave of nausea swept through Linda, and her lips quivered as she fought back tears. They had opened an ailing wound that would never heal. She snapped. "I'm here to help the police find Beaulin's killer, but you're wearing my patience."

LaFee gulped the last of her coffee and dropped the cup into a small trashcan. "You were born Linda Fluger. Why the name change?"

Linda blurted, "I have a right to change my name. That's none of your business." Changing her last name had mitigated the damage Helena and Adler Fluger had caused her. The detectives must have known that warrants were still valid for their arrests in the state of Florida. She huffed, feeling trapped. "Am I a suspect?"

Jansen relaxed his hands on the back of his chair and flashed a crooked, arrogant smile. "Until we determine you're not. We like to know who we're dealing with when solving murder cases. It's nothing personal."

Fuming, Linda stared from one detective to the other, her eyes bulging, her insides twisted into knots. She'd heard about the police framing citizens. Could it be happening to her? Everything felt surreal. "So, I'm guilty until proven innocent."

"Did you know Mr. Bartell left you his entire estate? Money, insurance, real estate?" LaFee asked.

Linda shrugged. "Yes, but he didn't have much."

LaFee's brown eyes gleamed like a serpent. "A half million in life insurance, two thousand acres of prime land in Tennessee, and $3.5 million in stocks and cash. People have murdered for a lot less."

The idea that Beaulin had so much money made her numb, leaving her at a loss for words. He'd given her the impression he had nothing. "He never told me he had an estate worth millions. I'd never kill anyone for money, and his murder occurred while I was out of the country."

Jansen nodded in agreement, dark eyes trained on hers. "Indeed you were."

LaFee held her cold stare. "There were no signs of breaking and entering."

Linda scooted her chair against the wall, nerves tighter than a steel guitar string. "He could have let someone in. Do I need a lawyer?"

Jansen's jaw twitched. "We don't know. Do you?"

Linda stood, her mouth as dry as flour. "Am I under arrest? If not, I'd like to leave."

LaFee pushed back her chair. "Dr. Harrison, we just need some answers. Innocent people usually cooperate."

Linda draped her coat over her arm. "I'm not saying another word without a lawyer." She hadn't received the good cop/bad cop routine. Both had been rude and insulting. She threw open the door and stormed out.

LaFee's voice echoed against her back. "We checked on your trip to Germany. You were on medical sabbatical for six months. Why did you leave after two?"

Linda didn't respond.

LaFee caught up with her just outside the interrogation room. "I'll need to escort you downstairs."

Jansen followed them outside. "I've met women like you," he said. "Smart. Pretty. The type men are afraid to ask out." He snorted. "What you need is a man in your pants."

Rather than coming to Linda's defense, LaFee smirked.

Linda growled in disgust. "You pig." Turning on her heels, she slapped Jansen's face so hard he fell against the wall.

"That's it," LaFee warned, gripping Linda's wrist. "You're under arrest for assaulting an officer." Rather than handcuffing Linda, LaFee tried tackling to the floor. Linda went into a karate defense mode, changing her stance and preventing the detective from taking her down. "What are you doing? I'm not resisting arrest."

Both detectives grabbed Linda's arms and body-slammed her to the floor while LaFee read her the Miranda rights with a knee digging into Linda's spine.

"You're hurting my arms." Linda yelled, her heart beating a million times a minute.

The cold, steel handcuffs secured Linda's wrists while the two detectives jerked her to her feet and practically dragged her down to the secured area. They planted her in a seat before an officer who booked her and placed her in a cage with the elderly shoplifter she'd seen earlier.

Linda paid a $5,000 bond that day and returned to her hotel room. Since the discovery of Beaulin's body, the police had seized her apartment and barricaded the door with crime tape, preempting her plan to search for her real parents. Had they given her up for adoption? Had they assumed she was dead and stopped searching? She could've had a normal life like most children.

She had the remainder of the week off from work but concentrating on Beaulin's cremation and having her apartment renovated took up most of her spare time.

***

At the clinic the following Monday, a nurse stopped Linda outside examination room 4. "Dr. Harrison, there's a Detective Coombs waiting to see you."

A lump filled her throat. "I'm not in."

The nurse covered her mouth with a hand. "Oops."

"Great," she said under her breath. "Have him wait in my office."

Linda saw another patient, grabbed a fresh cup of coffee, and headed for her office. A growl rose from the pit of her stomach—hunger pangs. But still, she couldn't eat.

When Linda entered her office, Coombs jumped to his feet, leaving a dismembered model of the female reproductive system rocking on her desk. The ovaries were missing, probably in the hand behind his back. "I'm sorry for disturbing you at work," he said.

"I understand you're off Beaulin's case. So why are you here?" Linda asked.

"I dated a victim once, almost lost my job in the process. LaFee thinks I flirt with every woman I meet. She got me off your case."

Linda placed her laptop on a two-drawer file cabinet. When she turned, one of the missing ovaries rolled across her desktop, and the other bounced across the floor. She retrieved them. "Maybe she's in love with you."

"LaFee has been my partner for two years. The woman is strange." He nodded at the model. "Sorry about that. I got bored." He let out a nervous chuckle, like a teenage boy being caught peeking in the girls' locker room.

Linda placed the cup of coffee on her desk but didn't sit. She stood face-to-face with Coombs. "My attorney advised me not to talk to the police. Do you enjoy harassing innocent people?"

"During a murder investigation, everyone's a suspect

until we rule them out," he said. "Sometimes it's the person we least expect. Let's talk, just you and me. Attorneys only hinder investigations. We want to find out who killed your friend. Don't you? You're the only person who can help us. My visit here is strictly off the record."

She snapped, "They asked things about my childhood."

He scanned her office. "We find out a lot by digging into people's pasts."

Linda didn't have photos of family, friends, or pets scattered about her office—only medical certificates. "So I've been told."

"Some questions may sound redundant. Let's talk about Beaulin again. Did he discuss his family with you?" he asked.

She looked at her wall clock. "A few things. Why do you ask?"

"We contacted his family about his death. They refused his body. Talked like they hated him, even after we said he had more than enough money to cover his funeral expenses."

Linda knew that Beaulin and she had similar backgrounds—no relatives, no one to mourn their deaths or take care of their remains. He'd had her. Now she had no one.

"He said they hated him," Linda replied. "He last saw them over twenty years ago. Maybe I should contact his family, talk to them myself. Twenty years is a long time to hate."

"I don't think that's a good idea," Coombs said.

Linda took a sip of coffee. "They must have simmered down by now. At fourteen, his family disowned him because of his sexual preference. Said he was an embarrassment to their family, manhood, or something like that. According to him, they were backwoods hill people who threatened to kill him if he returned home. Four years ago, I met him while I was attending an oncology seminar in Los Angeles."

He frowned. "You met him at a medical conference?"

"I glanced out my hotel window one night, saw four guys pounding on a large man in the alley, and called the cops. The victim turned out to be Beaulin. He spent four days in the hospital. I visited him every day. We've been friends since that incident." Linda took a seat behind her desk. "Have a seat."

Coombs took the chair directly in front of her. "His real name was William Joseph Bernard."

"Billy Joe," she said. "They called him Billy Joe when he was a kid."

That warm feeling from when she first met Coombs had returned, and she began to trust him again.

"May I ask you a personal question?" he asked.

Linda took another sip of coffee, then set the cup on her desk. "You already have."

He scratched the back of his neck and cleared his throat. "We didn't find a man in your life."

She leaned back and crossed her legs. "Is this a professional or personal question?"

"Both." He blushed.

"Don't you people do a thorough job when checking out suspects?"

"We didn't find anyone," he said.

She leaned forward. "Then why ask?"

"Because you're smart, beautiful." He shifted in his chair. "You don't like men?"

Linda's temper flared. "Did you get that from my coworkers?"

"When a good-looking woman dislikes men, people talk."

She scooted to the edge of her chair. "Is that what my coworkers said? That I hate men?"

He paused. "Ah … yes, but I understand why."

Coombs had read her adolescent cases, her darkest secrets, and she want to crawl under her desk.

"I heard about your incident with Jansen. Before your court hearing, ask your attorney to get a copy of the surveillance tape. He won't stand a chance."

Her gaze went to the floor. "It happened outside the interview room."

He chuckled. "There's an audiovisual system outside the door. You didn't hear it from me."

She picked up her cup. "If the judge hears what he said …"

"Sometimes Jansen can be a jerk," he admitted.

She gulped coffee. "You have some strange colleagues."

His face became stern. "I have some bad news. Bob Maggorani is dead."

The name didn't ring a bell. "Who?"

"You know ... the security guy who worked in your building. A waste management crew found his body in an alley about five this morning."

Her cup hit the top of the desk with a thud. "How? What happened?"

"Bullet in the head. He called LaFee yesterday afternoon, scared out of his wits. Said two mobsters paid him to have access to the side entrance of your apartment building while you were in Germany. He believed they killed Bartell. Was babbling something about witness protection when his phone went dead."

Linda scooted back in her chair, heart pounding. "And you think those guys—"

"A well-known mob attorney has been poking around, trying to find out who Beaulin's beneficiaries are."

Her heart dropped. "Am I in trouble?"

"It's possible. Do you know anything, Doctor? My department believes you do."

"No ... no. I don't."

He glanced at his watch, stood. "I know you have patients. Can we talk later?"

She nodded. "Next door, in the hospital lunchroom. It's in the basement, just follow the signs. 5:30."

"See you after work," he said.

Linda's mind surged after Coombs left. Her stomach felt uneasy. Had someone silenced Bob because he could identify who'd murdered Beaulin?

***

When Linda entered the cafeteria, Coombs was there already, sitting at a table and reading the hospital news bulletin. The place only served breakfast and lunch, leaving the thirty or so tables empty at this hour. Two nurses sat next to a window, sipping coffee. Six vending machines filled with drinks, snacks, and cold sandwiches catered to the late shift.

Linda approached Coombs's table, pulled out a chair, and took a seat.

"Hello, Dr. Harrison. You off duty?" he asked.

She scooted her chair under the table. "No, I'm never off work. Sometimes I assist in the emergency room."

"I think you're innocent," he blurted out.

A wave of hope uplifted her. "You don't know what that means to me. Your colleagues think I'm guilty."

"Bartell didn't get that kind of money from nightclub acts."

Linda said, "I've checked his assets. They looked legit to me. He did well in stocks and real estate. I've passed his financial records over to my CPA."

Four employees entered the cafeteria and bought drinks from the vending machines.

Linda leaned in and whispered, "If he had something people wanted, they'll be searching for it, right?"

Coombs cocked his head, eyes beaming as if he'd hit the jackpot. "Exactly."

"Maybe I should donate his assets to charity," she said.

As he settled back in his chair, the light faded from his eyes. "If it's the Mob's money, they won't be happy about that." He removed a card from his pocket, jotted numbers on the back, and slid it across the table to her. "If anyone contacts you about Beaulin, my private number is on the back."

A couple of coworkers took seats at the table behind them.

Coombs glanced over his shoulder. "How about a glass of wine? There's a place down the street."

"Ah … I don't know," she said.

"I'm a detective. You couldn't be safer," he said, rising from his chair.

She wanted to know more about the murders and if she was in danger. "One glass."

***

Linda trailed Coombs into a small restaurant and took a table near a window. They removed their coats and placed them on the empty chairs at their sides.

He never looked at the menu. "I'm having a cheeseburger and fries. I don't eat as healthy as I should."

"You're in great shape," she casually commented.

He smiled. "I have to be. Chasing criminals requires lots of energy."

She laughed. "I'll have the same."

"You've done pretty well for yourself, I mean, being alone in the world. No parents or relatives to support you, mentally or financially."

She forced a smile. "I've gotten used to the idea."

He reached across the table, touched her hand. "I'm sorry about what happened to you when you were a child."

Withdrawing, she placed both hands on her lap under the table. "I survived. My doctors influenced me, encouraged me to help people."

He smiled. "I just read a bulletin about some of your accomplishments."

Flattered that he'd shown interest in her success, she flashed a warm smile. "Becoming a doctor has been my greatest achievement in life."

"What motivated you? It must have been hard."

"I ended up alone in the world, was nobody, had no one. I didn't want to end up a loser, feeling sorry for myself. Fortunately, I didn't have concentration problems like most people who suffer traumatic experiences like mine. During my stay at the mental institution, my only mentors were doctors, and they encouraged me to become a productive citizen in society, to help others as they'd helped me. The doctors and staff were excellent.

They were my family. I'm ambidextrous, have the hands for surgery. I like oncology, but it's difficult telling patients how long they have to live."

He grinned. "I bet you save most."

"If they seek medical attention in time. Some patients ignore all the warning symptoms, see a doctor as a last resort." Linda unfolded her napkin and placed it on her lap. "How did your department get my adolescent records?"

"Networking. We don't contact the courts but rather the detectives who worked the cases. They usually give us a summary of their old notes."

"Why check out my background?" she asked, now grilling him.

"We got curious about the name change and checked out Linda Fluger."

"Can anyone do that? Find out about my past, I mean?"

"Yes, your case made national news. Child Protective Services should've changed your name when you were a kid."

Linda no longer listened to Coombs. She was becoming engrossed in thoughts about her past.

He snapped his fingers close to her face. "Hey, cheer up."

She blinked rapidly, fighting back the tears. "I'm not hungry anymore."

"Hey, don't worry about it. Someone would have to know your name used to be Linda Fluger to check out your background."

CHAPTER 4

THE STASH

Three weeks after Beaulin's murder, Linda stood in the living room of her apartment.

The maintenance men had left open the curtains she always kept closed because of the neighboring complex directly in front of her windows. The place stood cold, damp, and lonely. Cleaning detergent and fresh paint had replaced the odor of decaying flesh. The old carpet and padding were gone, and new rolls were stacked in the living room, along with most of her furniture.

She spent time checking out her new hidden security camera, then walked through each room, as if becoming familiar with the place again. Just outside the doorway of the guest bedroom was a bleached stain on the plywood floor where she'd found Beaulin's body. Searching through his belongings, she'd found nothing out of the ordinary: flashy, large dresses, high-heeled shoes, make-up, wigs, and jewelry—what she'd expected. A stack of papers lay on the floor. Among them were an airline ticket from New York to Los Angeles, a card from a lover, a work contract, and credit card statements addressed to a post office box in Chicago. Linda disliked going through his things, intruding into his personal life, like a thief stealing memories.

She decided to check the only place Beaulin could have hidden something in her apartment. She emptied his closet and stacked clothes and luggage on the bed. Removing the light switch cover, she pushed a button, activating a hydraulic lift that created a mechanical hum. The floor rose, exposing clandestine darkness below.

At the bottom of six steps, she groped for the overhead string dangling above her head. Pulling it caused the space to light up and revealed a six-by-six solid concrete storage room with a slightly acrid odor. Three stacks of five two-by-two-foot cardboard boxes—that were not hers—lined the walls. Linda stood, eyeing the boxes, as her mind went into overdrive.

She'd never seen Beaulin bring boxes into her place.

Clumsy fingers clawed at the transparent tape on the first box, but it didn't budge. Using her keys, she ripped away the tape, anxiously opened one box, and then another. Quart-sized bags of white powder filled each box. She guessed the substance was some kind of drug, but she had no way to be certain. As she stood back and studied the loot, everything became clear—the murders and the destruction of her apartment. In the last box, she found a standard white envelope on top of the bags.

Taking a seat atop a box, and resting her back on the cold concrete wall, she ripped open the envelope with trembling fingers and studied its contents. Except for a business card with the phone number of the mobster, Teddy Mudici, everything was in code.

When Linda released the two pages, they fanned to the floor. She had trusted Beaulin. How could he have endangered her life like this? Everyone who'd ever befriended her had betrayed her. First her parents, then her psychiatrist during her stay in juvenile detention, and now Beaulin.

She buried her face in her palms.

Nauseated and dizzy, she dragged herself back upstairs, locked everything up, and went back to her hotel room. She spent the entire weekend brooding over the matter. If she disposed of the drugs, the Mob might come after her. Turning them over to the police was the best option, but they might arrest her as an accessory. After all, how could she explain drugs stored in her apartment without her knowledge? The detectives had already flagged her as the prime suspect in Beaulin's murder, and she didn't want to give them additional ammunition.

But how long would it be before the Mob came for her?

＊＊＊

Early that morning, Linda and her attorney, Mark Brody, waited in a conference room in the assistant district attorney's office. Although freshly brewed coffee permeated the room, none was visible.

Brody was tall and bony with short salt-and-pepper hair. Her CPA referred to him as the Perry Mason type. He was pleasant, professional, and friendly.

When the door opened, Linda remained seated while Brody rose to his feet. He extended his hand to the assistant district attorney, an older woman with short gray hair. Linda had expected someone much younger.

"Hello, Ms. Parker. I'm Mark Brody, Dr. Harrison's attorney."

She pumped Brody's hand. "I remember you. Have a seat, Attorney Brody." She took a chair on the opposite side of the table from them and peered over her reading glasses at Linda.

"Dr. Harrison, Detective Jansen's attitude was rude and chauvinistic, but that didn't give you the right to strike him. In addition, Mr. Brody, you're practically blackmailing the police department, threatening to air the videotape on the evening news."

Brody folded his hands on top of the table. "Sorry. It gives us the upper hand."

Parker groomed her short hair with small fingers. "We understand your client may have some information concerning a homicide case," she said.

Linda's attorney shoved the envelope across the table to Parker. "Yes, or at least we think it might have some bearing on Mr. Bartell's murder investigation."

The ADA retrieved the pages with liver-spotted hands. "I'm sorry if your client doesn't like our tactics when dealing with this case, but murder is an ugly business, and we treat it accordingly."

Brody waved a hand. "Dr. Harrison discovered those in Mr. Bartell's belongings."

The room stood silent while Parker took her time reviewing the information. After a few minutes, she glanced at them over her reading glasses. "I'd like to know exactly where you found these, Dr. Harrison. My people do a thorough job when they search. You're telling me they missed this?"

Linda had never been a good liar. "Ah ... well, yes. I found it in the bottom of a cardboard box in the guest closet."

Parker peeked over her reading glasses again. She frowned at Brody. "It's in some kind of code."

Brody said, "We noticed."

Parker shuffled the papers, raised her narrow face, and removed her glasses. "Did you two look at this?"

"Yes, we did," Linda's attorney said. "We made copies."

"Mr. Brody, what's your conclusion about the contents?" Parker asked.

"I believe Mr. Bartell was involved with the Mob. Unfortunately, we don't know how or to what extent."

Parker eyed Linda. "If you know anything, Doctor, I suggest you spill it." She shook her head. "These guys don't play nice."

Linda thought about the drugs stashed in her apartment—and how to get rid of them. "I've given you all the information I have."

Parker shoved the papers back into the envelope and stood. "Give my team time to analyze this. I'll get back with you. If the victim's assets are drug-related, the IRS will seize them. Dr. Harrison, the department won't be pressing charges against you for slapping Detective Jansen's face." She smiled. "He deserved it."

To ensure her safety, Linda now knew she had to give the drugs back to Teddy Mudici.

CHAPTER 5

DETECTIVE COOMBS

Detective Coombs asked Linda to meet him for lunch one Saturday. Entering a dark, crowded restaurant, she glanced around the area, trying to distinguish him from the other men. The place reminded her of a hideout for couples who rendezvoused in secret.

With Beaulin gone, she needed a friend. Coombs informed her about his department's every move, and his actions made her cautious, leery.

He stood and waved. She approached his table, and he helped her out of her coat. Linda removed a thin pair of gloves, cupped her hands together, and blew a warm breath into them.

Coombs pulled out the chair opposite his. "Have a seat and a drink. You'll warm up soon."

Linda laid her coat over the chair next to her. "I had to park four blocks away. Why are we meeting here?"

He took his seat. "If I'm seen socializing with you, I could lose my job."

"So why do it? It's not worth it."

"It is to me."

The waitress lit the candle and placed a menu in front of Linda. She ordered a Bloody Mary. Coombs requested the house amber.

She scooted her chair under the table. "I've tried contacting Beaulin's family, but I didn't find a phone number on the internet, nothing. I'm taking a trip down there next weekend."

"How do you know where they live?" he asked.

"His parents have lived in the same place all their lives. If I meet them in person—"

"I don't think you should go there."

"They haven't seen Beaulin in over twenty years. Talking to them in person is the best way to deal with this situation. His relatives should be his beneficiaries, not me. Maybe they don't have the funds to bury him."

"My department told them he had money, not how much," Coombs said.

"I still think they should have his assets," Linda said.

"I know you didn't have anything to do with Bartell's"— he lowered his voice—"demise, but I think you know something."

When the waitress delivered their drinks, Linda stirred hers with a piece of celery.

Coombs coughed into his napkin. "My department

doesn't believe your story about where you found those papers. No way would our team have missed them."

"I didn't know Beaulin was involved in drugs, and the papers were exactly where I said they were," Linda said.

Coombs cocked his head, looked at her askance, and held his mug in midair. "I never said he was involved in drugs."

Her response was a mistake, and she needed to recant it. "What other dealings could he have had with the Mob?"

"Many. So why assume drugs?" he asked.

She shrugged. "Just a guess."

When the waitress returned, Linda ordered a Caesar salad with blue cheese dressing. Coombs requested a turkey sandwich and fries.

The detective gawked at a woman sitting at the next table, who clearly had breast implants.

Linda recognized this trait. Coombs was a womanizer, a skirt-chaser, a woman's man. She didn't deem him so special anymore.

Linda shook her head and sighed. "I can hear your arteries clogging."

"I work it off." He gulped beer. "My department broke the code."

She gripped her napkin. "What did it say?"

Coombs glanced at the woman with the breast augmentations again. "I shouldn't tell you, but it's drug related."

Linda scooted to the edge of her chair, eager to hear the news. "So I was right. Can you give me a hint?" she asked. "What about the mobster's name and phone number?"

"Two top mob bosses' private cells. Bartell has millions of dollars in cocaine stashed somewhere. At least we know it's not at your place," he said.

Linda's knees involuntarily bounced up and down. She planted her feet flat on the floor to stop the motion. Sweat formed on her forehead, and she dabbed it away with a napkin. "The information I gave to the ADA had only one contact: Teddy Mudici."

"Bartell dealt mostly with the Mudici family. The other mobster's name was in code: Al Selva. Why are you trembling?"

"I'm still cold," she lied. "Do you think they'll be coming after me?"

"I don't want to frighten you, but if they think you know something—"

She reached for her drink with a shaky hand. "But I don't."

"Relax. I believe you." He changed the subject. "Did you go to any of Bartell's shows?"

"Yes," she said. "He sang like a professional, and I never saw him practice. We enjoyed the opera, the theater, dining out, museums, and shopping. A huge six feet two man has no problem finding his size in dresses and high heels in the Big Apple. He gave me a makeover once, and I got many compliments from coworkers."

"I noticed that you don't wear makeup. Not that you need it."

"Thanks for the compliment." She changed the subject. "Beaulin never told me where he lived. He gave me the impression he didn't have a permanent address."

"He didn't," Coombs said, then excused himself and left the table.

Linda's eyes had finally adjusted to the dark. Looking around the place, she wasn't impressed with the crowd. A middle-aged man with a bushy beard, wearing a bright red suit, entered the restaurant with a woman on each arm. When the waitress returned, she ordered another drink for Coombs and herself.

Moments later, Coombs returned and slid into his chair. His voice was soft, cajoling. "Linda, there's something special about you."

The hound was coming on to her as if she were a naive high school girl. Did he flirt with other women he met on the job? "Special? How?"

His right index finger ran up and down the handle of his mug. "I've never met a woman like you. You're beautiful, intelligent, a doctor."

Yuck. "There are lots of pretty, smart women out there. I don't know anything about you, and I'm not interested in a relationship."

He gave her the spiel about being a police officer for eight years—how he'd earned his master's in political science before transferring to homicide.

"Call me Rick," he added.

Linda speared her fork into her salad. "I prefer to remain formal, Detective. Do you like your job?"

He studied the waitress's rear end as she passed. "Sometimes it gets to me. The way people murder each other, parents killing their kids and vice versa. We live in a sick world."

Linda turned and glanced at the woman, trying to determine what interested him. She guessed it was a guy thing. "Thought about making a career change?"

He took a sip of beer. "I'm a cop. I don't know how to do anything else."

"At least my clients are alive," she said. "I operate on them and monitor their results. A few go to hospice."

Coombs took a giant bite of his sandwich, chewed, and swallowed hard. "Our jobs are just the opposite. I deal with them after they're dead. At least your patients have time to prepare."

They chatted for over two hours. He claimed he wasn't dating anyone, had never married, didn't have kids, and didn't want any.

Before Coombs walked around the table, Linda quickly slid into her coat.

"My car is parked outside. Let me give you a lift to yours," he said.

"Thanks, Detective Coombs, but I prefer to walk," she said. She silently scolded herself for having believed he might be different.

CHAPTER 6

THE MOBSTER

When Linda entered Teddy Mudici's restaurant that afternoon, a soft soprano voice echoed in the background.

The man at the host station wore a black tuxedo and looked like a retiree. "How many are in your party, madam?" he asked.

"One. I don't need a menu. I prefer to sit at the bar," Linda said.

"This way." He shuffled about ten feet from where they stood. "Sit wherever you please."

A banister separated the bar area from the dining room. The restaurant was crowded with Italians. Some spoke in their native language. Tables seated two to eight customers, who laughed and ate as if life were one hilarious journey.

An old man with an irritating hyena laugh and skin like leather occupied a table with three middle-aged women. His bald head shone like a mirror, and his most prominent feature was his arching forehead, which was furrowed in deep wrinkles. A white cake with blue trim sat before him. Crowned with candles, it blazed like a forest fire.

Linda needed a drink. She removed her coat and took a seat at the far end of the counter, away from a lone man, putting as much distance between them as possible.

The bartender looked about fiftyish and like a body-builder, with salt-and-pepper hair slicked back in a ponytail. "What can I get you?"

She slid onto a stool at the counter. "A glass of chardonnay please."

The customer at the bar moved in on her like a vulture over a fresh kill. He stood tall and was lean, and he was clean shaven with manicured nails. Every strand of his light brown hair looked glued in place.

"May I buy you a drink?" the intruder asked.

Linda glanced at him, then diverted her attention to the glass the bartender set before her. "No. I'm waiting for someone."

"If he doesn't show"—he waved a hand—"please, join me."

She didn't respond, just shunned him. After two glasses of wine, a burning sensation settled in her stomach. A buzz was setting in. She tipped the bartender a twenty. "I'm here to see Mr. Teddy Mudici."

The man mopped the counter with a white rag. "Who's asking?"

"Dr. Linda Harrison. He's expecting me," she said.

The bartender hailed a young waiter who was walking nearby and gave him Linda's name and request. The young man passed through the dining area and exited through a side door near the kitchen. A few minutes later, he returned and asked her to follow him. The kid led her past the laughing hyena, through the exit where he'd disappeared earlier, and made a right turn that ended at a closed door. The waiter didn't knock, just opened the door and stepped inside. Four men sat at a table, stuffing their faces. Other than on television, Linda had never seen men with napkins tucked inside their collars. The waiter announced her and left the room, closing the door behind him.

The Smith & Wesson .357 Magnum crammed into her purse with extra rounds gave her some comfort.

Had she been watching too many gangster movies?

Teddy Mudici looked exactly like recent photos Linda had seen in newspapers and on the internet. His weathered brown eyes caused her to stiffen. His thick gray hair matched his eyebrows. Not certain what to say, she stood there without uttering a word.

"Hello, Dr. Harrison." He spoke with a slight Italian accent. "I'm Teddy." He stood taller than she'd imagined, walked to her, and extended his hand.

Linda hesitated, then reluctantly gave his soft hand a weak shake with her sweaty palm.

"Thanks for meeting me." With a wave of his hand, he said, "This is my youngest brother, Ralph."

The brother occupied the chair on Teddy's right side. He was shorter and had smooth skin and a meek face that made him look more like Teddy's son. "Pleased to meet you, Doctor."

"My grandson, Billy," Teddy said, motioning again to his right.

Billy sat next to Ralph and looked about Linda's age. He tried to conceal the bulge under his jacket by pushing it farther under his arm. He flashed perfect white teeth and waved. "Ralph's my father."

Teddy introduced the third man. "And my grand-daughter's husband, Swift."

Swift, who sat on the other side of Teddy, didn't acknowledge her but shoved food into his mouth, his face stoic. Unlike Billy, he didn't try to hide the bump under his jacket.

Teddy put a hand on Linda's shoulder and nudged her forward. "Have a seat. How about lunch?"

Her voice trembled. "No, thanks."

He gestured to the chair next to Swift. "Please."

Linda didn't move, just gawked at the group.

Teddy took his seat. "I understand you need some merchandise moved. I did a background check on you. It's amazing what we can do with computers these days." Teddy chuckled. "I'm computer illiterate myself. What's your mother's name?"

"I'm not sure," Linda said. "You tell me."

"Your mother's name is Helena. Her maiden name is Mudici. Don't you think that's quite a coincidence?" he asked.

Linda's temper flared, but the tightness in her chest contained it. "What does my genealogy have to do with this meeting? Many people have the same last names. No relation."

"Helena was born right here." He tapped the table with his index finger. "In New York City."

Linda had researched Teddy, but he'd done a more thorough job on her.

"So? I came here to ask you to remove your garbage from my place, not to discuss my family tree."

"Straight to the point," the old man said, shoving a forkful of food into his mouth. He took his time chewing, then swallowed. "You're too uptight. Relax." He looked at Billy and waved his fork in the air. "What do you kids say nowadays? Chill."

"I'm being followed." She laid her coat over a nearby chair but remained standing. "Is it your people or the police?"

"Both. Seems neither party trusts you." Teddy laughed at his own joke.

She bit the inside of her cheek. "If you don't remove your junk from my apartment, I'm calling the DEA."

Teddy shook his head and wiggled a finger at her. "No. You don't want to do that." He stared into the distance.

"Maybe you already have. What if this is a set up? My guys show up at your place, get caught with illegal goods."

She gripped the strap of her purse, her fingernails digging into her palm. "I just want it out of my place, and I want it out now."

The old man shrugged. "Well, I guess we'll just have to move it, won't we?"

Linda retrieved two electronic keys from her pocket and held one between her thumb and index finger. "This is the building key. Use the side entrance. The blue one opens my apartment. The security system is off. Your stuff is stored under the closet floor in the guest bedroom. I left it open. I'll wait for my keys in the restaurant across the street from my place."

The old man shook his head. "Looks like you'll be staying for lunch after all. If the cops are there, I'd hate to imagine what would happen to you. Have a seat."

Swift wiped his mouth with his napkin. "It's too risky."

"Not as long as we have her." Teddy gave Linda a stern look. "My grandson-in-law doesn't trust anyone."

The skinny Swift stood, rising to a height of six feet four. He took the keys from her hand and studied them. "What if the police followed her here?"

"If the police are following her, they won't be watching her place," Teddy said.

Linda shivered. "I'm positive no one followed me."

"We'll have Jenny go in first," Swift said.

Teddy ran his fingers through his mop of gray hair.

"Take two of the guys. Make sure the cops are not following you. Billy, you'll stay outside in the van." He glanced at Linda's purse as if he had X-ray vision. "Why don't you sit? That gun you're carrying must be getting pretty heavy."

His words were electrifying, rattling every nerve in her body. How did he know?

Billy and Swift left, leaving her as Teddy and Ralph's hostage.

The old man patted the back of the chair next to his.

Linda held on to her purse, slid into the chair as if Teddy were a rattler, coiled and ready to strike.

The waiter opened the door and stepped inside. "Anything else, Mr. Mudici?"

"Yeah." He removed the napkin from his collar and tossed it onto the table. "We're done here. Bring this young lady a menu."

"No," she said. "I'm not hungry."

Teddy flashed a warm grin. "Do I frighten you? I'm as gentle as a lamb. Ralph and I are from the old country. We believe in family values."

Ralph didn't speak, just listened.

***

After three hours of sitting on the edge of her chair, Swift and Billy returned, confirming they had the merchandise. The psychopath, Swift, dropped her keys onto the table and took the chair next to her. Billy resumed sitting next to his father.

They had their drugs, and Linda felt safer, more confident. "Someone tore up my apartment."

Teddy cleared his throat. "Sometimes you have to pay for your mistakes—allowing strangers under your roof, I mean."

"Beaulin wasn't a stranger," she snapped at Teddy. The bitterness that rose in her throat died in fear. She softened her tone. "I mean, he was my friend."

"You promised to tell me about your parents," the old man said.

Linda said, "I made no such promise."

Teddy cocked his head. "You have a cousin about your age. You two are very different. Jenny's a party animal."

The old man seemed to be losing it. Linda gazed from Teddy to Ralph. Both stared at her, waiting for a response.

"What are you talking about? Helena never knew her relatives, and Adler's only brother lives in Germany."

Teddy lowered his voice as if talking to a child. "Helena was my daughter until I disowned her, and for good reason. I don't know if this is good news or bad, but I'm your grandfather."

Linda scooted her chair away from the table—the madness. "I don't believe you." The possibility made her stomach churn. "Without a DNA test, no way. You're—you're—"

"Say it. You can't insult us." He pulled a piece of paper

from his pocket, unfolded it, and tossed it to her. "Here's the DNA test."

She snatched up the paper and scanned the results. Her shoulders slumped. A legitimate laboratory had performed the test. "Where did you get my DNA?"

"We can get tested together if you don't trust this report," Teddy said.

Swift's face remained emotionless. Ralph smiled.

Billy laughed. "Welcome to the family, cousin."

At a loss for words, Linda stuck her shaking hands under the table. Teddy was right about two things—her adoptive mother's maiden name was Mudici, and she had grown up in the city. At this point, she didn't know what to believe. These people could be her relatives. Being ridiculed, humiliated, and teased was more than she could endure though. She rose from her seat. So did Swift. He blocked her move, stepping in front of the door.

She brushed a tendril of hair from her face. "Excuse me."

Swift didn't move, nor did he say a word.

The group continued their display of amusement, letting the news sink in. The Mudici family could have gotten her DNA from something in her apartment or followed her to a restaurant or the cafeteria at the hospital. If Teddy had this information, he must have known about her past. As a kid, Linda had dreamed of having relatives, but the idea of a mob family made her cringe.

She turned to Teddy, her upper lip trembling. "You have what you want. Let me go."

Billy said, "Come to Uncle Teddy's house tomorrow for Sunday dinner. Meet the rest of the family."

Linda tucked the paper into her purse. "No thanks."

Ralph spoke for the first time, and his eyes welled up. "What did Helena and her husband do to you? We would have come for you if we'd known."

She was adamant. "I don't want to talk about them, ever."

Ralph stood, walked to her side, and gently touched her shoulder. "I'm your mother's uncle."

Teddy slid a card across the table. Ralph picked it up, placed it in her hand, and gently closed her fingers. "We have dinner every Sunday, five o'clock sharp at Teddy's house. The rest of the family would love to meet you. Call or just show up at this address."

"I have a very prominent practice. I can't be seen associating with your family," Linda said.

"No one needs to know we're related," Teddy said.

"I must say farewell, Mr. Mudici and family." Linda plowed into Swift. As he stepped aside, she threw open the door and stormed out.

Teddy shouted at her back before the door closed, "Grandpa ... call me Grandpa."

***

Linda walked aimlessly along the street, head down, staring at the sidewalk, bumping into people. Her mind replayed the news of her possibly being the granddaughter of a mob king. Her life was surreal, never normal like other people. Why did all these bad things happen to her?

A man stumbled and barked, "Hey, lady, watch where you're going."

Keeping her head down, she said, "Sorry."

Two blocks from her apartment, a voice echoed behind her. "Dr. Harrison?"

She turned. "Do I know you?"

The shorter of two men repeated her name. "I'm Selva, Mr. Al Selva. I understand that Bartell was killed in your apartment." He didn't bother to introduce the good-looking muscle man by his side.

Her eyes narrowed. "Yes."

Selva had a well-trimmed beard and wore sunglasses and a hat. He was short and plump. Linda recognized him from newspaper pictures. He made Teddy Mudici look like Mary Poppins. A mile-long trail of unsolved murders followed his path. She shivered. What could he want from her?

Selva folded his arms. "Bartell had stuff that belonged to me."

Linda's blood turned into ice. "Stuff?"

"Packages in cardboard boxes." His voice became cold, demanding. "I want them back."

She imagined hollow eyes behind his sunglasses. Her legs weakened and threatened to buckle. Had she given the drugs to the wrong mobster?

"I don't … know what you're talking about."

She began to breathe hard. Teddy Mudici had never admitted the junk belonged to him, but he'd pretended it did. He claimed to be her grandfather, yet he'd put her life in grave danger. Her days were numbered. She knew it.

"The police searched your place. Did they find anything?" Selva asked.

Stay calm, she told herself. He doesn't know a thing. "No, nothing like that in my place. The police tore it apart, but only after someone else already had. I never saw Beaulin with anything except luggage. What's this stuff you're referring to?"

She'd never imagined the safest place to hold a private conversation was on the streets of New York City. Pedestrians traveled past them like a herd of sheep. No one seemed to notice them. "When I returned from Germany, I discovered Beaulin's body, and my place had been ransacked."

Selva pulled a cigar from his pocket and stuffed it into his mouth but didn't light it. "How long were the cops there?"

"I don't know. I moved into a hotel for a month, until contractors cleaned and renovated my place."

"Did you examine the body?" he asked.

His question brought back the gruesome picture of her friend's body, the stench, and the blood spatter on the walls. "Not really. I saw lots of bruising. He'd been tortured. Throat cut—carotid artery. I think that's what killed him, but only the medical examiner who performed the autopsy can confirm his actual cause of death."

"They forced him to talk," the muscle man said.

Maintaining her gullible composure, she asked, "Exactly what is in these packages?"

"That doesn't concern you," Selva said. "Did Bartell have a storage locker?"

She knew Selva sensed her fear like a bloodhound. "I don't know." She searched through her purse and offered him a chain with multiple keys. Her hand shook so badly they rattled. "These belonged to him."

Selva opened a hefty paw, and she dropped the keys into it.

He held the keys in his palm but didn't close his fist. "Did he get mail here?"

"No. He only stayed with me three, maybe four times a year."

He dropped the keys into the pocket of his pants. "What did the cops ask you to do?"

Stuck between two mobs, she regretted not going to the feds. With the drugs now gone, the detectives wouldn't believe her story. How could she explain not informing the authorities?

"They attached crime tape to my door and told me to leave," she said.

"Good day, Doctor. I'll get back in touch if I have more questions."

Linda watched their backs disappear into the crowd.

She fought back the tears as she mimicked, "Get back in touch."

Digging into her purse, frantically searching for Teddy Mudici's card, she rushed down the street in search of a payphone. She found one two blocks away, but a man was on it. After fourteen agonizing minutes of waiting, she dialed Teddy's number. He picked it up on the first ring.

She cried into the phone, "Al Selva just left me. He said the stuff you took belonged to him. How could you do this to me? You're a liar, a crook, and a drug-dealing murderer."

The old man chuckled. "Calm down. You ordered me to get it out of your place. I never said it was mine."

Linda yelled into the phone, "Give it back."

He remained calm, like a cat who'd eaten a canary and gotten away with it. "No way. Do you know the street value of that stuff?"

"If this guy doesn't find his junk, he's going to kill me."

"Why don't you meet me at my house for dinner tomorrow?" Teddy asked nonchalantly. "We'll discuss the situation and schedule that DNA test. Everything will be resolved, I promise."

People stared, but she continued her desperate rant. "My life's on the line. You're talking about food and a stupid test. I don't care if I'm related to you or not. You get this mess straightened out—or I'm going to the cops."

"Be at my house tomorrow at five." Teddy hung up.

***

Back in her apartment, Linda sat in front of the TV, staring at the black screen, when the doorbell rang. She checked her surveillance video and saw two men standing outside.

Linda opened her door. "May I help you?"

An African American man produced an FBI badge and said, "Dr. Harrison, I'm Agent Jackson, and this is Agent Truet. May we come in?" He looked fiftyish and had graying hair around his temples, as well as a belly that slightly hung over his slacks.

She became as stiff as a board. "Who?"

"We'd like to have a word with you please," Jackson still held his badge.

Linda opened the door wider and stepped aside.

Jackson entered, followed by Truet.

Truet looked to be right out of college—a brainy geek with acne and wire-rimmed glasses. He wore a black suit too large for him and a green tie with a yellow elephant embroidered on it, seemingly the handiwork of his grandmother.

"What do you want?" she asked.

"May we have a seat?" the younger man asked.

Linda sat on the loveseat, and the agents took seats on the sofa.

"We are interested in Mr. Beaulin Bartell and his ties with the Mudici and the Selva families. We know that you're Mr. Teddy Mudici's granddaughter. Do you know what he does for a living?"

"You mean being a mob boss?" she asked.

"Yes," Jackson said. "Our sources informed us that you're new in the family. How close are you to them?"

"Ah, I don't know them at all."

"We think Mr. Bartell was involved in drug deals with both families. Do you know anything about that?"

"Ah—no. No."

I should have turned the drugs over to the feds. I made a big mistake. Is there a way out now?

Linda's heart started palpitating, and her body shook.

"Dr. Harrison," Truet said. "Are you all right?"

"I don't feel well," she said.

"Shall we come back another time?" Jackson asked.

"No. I'll feel better in a minute," she said. "I don't know anything about the Mudicis, and Beaulin didn't visit me that often. He never discussed his business with me."

"How did you learn that Mr. Mudici was your grand-father?" Truet asked.

"He told me."

"Where did you first meet him?" Jackson asked.

"At his restaurant. I insisted on a DNA test."

"Do we frighten you?" Truet asked.

"I don't have the FBI knocking on my door every day." Linda stood.

"Innocent people cooperate with us. You got some-thing to hide?" Truet asked.

"No. I just don't have anything to tell you. Please leave."

"I'm leaving you my business card," Jackson said. "If you feel like talking, just call me."

CHAPTER 7

DARKEST SECRETS

The next day, against Linda's better judgment, she asked Coombs to meet her at the café across the street from her apartment building. She hadn't planned to associate with Coombs again, but after yesterday's events, she was about to pull out her hair. She couldn't tell him about the drugs, Selva, or her newfound family, but she needed someone to talk to—about anything.

When Coombs joined her, an hour late, Linda was sipping on her fourth beer—or was it the fifth?

He eyed an empty mug. "Happy hour?" he asked.

"No. Just thirsty," she said. Bad news caused her to drink more than usual, and she needed to stop it.

He took a seat. "Didn't think you liked beer."

She picked up her mug and took a sip. "I usually don't."

He frowned. "What's wrong?"

She shook her head. "Not a thing."

"You didn't ask me here for nothing."

They both sat in silence for a few moments. Coombs ordered his usual sandwich and a beer. He gawked at the waitress's chest while she jotted down his order, then turned and watched her rear end as she walked away. He checked out other women in the restaurant as he spoke. "Our detectives have been following you. So has the Mudici family."

The beer made her hot and anxious, but she continued drinking. "I know someone has been following me."

"My department said you met with Al Selva yesterday. Is that true?" His words echoed between them.

Linda hadn't planned to mention her recent visitor. "He said Beaulin had stuff that belonged to him. He's searching for it."

"He meant drugs?" Coombs asked.

After repeating Selva's conversation, she said, "Excuse me. I need to visit the little girls' room."

Her stomach churned as she rushed into the ladies' room, gripping both hands over her mouth. The stalls were full, so she threw up in a sink, and then she studied her reflection in the mirror. Her face was a clammy red; her eyes were puffy. When she swayed back into the restaurant, the crowd moved in waves.

Coombs had started on his lunch. "How many beers have you had?"

She cleared her throat. "I'm not counting so why should you?"

He summoned the waitress and asked her to bring Linda a chicken salad.

"How much do you know about my past?" she asked him.

Coombs picked up the salt shaker and sprinkled it liberally over his fries. "Your records are sealed. Like I said, we don't get court reports, just a summary from the cops who worked your case."

"A man raped and tortured me for days after my thirteenth birthday. I spent a year in a mental institution. I didn't want to be a teenager but a little girl again."

He picked up two fries and shoved them into his mouth. "I know. I'm sorry about what happened to you. You're a very determined woman. I praise you for your success."

"My past made me strong. I could deal with anything after that."

Other than her childhood psychiatrist, she'd never confided in anyone about her early life trauma. She gave Coombs the entire story, excluding the shocking, gruesome details of her rape. When she finished the part about her abduction, his eyes looked glossy, almost teary.

He reached across the table and touched her hand. "I don't need to know any more."

His warm touch comforted her, and she didn't shun him. "They said I stabbed my abductor sixty-seven times. During my stay in the hospital, my attending psychiatrist helped me with my studies. She pretended to be my friend until she started sexually abusing me."

Coombs slid to the edge of his chair, leaned in. "Did you report her?"

"She was my doctor, said she could make my life miserable and promised to get me into the university. She did teach me a lot about medicine, gave me books, weekend passes."

His eyes widened. "Passes to where?"

"Her house, mostly. She got me out of that place. The other girls were jealous. She dined with me at nice restaurants and took me to the movies. I had my own room, a color TV."

Coombs scooted back in his chair as if the moment had become too intense. "Did the other girls know?"

She looked into the distance. "They weren't sure until she propositioned another girl. I never saw her after that."

"Why didn't you turn her in to the authorities? Let the system deal with her?"

"I was a mental patient." Linda checked her watch. "When you have no one, you do whatever it takes in order to survive. That's what it's all about—self-preservation. I've been there, lived it. Most of the girls were older than me, and she stopped them from bullying me."

"You shouldn't have been put in that position."

"Life is not always fair," Linda said. "The board asked me if she'd abused me. I denied everything."

"Why? You were a minor. She threatened you."

"I didn't want to end up in the national news again. I'd had protection since I was a kid, but some agencies found ways around the barriers."

Coombs drained his mug and ordered another beer. "How old was she?"

"About forty." She could no longer hold back the tears. "I had a great childhood, didn't I? Citizens nationwide put money into a trust fund for me after they discovered my parents ordered my kidnapping and murder. I had enough funds to pay for my private hospital care, college, and then medical school."

"You received that much money?"

"If the authorities had checked out my finances, they would've found that I have much more money than Beaulin left me."

"That might have put a halt on everything, eliminated you as a suspect," he said.

"After the mental hospital, I went into foster care. The couple's son groped me, and I beat him with a metal pipe. He went into a coma—brain dead. His parents took him off life support, and the local authorities charged me with manslaughter. They threw me into juvenile hall until the age eighteen."

He slapped his palm on the table. "Hey, I remember that story from years back. You were that girl?"

Patrons stared at them, so they both lowered their voices.

Linda glanced at her watch again. "I got offers from prestigious colleges all over the States, but the parole board restricted me to the state of Louisiana. I never squandered money on cars, jewelry, or fine clothes. I invested my funds—had more than three million dollars when I finished medical school."

Coombs asked, "Did you ever see your parents again?"

Linda cleaned her face with a napkin, tension rushing through her like a tornado. She repeated the experience with her parents in Germany.

Linda glanced at her watch yet again. "I don't know who I am. I had planned to start searching for my birth parents when I returned, but then I found Beaulin's body, and my place became a crime scene."

"Why do you keep looking at your watch?" Coombs asked.

Linda combed fingers of both hands through her hair, trying to determine how to lose whoever was tailing her. Coombs offered to drive her to wherever she was going, but she declined.

After taking four different taxies, Linda got off in the middle of a street at a stoplight. She entered a public ladies' room, removed her skirt, and slid into a pair of stretch pants. She covered her hair with a scarf and turned her coat inside out. There was no way the cops could identify her now, among thousands of commuters.

***

Teddy Mudici's plush home stretched across half a block in the suburbs. When Linda rang the bell at the gate, she was forty minutes late. A man as large as a gorilla, wearing a suit, came outside and greeted her.

"I'm Dr. Linda Harrison. Mr. Teddy Mudici invited me to dinner," she said.

The man smiled and stuck out a big paw. "Glad to meet you. Don't call him mister. He's your grandpa." The big ape led her into the house and yelled, "Teddy, your granddaughter's here."

The place looked better than a palace. Linda's feet sank into thick blue carpet as Teddy and Ralph greeted her in a living room almost the size of her apartment, grinning like a couple of clowns.

Ralph beamed. "We're glad you could make it. Come in and meet the rest of the family."

A short, chubby woman rushed in behind them, gave Linda a tight squeeze, and planted sloppy kisses on both cheeks. "My grandbaby. I'm Isabella." She held Linda back at arm's length, looked her over, and bear-hugged her again. "Welcome. You're beautiful. Have you been crying?"

Linda sniffed. "Had a bad day."

Another woman hugged Linda. "I'm Christina, your Uncle Ralph's wife. Glad you could make it."

Ralph said, "You're going to love our food—old Italian recipes."

Linda didn't like pasta, but she simply said, "Thanks for inviting me."

Teddy wasn't the hugging type. "You smell like a brewery. What made you change your mind?"

As if he didn't know. "Selva," Linda said.

Teddy and Ralph locked eyes.

Teddy said adamantly, "We don't discuss business during dinner."

Linda's words rushed out in a panic. "But I'm in trouble. Selva—"

Teddy put a finger to his lips. "I don't want to hear it now. Let's get acquainted."

She followed the group into a large dining area, where Isabella introduced her to everyone. Billy and Swift were there with their wives. Both couples had a boy and a girl who were about middle-school aged.

Dishes of meat, vegetables, pasta, and bread lined the center of a long mahogany dining room table. Beautiful oil paintings of fruits and vegetables covered the walls. A china cabinet stood behind the tables, along with a matching wine cooler and another cabinet filled with crystal glasses. A large window overlooked an inactive water fountain in the backyard.

Isabella ushered Linda into a chair next to Jenny. The name stuck in her mind because she'd heard it at Teddy's restaurant. Jenny's eyes were narrow, glassy, and distant. Seated, she looked about five feet ten and a hundred and twenty pounds. Her breast implants, which were out of proportion with the rest of her body, must have been a size D.

Thinking of food made Linda sick. "The table looks great, but I can't stay."

Isabella joyfully passed dishes around to Linda. "You're too skinny. We need to fatten you up."

The pressure in Linda's head grew by the second, and she had to purge it. Jumping to her feet, she said, "Mr. Mudici—"

"It's Grandpa. Have respect for your elder," he shouted.

Linda's fiery voice erupted. "I'm not calling you Grandpa. I don't know who you are."

The old man said, "I called in today and scheduled a DNA test for noon tomorrow near your office."

"I don't care what the DNA results say," she said. "And today is Sunday. How did you schedule a test?"

"Have a seat," the old man said. "Whatever is bugging you can't be that important."

Linda held onto the back of her chair. "If you don't leave this table, I'll discuss it here and now."

Teddy tossed his napkin onto the table and stood, his mouth stuffed with food. "This had better be important." He led her into an office that contained a desk and seven chairs, closed the door, and threw his hands into the air. "Now what's the rush, huh?"

Linda shouted, "Al Selva. I told you about his visit. The merchandise you took belongs to him."

"Keep your voice down," he said.

She stood on the verge of death, or worse. "You took stuff that belongs to Selva, and now he's looking for it."

The old man shrugged. "I'll take care of it."

She yelled louder, "Are you going to tell Selva you have it?"

"I said keep your voice down," he warned.

She could accept death, but not torture. She'd been there. Standing almost nose to nose with Teddy, she shouted, "Return it."

Teddy grabbed Linda's shoulders with both hands and shook her. "You asked me to move it."

"Because I thought it was yours." Linda thumbed her chest. "I'm the one he's coming after, not you."

"Selva thinks we took the stuff. You're family. You have our protection. Eat something and sober up." Teddy threw open the door. "My dinner is getting cold. We'll finish this conversation later."

She followed Teddy back to the table, head down like a whipped dog. Isabella chuckled and passed food Linda's way. Linda slouched in her chair as an agonizing end flashed through her mind.

Isabella said, "How about some wine?"

"She doesn't need any," Teddy barked. "Get her a cup of coffee, Jenny."

Jenny giggled as she stood. "Looks like someone can't hold her liquor."

Other than having brown eyes, Linda didn't resemble any of the Mudicis. Her small, straight, reconstructed nose did not resemble the family's prominent hawk nose. She also didn't have a dimpled chin like Teddy and Ralph. Her old jutting chin had been replaced with a cute and perfectly round one. She'd probably inherited her petite figure from her biological mother. She didn't share Jenny's big-boned look.

Linda's mind drifted back to Selva. "I usually don't eat Italian food."

Isabella gasped, "What."

"Not only will you love Italian dishes, we'll teach you how to make them," Christina bragged. "Have you been to Italy?"

Linda stammered. "Ah … no."

Isabella said, "You've been to Germany but not Italy?"

How did they know about her trip to Germany? "Father—Adler taught me German. I don't think Helena spoke Italian."

Isabella eyed her husband. Her voice grew low and deep. "Helena ever talk about us?"

Linda wanted to end the conversation. "Mother— Helena—said she grew up in foster care—no known relatives."

Jenny placed a cup of coffee on the table next to Linda, took a seat, and nibbled her food like a rabbit.

Everyone accepted her except Swift—the sociopath. He rarely acknowledged her or anyone else.

All through dinner, Linda kept thinking, Selva is going to kill me.

Isabella frowned and squinted. "Are you always so sad, darling?"

"Only when my days are numbered," Linda snapped.

Teddy washed his food down with a gulp of wine. "Hey. Don't speak to your grandmother like that. Who raised you to behave like a moron?"

Like a child, Linda said, "I'm sorry, alleged Grandma."

"Tomorrow you'll know for sure," Teddy said.

Linda's mind surged like a swollen river. Nothing could cheer her up or make her forget her problem. She needed either Teddy's or the police's protection from Selva. Waving her coffee cup in the air, Linda interrupted the family conversation, stating that she had to work the next day.

The old man stood. "Linda, come to my office. We need to talk."

Linda wanted to discuss her problem privately with Teddy, but Ralph, Billy, and Swift came along. Teddy patted her on the back as she walked through his office door. After a short conversation, he smiled and reassured her that Selva wouldn't contact her again. Teddy advised Linda to go home, get a good night's rest, and concentrate on her morning patients.

**

Linda lied in bed, sipping hot tea. The evening news was broadcasting a special report: "*An unknown assailant gunned down well-known mob boss, Al Selva, and one of his bodyguards as they exited their vehicle tonight.*" Pictures of both victims aired on the news. It was Selva and the man who'd stopped her on the street after her first meeting with Teddy. "*If anyone recognizes this man, call …*"

The sketch of the perpetrator flashed on the screen. He had a narrow face with an average nose and thin lips. Linda gasped, "Swift." He wore a hat, earrings, and a fake mustache.

She spilled her tea, jumped off the bed, and paced around her apartment. The old man had promised to take care of Selva, but she'd never suspected a hit. Would she now be in his debt forever? She was a doctor. What could he possibly want from her?

***

DNA results confirmed that Teddy and Isabella Mudici were Linda's grandparents.

Grandma invited her to dinner until she ran out of excuses. The old lady's sweetness and concern for her wellbeing were creating a soft spot in Linda's heart. Grandma worried because Linda spent long hours working with practically no social life.

Never in her life had anyone hugged and kissed her as Grandma did. Linda cherished her warmth, love, and closeness, and she welcomed the attention. Loneliness and a desire to belong began to tear her apart inside. Just because they are mobsters didn't mean I have to be one too, she thought. Linda promised Grandma she would have dinner the next Sunday with the family.

After all, what could it hurt?

***

Grandma planted sloppy kisses on Linda's face at the front door that Sunday. "Welcome. We're so glad you came." She led Linda into the dining room and seated her two chairs down from Grandpa, who headed the table. He was the only one wearing a suit.

Grandma occupied the opposite end. Swift and Billy attended with their wives but not their kids.

Linda greeted everyone. "Thanks for inviting me."

Jenny's eyes were red and distant, and her pupils were dilated. She didn't make eye contact but said, "We knew you couldn't keep away from us."

"The table looks marvelous, Grandma. I can't believe you don't have a maid or at least a cook."

"We don't want strangers in our house, dear." Grandma passed a dish to Christina, who sat next to her. "I had part-time help once. She worked here every Saturday for extra money."

Linda placed a napkin in her lap. "What happened to her?"

Grandma shook her head. "She's dead. Committed suicide over a man who's not worth the dirt under my shoes. Nice girl. I'll tell you about her later."

Christina took a heaping portion from a dish of meat and passed the platter to Ralph. "Why don't you have a boyfriend?" she asked imprudently.

Linda poured a glass of wine. "Haven't found the right man."

"What about Coombs?" her aunt asked.

"He's just an acquaintance. It's been a month since Beaulin's murder," Linda said. "Coombs said they've cleared me as a suspect, but I still want to know what's going on with the cases. Besides, he's just an acquaintance."

"Keep it that way," grandpa warned.

After dinner, Swift and his wife left. The remainder of the family moved into the living room for tea or coffee.

Linda sat on the sofa next to Billy and his wife. "Who are my real parents?" she asked.

Grandpa's eyebrows went up in question. "Did Helena say she wasn't your mother?"

"No, but I know," Linda said.

Grandpa occupied another sofa with Grandma and Jenny. His voice carried a hint of rage. "Helena was once close to our son, Tony, and his wife. When they died in a car accident, Helena claimed legal guardianship of you. Shortly afterward, I kicked her out of the family. She left, taking you with her. She loved you."

Linda held her coffee cup in a saucer over her lap. "Strange thing is, I don't remember her love."

Grandma walked to a cherry wood cabinet, opened a door, and pulled out a large photo album. "We're so sorry about what they did to you. Come, sit next to me."

Jenny had cuddled up next to Grandma and seemed irritated that she had to move. Linda took her cousin's place on the sofa next to Grandma.

The old woman placed an album in Linda's lap. "These

were your parents. They made a lovely couple, didn't they? This is your mother, Maria, and your father, Tony, holding you at ten months old."

"Maria and Tony," Linda repeated the names. "How old was I when Helena took custody of me?"

"Fourteen months," Grandma said.

Linda removed both photos from the album and held them in her hands. Her fingers caressed the glossy surface of the pictures. How would her life have turned out if her parents had lived? Would she have been more like Jenny, or would she still have been driven to become a doctor? "May I have copies?"

"Yes, we've already made duplicate photos for you to keep," Grandma said, turning a page. "There you are on your first birthday."

Linda began to relax and smiled. "Cute, wasn't I?"

Jenny sat on the arm of the sofa next to Linda and leaned over her shoulder, forcing her closer to Grandma. She dropped a large envelope into Linda's lap. "I had these made today."

Linda didn't open the envelope. "Thank you, Jenny. You've all been so nice to me." She glanced around the room. "I don't know what to say."

Grandma put an arm around Linda's shoulder. "Just get to know us, dear. Don't be too judgmental."

"Do I have siblings?" Linda asked.

"No. Maria was three months pregnant when the accident occurred."

Linda's voice lowered. "Why didn't you all come for me, Grandma?"

"We heard about a young girl whose parents had paid someone to kill her, but we didn't know it was you. Helena had married, changed your last name."

"Why did Grandpa kick Helena out of the family?"

Grandma placed a hand on her throat. "Well—"

Grandpa intervened. "We don't care to talk about that."

Linda dropped the subject and concentrated on her parents' pictures. Aunt Christina sat at the piano, thumbing through music books. Although the Mudicis had inducted her into the family, Grandpa still frightened her.

***

Over time, Linda began spending more of her Sundays at the Mudicis' home. For the first time in her life, she had a loving family to call her own. She now yearned for their presence in her life. Often, she wanted to ask Grandma why she'd stayed with a man like Grandpa. She must have known what he did for a living, but she looked the other way and remained faithful to her husband. Linda came to love Grandma, Uncle Ralph, and Billy. The rest of the family she could live without, but they came as part of the package.

CHAPTER 8

HILL PEOPLE

Linda flew into Lexington, Kentucky, rented a Dodge Ram 1500, drove south on Interstate 75 to Richmond, and took Highway 52 to Lance. When she drove through the town, a sign read: "LANCE, POPULATION 20." Not a traffic light, general store, or post office in sight. The only business alongside the highway was an old combination service station, garage, and deli.

She loved the countryside, the open space, the freedom. That was the only thing she missed about growing up in the South.

As Linda drove along the blacktop roads, her mind drifted to Beaulin. At age fourteen, his relatives had disowned him, kicked him out of their family, and threatened to kill him if he returned. She could relate to him, because her parents hadn't wanted her either. Maybe that was why she cared so much about Beaulin and had always been eager for his visits to New York.

Directions to the Bernard homestead cost her two pieces of greasy chicken and a drink from the deli, with a strict warning not to go there if it concerned William Joseph Bernard, a.k.a. Beaulin Bartell. Linda ignored the warning, wrote down the directions, and headed northeast past Lance and through provincial hilly terrain before making a right turn onto a country road.

She drove six miles and made another right turn onto a narrow dirt path covered with a thin layer of snow and patches of ice. A yellow road sign read: "DEAD END." The farther she traveled, the sparser the houses became.

After passing a few ramshackle homes, she spotted a mobile home sitting next to a modern two-story structure. She drove ten more minutes before seeing another house. Cows dotted pastures on both sides of the road. Around a curve, two wild turkeys startled her as they took flight over her vehicle.

Four abandoned vehicles covered with dust were parked at the end of the road and near them, about two feet off the ground, stood two unpainted homes with tin roofs. Three outbuildings could be seen near the backs of the homes, and they were in the same condition as the main structures, only smaller. Linda hadn't seen an outhouse since her childhood, but the one between the homes captured her eyes.

Except for the new Ford 250 pickup truck parked in the yard of the far house, Linda felt she had stepped back in time. A huge woodpile was stacked on the south side of the property. Five dogs tied to separate nearby trees howled, making the place sound like a dog pound when an emergency vehicle would pass. Two pit bulls ran out from under one house, lips curled back in snarls, exposing teeth as saliva dripped from their jowls. Remaining in her vehicle, Linda blew the horn.

A tall, lean man about thirty, with a scraggly beard, came out of the closest house. A cold breeze fanned his thick brown hair. He wore blue jeans, high-top boots, and a brown Carhartt jacket. He tied ropes around the dogs' neck and secured them to the front porch.

Linda had come on a mission. She wanted Beaulin's family to have his estate, and it looked like they could use it. Maybe his estranged family had learned to accept his sexual preference and no longer hated him—she hoped. She stepped out of her truck, stopped next to a small woodpile, and extended her hand. "I'm Dr. Linda Harrison, a friend of William Joseph Bernard."

The man held a stick in his right hand and refused to shake hers. He spat tobacco on the ground near her feet, squinted, and tilted his head. Red-veined eyes scrutinized her from head to feet, and he reeked of marijuana. His deep voice vibrated. "You one of them freaks?"

She gritted her teeth. "Freaks? You mean homosexuals. No, I'm not."

He wiped his mouth with the back of his hand and leaned on the stick, as if he needed it for support. "Then how did you come to know Billy Joe?"

Her stomach knotted in apprehension as she sucked in a deep breath. "I saw four men beating him in an alley from my hotel window during a medical conference. I called the police and went to his aid."

He snorted, and his jaw hardened. "They shoulda kilt him."

A lump filled Linda's throat. "Why? I found him a rather pleasant person."

"What kind of doctor are you?" he asked.

A gust of wind sent a pile of leaves into a whirl. "A surgical oncologist," she said.

He coughed up mucus and spat it on the ground. "Oncolist? What's that?"

She noticed someone peeking through a curtain from the other house. "I treat cancer patients. Anyway, after Billy Joe's murder, your family refused his body. I'm here to speak with his parents."

"I hate to admit it, but Billy Joe was my older brother. My folks'll tell you the same thing. We don't want his name mentioned here, ever. Everyone in the county knew about his evildoing except us. Folks were laughing behind our backs because of him."

"But you must be concerned about his murder and want to find out who killed him. He left me his estate, but I'd like his family to have it. Certainly you'd want his things."

"Ma. Pa," he shouted over his shoulders. "Get out here. There's some nosy female doctor poking around. Wants to talk to y'all about Billy Joe."

An elderly couple stepped onto a rickety porch, and Linda noticed that the boards bowed under their weight. She walked toward them.

"You knew Billy Joe?" the toothless woman asked. She wore glasses and a faded, dirty dress.

The father wore coveralls, probably purchased from Sears. He exposed a few tobacco-stained teeth. "We ain't seen Billy Joe in years. Glad someone kilt him. Should've happened sooner."

Linda had expected them to be concerned, caring. "Billy Joe left everything to me. Said his family hated him, but I want you all to have his personal things and his estate."

"Estate." When the old man laughed, brown spit dribbled down the side of his mouth. "Why, you act like he was a Rockefeller."

"We don't want anything from that fairy. Now git— and don't ever come back here," the old woman said.

"But he has money," Linda said.

Beaulin's brother laughed. "Probably enough to buy a box of see-gars."

"But he's your son." She turned to Beaulin's brother. "Your brother. Nothing can change that. He couldn't help the way he was born."

As the tension mounted, the warning the service station worker had given her bounced around in Linda's head. Only he and Coombs knew her whereabouts.

"Get away from here," the old woman yelled. "If you come back, you'll be sorry."

Beaulin's brother then spat tobacco on a piece of near-by wood, and it spattered on Linda's shoes and the legs of her pantsuit. "You heard her. Now git, or I'll sic the dogs on you." He turned toward the growling beasts.

Hastening to her vehicle, she jumped inside, slammed her door, and locked it. The dogs began howling again. She backed up, turned around, and drove off. The annoying animals followed her quite a distance before retreating.

Now she understood why Beaulin had severed all ties with his family.

CHAPTER 9

HIT AT THE BLUE PARROT LOUNGE

Coombs and LaFee entered the Blue Parrot Lounge, a gentleman's club catering to the elite. Young, exotic strippers brought in extravagant customers, and money flowed like water. Coombs had visited the place a few times as a guest, but he couldn't afford it on his budget.

Practically empty—absent of pole dancers, customers, flashing lights, and seductive music—the place reminded him of a movie theater after a Tuesday matinee.

A cop met Coombs and LaFee just inside the door. "Detectives, we've questioned the manager. He has been uncooperative. Claims that he doesn't know any of the customers who were here tonight, or any other night for that matter. The victim's this way. Gunshot to the head."

Coombs scanned the club. "They must have regulars."

"We have nothing on this place or the manager," the officer said. "From the what we gathered from a waitress,

122 | EDMANTHA HALL

the perpetrator fits the same description of the man who gunned down Selva and his bodyguard."

Coombs glanced at a dancer, noting how attractive she was. "Where's the witness?"

"She couldn't tell us much. Paramedics took her to the hospital. The bullet exited the victim's head and nicked her shoulder. Nothing serious," the cop said. "You should be able to question her."

"We have an idea who the shooter was," Coombs said. "Teddy Mudici's grandson, Swift. He's careful, doesn't leave evidence, and always comes up with an alibi. Disguises himself so well his own mother wouldn't recognize him."

LaFee stopped at a nearby table and spoke with the manager.

Coombs donned gloves and stepped under the crime scene tape. A male victim lay sprawled on his stomach, head twisted to one side, with one arm displayed at his side and the other folded under his body. A dark pool of blood soaked the carpet around his head.

Coombs couldn't check the victim's wallet without disturbing the crime scene, so he left the area and joined LaFee. "Got anything?"

"This is the manager, Mr. Bradley," LaFee said. "He was closed up in his office when the incident occurred. Customers fled this place as if it were ablaze. So did most of the workforce. Only three employees stayed."

The casually dressed man wiped sweat from his face

with a handkerchief. He was about ten years Coombs's senior with a thin mustache, receding brown hair, and a shiny forehead.

"Mr. Bradley," Coombs said, "the officer said you refused to give him information concerning your customers."

"I've told the police everything I know," the manager barked.

"We'll contact the DA, get a subpoena, shut this place down, and spend two weeks going through your credit card records," LaFee threatened.

"Why doesn't this club have surveillance?" Coombs asked.

The manager stood with the assistance of a handcrafted walking cane and limped toward a young girl who looked about sixteen. "We don't have cameras because patrons don't want them. This is Genie. She was on stage during the shooting."

The young woman wore a flashy silver thong and a matching top that barely covered her breasts. She looked gorgeous, well built. Red, puffy eyes indicated that she'd been crying. "The victim was Robert," she said.

As the interrogation continued, Coombs thought about how he could give the girl his phone number without his partner knowing. He asked, "What's the victim's last name, Genie?"

The girl sniffed. "I don't know. He tipped well."

"How old are you, Genie?" LaFee asked.

Genie donned a robe. "Nineteen."

"Can I see an ID?" LaFee asked.

"Sure. This way." The girl led LaFee toward the back.

Coombs grilled the manager. "Why did you let your employees and customers leave?"

"I couldn't hold them here." Other than irritation, Bradley showed no emotion.

"What about the victim? According to Genie, he was a regular."

Bradley leaned on his cane. "He may have been here a few times."

"I don't like deflection. Was he a regular or not? That's a direct question. If you don't cooperate with us, we're charging you with obstruction."

"Yes, he was a regular, but I never knew his name, just his face. I'm not on a first-name basis with the customers."

A man sat on a barstool facing them with his back pressed against the counter, and a woman occupied a nearby table, her face buried in her palms.

"Are those your other employees?" Coombs asked.

"Yes." Bradley limped to the bar. "This is Jack, one of my bartenders."

"Hello, Jack, I'm Detective Coombs. What did you see?"

Jack sat up straight. "All I can tell you is the shooter was a tall, thin man with a beard. Couldn't see his face. When I heard gunshots, I dropped behind the bar."

"What about his clothes? Did you see what he was wearing?" Coombs asked.

Jack shrugged. "Long, dark coat and dark pants."

Coombs glanced at the back of the room, looking for Genie. "You see the gun?"

Jack frowned as if he'd been insulted. "You kidding?"

Coombs sighed. "Did you see which direction he came from?"

The bartender shook his head.

Coombs turned his attention back to the manager. "Look, mister. We need customers' names, credit card receipts. I need to talk to every employee who worked here tonight. As a matter of fact, you make some calls, get them all back here now."

LaFee returned. "I didn't get much. Strobe lights blinded Genie during her act. The man was tall and skinny with a beard. Sound familiar?"

"Seems that it was too dark for everyone except the shooter." Coombs shook his head. "He had no trouble finding his target."

Next, Coombs interviewed a Hispanic woman who spoke very little English—a janitor who'd heard a loud bang while cleaning the ladies' room.

Genie returned from the back. "Can I go? I have a class early in the morning."

"Just one more question," Coombs said. "Do you know other regulars who visit this lounge?"

Genie laid her purse on a table and slid into her coat. "Sure, almost always the same crowd. I know some by their first names—if those are their real names. Strippers have stage names, and customers give false names too. Some are politicians, judges, wealthy men who don't want anyone to know they frequent this place."

Gee, she is gorgeous, Coombs thought. "How do you know their backgrounds?"

"Hello?" The young woman removed her heels and stepped into a pair of jogging shoes. "I watch the news, read the newspapers. I need to go." She glanced at her boss as he approached them. "I don't want to lose this job. I make thousands here on the weekends."

Coombs pulled a business card from his pocket, but LaFee intervened, giving Genie hers instead.

"We'll talk tomorrow, at the precinct. Just us girls," his partner said.

Two women from CSU appeared with equipment in hand. They took photos, collected evidence, and turned the body over. The older of the two retrieved the man's wallet, checked out its contents, and passed it to Coombs.

He removed the man's ID. "Mr. Robert Angiletti—Selva's brother-in-law. Let's see what else we've got here. Credit cards, family photos … a wife and two teenagers."

"Let's pay the widow a visit," LaFee said.

CHAPTER 10

BLIND DATES

Linda heard her phone ring over the whirring of the blender. She turned the machine off. "Hello, Grandma," she said.

"I'd like you to meet some doctors we know."

Linda rolled her eyes. "I said no, and I meant it."

"Okay," Grandma said. "How about you just meet four? If you don't like them, we won't bother you again."

Linda licked the strawberry juice from her fingers. "I won't like them."

"Amuse an old lady. It's not as if you have a life. What do you do with your leisure time? Read, write, watch TV, and eat alone."

"Grandma, I'm satisfied with my life."

Her voice became cajoling. "Please, Linda."

Linda gave in, because she felt she owed the family for saving her life, and she didn't want to disappoint Grandma. "Only for you."

"You have a date tonight with Dr. Chris Wells."

"I can't go tonight, Grandma."

"You have nothing else to do. Be at Teddy's restaurant at six. Bye." She hung up.

Great. Now Grandma was trying to get her hitched to one of her mobster friends.

Linda sat on the sofa, drinking her shake and watching the news. For the second time that day, she heard about the murder of Selva's brother-in-law, and then a composite sketch of the killer hit the screen.

Swift.

He was killing people, and she didn't know what to do about it. Wearing rubber gloves, she typed an anonymous letter on her computer, and mailed it to the police department.

***

Linda wore a black business suit and a high-neck pink blouse, not wanting to give the guy the wrong idea. As she sat, she checked the closing stock prices for the day and observed patrons around her.

Finally, she caught sight of Grandpa. He was escorting a six feet four, clean shaved, brown-haired man to her table. His navy-blue suit a striped, two-tone blue tie gave him the appearance of elegance. His shirt sparkled so white it almost glowed. Swaggering as if he owned the place, he strolled at her grandfather's side.

They were twenty minutes late.

Linda's eyes bulged as she realized that the man was the jerk who had tried to pick her up the first time she'd visited Grandpa's restaurant. The man wasn't handsome but carried himself as if he were a prince.

Grandpa made a brief introduction and left in haste.

Dr. Wells took Linda's right hand in his and gently kissed it. "Dr. Harrison, I'm sorry for being late, but I didn't trust the valet with my car. Can you imagine an eighteen-year-old behind the wheel of a Ferrari?" He chuckled and perched himself in the chair across from her. "I insisted on someone older."

"I'm off duty. Call me Linda."

His piercing eyes ogled her body. "I didn't spend years in medical school to be called Chris. You are lovely. I expected someone homely."

Linda pondered his word. "Homely?"

He smirked. "Yeah, blind dates usually are. I guess that's why they're called blind." He concentrated on her face. "Did I say something wrong?"

"If you can't figure it out, I can't tell you. How do you know my grandmother?"

As he talked, his eyes continued roaming her body. "Actually, your uncle contacted me. He used to bring his daughter to my practice."

He's lying. He's only slightly older than Jenny. Why would he lie?

"I'm a pediatrician. And you?"

He clearly didn't recognize her. "Surgical oncologist."

Their server arrived with a wine menu.

Linda began, "I'll have a glass of—"

"Two glasses of Ferrari Perle Rose please."

"I prefer a chardonnay," she said to the server.

The confused waiter tugged at his tie and trotted off.

"Have you traveled much?" he asked. "I've been to just about every country in the world. Some I didn't know existed until I needed a visa."

"I've only been to the Americas and Germany."

He turned up his nose and shook his head as if she were a disappointment. "I have my own practice. How about you?"

"I work at Presbyterian Hospital Clinic," she said.

"Presbyterian Hospital chooses only the best doctors. You must be proud."

Linda opened her menu. "I'd feel equally proud if I worked at another hospital."

Wells never looked at his menu. "I love kids but hate their mothers. They ask the dumbest questions. What can I do but keep smiling and deal with them?"

"When kids are sick, I'm certain their parents are concerned."

"I had one mother bring in her six-month-old daughter because she was bald." He laughed. "Can you believe that?"

He's so full of himself.

Their server returned and poured their wine. "Would you like additional time?"

Linda glanced at Dr. Wells, then back at her menu. "Have you decided what you're ordering?"

"Yes, we'll both have the smoked duck breast," he said.

He was really pushing her buttons. "I'm having the salmon," she said to the waiter.

"I dine here often. You're going to love the duck," Dr. Wells insisted.

The waiter logged their order on an electronic tablet. "Two duck breasts. What kind of soup and salad?"

"Sorry, I don't care for soup or salad," Linda said tersely. "I ordered salmon."

Wells chuckled. "Oh, come on. Eat with me. I'd like the garden salad with blue cheese dressing and the split pea soup. She'll have the same. I'm footing the bill."

The server looked from Linda to Wells. "Two of the same?"

Linda repeated, "I'll have the salmon. No soup or salad. Separate checks please."

The server punched keys on his electronic menu as he walked away.

Wells's face turned as red as a lobster. "Why did you embarrass me like that?"

Linda took a sip of wine. "Like what?"

He poked a thumb at his chest. "I ordered for us. Why did you change it?"

Linda held her breath. Is this guy for real? "I'm not a child. I order my own food, thank you."

His brows furrowed. "I always order for my dates."

Linda removed her napkin from the table, unfolded it, and dropped it into her lap. "Maybe that's why you're still going on blind dates."

"I was doing you a favor," he huffed, his eyes savage. "You don't talk to me this way."

Linda stood and pushed her chair under the table, retrieving her glass of wine. "This isn't working. I think we should go our separate ways."

A wave of relief swept through Linda when she walked away from the table. It was times like this that made her think of Dr. Eber Bauer. He seemed so kind and gentle. She wondered if she'd ever meet him again.

As she sipped her drink at the bar, a stranger approached her.

"Hello," the man said. "I saw you leave your gentleman friend. May I join you?"

"Sure, why not?"

Usually she'd say no or get lost.

"A blind date?" the man asked.

"My grandmother insisted," Linda replied.

"You don't look like you need help finding dates. I'm Drake." He extended his hand.

She smiled. "Hello, I'm Linda."

"He likes to be in control, doesn't he? Bet he drives a sports car," Drake said.

Linda's temper rose. "Are you spying on me for Grandpa?"

"Of course not. I don't know your grandpa," he said.

She blurted out, "Teddy Mudici."

He stood. "Nice meeting you, Linda. Have a good night."

Linda held her chin high, grinning. Grandpa had influence. All she had to say was "Teddy Mudici," and everyone shivered.

***

Linda promised Grandma she'd go on just one more blind date. This time, she sat in a lounge chair in the restaurant's lobby. Her date would recognize her by the color of her clothes, and she would be reading a book.

Servers milled around the restaurant in black suits, white shirts, and black ties.

"Dr. Linda Harrison?" A British accent alerted her.

"Yes." She stood face-to-face with a man dressed in faded jeans and tattered loafers. He looked more like a homeless person than a doctor.

"Dr. Ian Worthing. Sorry I'm late." The stocky British man with long, frizzy red hair tied back in a ponytail stuck out his large paw and gave her hand a firm grip, pumping it twice.

She closed the book and placed it in her purse, appalled at the sight of the man before her. "Nice to meet you, Ian. I'm Linda."

His face was nearly the color of his hair. "I had a difficult time finding this place. Had to park a few blocks away and hustle."

The host approached Ian. "May I help you with something, sir?"

He flashed teeth as yellow as corn. "A table for two."

The host's eyes widened, and he shook his head. "I'm sorry, sir, but we have a strict dress code here."

Linda said, "Thanks. We'll try elsewhere."

The host said, "Take a right turn outside the door. There are a few places down the street."

Linda walked out behind Ian, her coat thrown across her arm. "Didn't you know about the dress code?"

He pulled a pair of gloves from his pocket and slipped them on. "Sorry. I wasn't expecting such a fancy place."

She said, "If you don't mind pizza or subs—"

He let out a nervous chuckle. "Allow me to treat you to dinner at your grandfather's place sometime to make up for tonight."

"Forget it." She slipped on her coat. "We probably won't see each other again anyway."

"You look familiar," he said, glancing at her. "Didn't you give a presentation at a medical conference in Chicago last year?"

"Yes, concerning early cancer detection," Linda said.

His frosty breath steamed from his mouth. "Why are you meeting men like this?"

"I've befriended a man my grandparents disapprove of, so they're setting me up on dates. They don't realize that I don't like the guy." She chuckled. "I'm sorry if they put you on the spot. How did they coax you into this date?" she asked.

"Your grandfather donates money to the clinic where I work."

"Grandma said you've worked in remote parts of Africa," she said, shivering. "And now for a free clinic. How do you support yourself?"

He slowed until she caught up with him, then they walked side by side. "We get some money from the government, charitable organizations, and private donations. What the clinic really needs are doctors. Most are not willing to work for free—not that I blame them."

"How many doctors are on the staff?" she asked.

"I'm the only full timer. We have a dentist who comes in on Friday or Saturday, two general practitioners one day a week, and a pediatrician once a week. Oh yeah, and we have four retired RNs. They're very experienced and sometimes do more doctoring than they should."

A gust of cold wind blew up Linda's skirt, making her wish she'd worn pants. "I sometimes work in the emergency room," she said.

"Maybe I can get you to volunteer a few days a month. With you being an oncologist, do you know what that would mean for us?"

She shook her head. "I don't know. This is kind of sudden."

"At least think about it," he said.

They found a pizza joint, walked in, and took a table

near the back. Ian unzipped a dirty navy-blue jacket, re-moved it, and hung it on the chair next to him. A red-and-white plaid flannel shirttail hung over his pot belly. Linda studied him from head to feet, then said candidly, "If you're trying to discourage women, you've certainly succeeded."

He blinked several times. "I usually dress like this when I'm set up. Women aren't attracted to me anyway, and I never dress right. I guess it wouldn't hurt if I lost a few pounds either. I didn't expect someone so lovely," he added.

Like other men, looks meant everything to him. "Does it matter how a woman looks?"

He blushed. "In a way, yes."

Ian ordered a large pizza with everything on it except the kitchen sink. He confided in her about why he'd left England. His parents were rich, privileged. He'd disap-pointed them by turning down prestigious assignments and dedicating his life to helping the needy.

When their dinner arrived, Linda took a slice, bit into the hot, gooey cheese, and chewed. "Tell me about Africa. I've never been there."

"When locals hear a doctor is in an area, they walk for miles to get medical treatment." He took a sip of soda. "I asked some of the women to help as nurses. They didn't know a thing about medicine. Sometimes I had to work without the correct instruments or enough medicine, es-pecially anesthetics."

"You operated without it?" she asked.

A piece of pepperoni fell on his shirt. "Sometimes I had no choice."

He talked extensively about doctoring in remote villages. His willingness to help the underprivileged made her proud to spend the evening with him. She'd decided to donate a few days to his clinic.

He finished the rest of the pizza, and they chatted until the restaurant closed. She'd become interested in him.

He reminded her of Beaulin.

CHAPTER 11

HIT AT THE LIBRARY

Coombs and LaFee arrived at the public library at the intersection of 5th Avenue and 42nd Street just after five. Emergency lights from a fleet of blue and whites lit the area. An officer approached them about ten feet from the entrance. Four others manned the front door.

"Detectives, I'm Duncan. I was at the circulation desk when I heard gunshots. This incident reminds me of the shooting last week. You know the one—lone gunman at the Blue Parrot Lounge."

Coombs pulled his notepad from his pocket. "Why were you here?"

Duncan glanced at the sidewalk. "Checking out books for my grandkid."

"Where's the library's security officer?"

Officer Duncan motioned for them to follow him, and he led Detectives Coombs and LaFee through the sliding glass doors.

The officer took wide strides as he talked. "The security guy was out when it happened. He's now checking surveillance footage."

Coombs walked through a group of cops milling around near the circulation desk. "Any shell casings?"

The officer led them to the elevator. "Didn't see any. Crime Scene Unit should be here any minute. Two people gave us a description of the perpetrator. It's on the wire. So far, nothing. Sounds like the Mudici guy. We'll contact local businesses when they open first thing tomorrow morning. They may have something on their cameras."

LaFee stopped. "What time did this happen?"

"4:40. Twenty minutes before closing," Duncan said.

LaFee turned to a nearby policewoman. "I'd like to check out the stairs. Show me the shooter's escape route."

"Where's the crime scene?" Coombs asked.

"Third floor." Duncan led the way.

The elevator doors clunked and clanged when they opened. Coombs looked for an inspection sticker. A posted sign read: "CHECK WITH THE BUILDING MANAGER."

After a few moments, the slow-moving lift squealed to a halt on the third floor. The doors opened, and Coombs and Duncan stepped into the vestibule.

"How did he get a gun past the security scanner?" Coombs asked.

The officer said, "I understand it hasn't worked in months."

Dull gray paint covered the walls, and the blinds were up on the few windows in the area. A small table with four matching chairs and a copy machine were nearby, and two orange lounge chairs had been placed near the first stack. Tall artificial plants stood on either side of the double doors.

Coombs donned rubber gloves and stepped under the crime tape. Two bodies lay on opposite sides of the table, and a third lay a short distance away, near a stack of books. The blood-soaked brown carpet made the floor appear black.

LaFee approached Coombs and Duncan from behind another stack of books. "Who are the witnesses?"

"A librarian and a Hispanic kid—about thirteen," Duncan said. "According to the boy, the shooter rushed down the stairs, forced his way past him, and knocked the kid down. The man crashed through an emergency exit on the first floor. The gunman either knew this place well or he'd staked it out."

Coombs glanced at LaFee. "Where are the stairs?"

She pointed. "Over there, behind the shelves."

He asked Duncan, "Where are the witnesses?"

"Ms. Wimberley is waiting downstairs. She was shelving books in this area when the incident happened."

LaFee stepped under the crime tape and joined Coombs. "Where's the kid?"

Duncan folded his arms behind his back. "Uh …"

Coombs didn't like the expression on his face. "You did detain him?"

"With all the commotion, I got distracted," Duncan admitted, blushing. "I told him to stay put, but he gave me the slip."

LaFee sighed in disgust. "Did you at least get his name and address?"

"Yeah." Duncan let out a deep breath. "Alan Smith."

"A Hispanic kid named Alan Smith?" Coombs glared at him.

"Sorry," Duncan said. "He gave me false information."

LaFee shook her head. "And his address is probably in the industrial area."

To avoid stepping in blood, Coombs maneuvered his way to the largest body and crouched beside it, then opened the victim's coat, removed his wallet, and flipped it open. "Vince Selva," he said. "Al Selva's nephew. They called him The Hammer. His fists won't be pounding anyone else."

Coombs's partner studied the second man's ID. "This was the youngest Salamici brother, Jimmy. Both were Selva's right-hand men. Gun never cleared his holster."

"Same here." Coombs approached the third victim, who lay on his right side near the first shelf. After searching through the zipped compartments of the kid's backpack, he found a student ID.

"What you got?" LaFee asked.

"College kid, freshman. Bullet through the heart and out the back." He held up a handful of bags containing white powder. "Drugs. My guess, dealer. But why were those two guys here?"

"Maybe they were waiting for someone," LaFee said.

The same two CSU women who'd processed the Blue Parrot Lounge scene arrived and started working the area.

"Duncan, contact local schools tomorrow. Try to locate that Hispanic kid," Coombs said. "We should have him on surveillance too."

Duncan said, "Word around the station is that there's a mob war between the Selvas and the Mudicis. The latter are winning."

The detectives took the elevator back down to the first floor, where the officer led them to a short African American woman with slicked back salt-and-pepper hair mounted in a bun. She sat with her back to them, watching a fleet of red and blue lights illuminate the night.

Two police officers stood nearby, discussing the incident.

Duncan gestured with his hand. "This is Ms. Alice Wimberley."

"Ms. Wimberley," Coombs said. "I'm Detective Coombs, and this is Detective LaFee. We need to ask you some questions about the shooting."

The woman continued staring out the window. In an almost inaudible, distant whisper, she slowly said, "I really didn't see much. When the shooting started, I dropped to the floor and remained behind the stack."

Coombs lowered his voice. "Ms. Wimberley, will you turn and face us? We know this ordeal must be difficult for you. Can you tell us what happened?"

Ms. Wimberley turned sideways in her chair, tears racing down her cheeks. Her glassy eyes didn't focus on either of them. The woman's voice quivered as she said, "A man approached the two men sitting at the table … started shooting. I only noticed him because he walked through the stacks and bumped into me. I didn't think he wanted the other men to see him."

Coombs nodded, jotting down notes. "An ambush?"

One of the nearby officers laughed about something, interrupting Coombs's train of thought. "Ms. Wimberley, can we go somewhere more private?"

"There's a vacant conference room around the corner," Duncan said.

Holding the woman's arm, Coombs helped her stand and walked her to a chair in the secluded room. "Will you wait outside, Duncan?"

The officer closed the door.

Coombs and LaFee took seats across the table from their witness.

"Can we get you something to drink?" LaFee asked.

"I just want to go home, hug my son," the woman said.

LaFee eyed her notepad. "Did the shooter say anything?"

"No. The two men he shot, they stood out," the librarian said.

LaFee cocked her head. "How so?"

"They were in the oldest section of the library. We keep items there that patrons normally don't use, such as old books, maps, and outdated newspapers. It's not a great place to hang out, cold during the winter, hot in the summer." The woman's eyes remained distant, rarely blinking. Her whisper continued. "Patrons normally go there, get what they want, and leave. Those two men sat there for about ten minutes, never removed their coats."

Coombs looked at LaFee. "The kids must have been standing at the shelf directly in front of the shooter."

The woman cleaned her cheeks with both hands and sniffed a few times.

Coombs imagined what the woman had endured. Three murders were a lot to witness. "Where were the two boys standing?"

"They were, ah … they stood in front of the gunman," she said.

"Can you describe the perp?" LaFee asked.

The woman blinked several times. "The what?"

LaFee rephrased her question. "The shooter. Can you describe him?"

"Tall, thin, with a funny-looking mustache."

LaFee raised her eyes from her pad. "Height?"

Ms. Wimberley wiped her cheeks again. "Six-four. Same as my son."

Coombs dropped his pad onto the table. "Six-four. You have a tall kid. What does he do?"

"He's in college. Got a basketball scholarship. He wants to play professional."

Coombs often used this tactic to get witnesses to relax, to feel more comfortable communicating with him.

LaFee managed a smile. "What's his major?"

"Computer science. He says it comes natural to him. He makes good grades."

"Do you have any other kids?" Coombs asked.

"He's my only child. I'm a single mother. I think I've done a good job bringing him up."

LaFee turned a page on her tablet. "You must be proud."

The librarian whimpered. "I am."

Coombs leaned back. "You said the man's mustache looked funny. How?"

"Fake. So did his long hair."

Coombs paused for a minute. "Color of hair? Mustache?"

The lady seemed to be returning to reality. "Both brown."

LaFee asked, "What about clothes?"

Her voice became stronger. "He wore a long black coat, wool, and a camouflaged hunting cap with flaps over his ears that tied under his chin."

"What about eye color?" Coombs asked. "Did you see his eyes?"

Ms. Wimberley shook her head. "No, I didn't notice."

He paused again, giving his witness time to think. "Did anything else stand out? Glasses, tattoos, or other distinguishing features?"

Ms. Wimberley frantically threw her hands into the air, frustrated. "One question at a time. Nothing else about him stood out."

"Did you see the gun?" LaFee asked.

"No, but the other boy might have. He ran down the stairs. The gunman ran after him. I thought he was going to shoot the kid."

Coombs stood, walked out the door, and beckoned Duncan. "We need to find that kid. Let me see your notes on this case."

While Coombs checked the officer's notes, LaFee walked the librarian back to the circulation desk and remained with her.

"If this is his address, he's far from home. No libraries in his neighborhood," Coombs said.

"You found drugs on the college kid. Maybe he was buying," the officer said.

"Do you have any idea how many thirteen-year-old Hispanic kids there are in this city? If you saw him again, could you identify him?" Coombs asked.

Duncan nodded. "I think so, Detective."

Disgusted with the officer, Coombs took a deep breath and let it out slowly. "Fake name, probably a fake address. How are those surveillance checks coming? Anything?"

The officer passed a small box to him. "The shooter is on two cameras with his head down. Cap's bib and earflaps hid his face. The kids are probably there, but the officers and the security guard concentrated on the killer. The surveillance is poor quality: black and white, grainy."

The librarian sat behind the circulation counter, her coat thrown over a chair, a purse in her lap.

Coombs approached Ms. Wimberley and remained standing. "Just one more question. Could you identify the suspect again?"

She shook her head. "I … can't. I can't identify him."

Coombs remained gentle but firm. "We'll take you to the precinct, have you look at some photos. Sometimes things click when people see a mugshot."

"I can't." Her voice trembled. "What if he comes after me? He killed three people. How can someone kill an innocent kid?"

Coombs said, "If we find him, he's going nowhere but jail."

"And what happens to me when he gets out on bail?"

"It's your duty as a citizen," LaFee said.

The woman gasped, "Duty? I'm alive and plan to stay that way. I read a lot, watch the news, and this hit reeks of the Mob. From the TV reports, this might be the third hit by this man."

Coombs noticed there weren't as many flashing lights outside. "You're a material witness. Officer Duncan will take you downtown and then give you a ride home."

The woman clasped her hands together, slowly stood. "Please, I don't want to get mixed up in this."

"Sorry," Coombs said. "We need your help to put this guy away."

CHAPTER 12

THE FAMILY

Linda arrived at the Mudici home earlier than usual for the family gathering. With each visit, she left her professional world behind and stepped into the role of being a granddaughter. She, Grandma, and her aunt cleaned up the kitchen after lunch while the men bonded in the living room. Helping the family prepare meals made her happy. Grandma's hugs were amazing, warm, and loving.

Aunt Christina left the room to answer a private cell phone call.

Linda loaded the dishwasher and turned to Grandma. "Why did Grandpa kick Helena out of the family?"

Grandma whispered, "Helena went into witness protection. She dated a detective who used her. She spied on our family operations and gave him evidence that sent Teddy's father, your father, Tony, and his twin brother, Danny, to prison for life. Danny's wife moved back to Italy. Swift is married to their daughter. Your great-grandfather died in prison."

Linda turned to Grandma, then froze. All feeling left her hands. She dropped the bowl she was holding, and it shattered on the floor. "My father's alive?"

"Quiet. They're in Leavenworth. We speak to them once a month," Grandma said.

Dazed, Linda asked, "Is my mother, Maria, alive?"

"No. She really died in the accident."

Like a zombie, Linda opened the kitchen closet, retrieved a broom and dustpan, swept up pieces of the glass, and dumped them into the trash. "I'd like to meet my father."

"Tony and Danny's birthday is in June. That's the only time we visit them. You're welcome to come with us," the old woman said.

"Why did Grandpa say Tony was dead?"

Grandma stepped closer. "He didn't mean to lie. He just couldn't tell you the truth. After Helena testified in court, the detective dumped her, called her stupid and boring. He got a big promotion, his picture in the news. It aired nationwide. Two weeks later, he married another woman. Teddy says the only reason she's still alive is that he couldn't find her."

Linda placed the dustpan and broom back into the kitchen closet. "So, that's why Mother—Helena—said she didn't have any relatives." I could've lived with my grandparents rather than in foster homes. Aloud, she said,

"Grandpa wanted to kill his own daughter? Why didn't you and Uncle Ralph help her?"

"Don't worry. Teddy has simmered down now." She shook her head. "My child, you don't understand the family."

What kind of a mother was Isabella? Didn't she love her daughter? "But you're her mother." Linda blurted out.

Grandma appeared rather nonchalant about the situation. "Helena disgraced the family. That's why Teddy hates cops so much. This one you're seeing—what's his name?"

Linda washed her hands in the kitchen sink. "He's just an acquaintance, Grandma."

"I hope he hasn't bedded you."

At a loss for words, Linda stuttered, "No ... of course not."

"Most men don't respect women who jump into bed with them without long courtships. Teddy and I were married first. Nowadays, women don't even know the man's name."

Linda wondered if Grandma ever had that conversation with Jenny. "I know." As her mind soaked up the information, she turned on her heels. "If Helena entered witness protection, how did we keep our names?"

"Teddy thought she went into witness protection because he couldn't find her. Actually, she hid out in Florida, never used her name on anything that would send up red flags."

Linda's mouth was agape. "She couldn't have done that without money and support from someone."

Grandma smiled. "Exactly."

Linda sighed with relief. At least Grandma wasn't so cold after all.

The old woman removed a flour container from the cabinet. "You're smart, respectable. I really like you."

"Grandma, these family gatherings mean so much to me. My parents—I mean, Helena and Adler—never hugged me, never shared their affection. Adler only showed interest when I studied German."

The old woman gave Linda a tight hug and patted her on her back. "I've heard about your childhood. If you ever need to talk …"

Other than her psychiatrist, Linda had only confided in Coombs. "No, Grandma. I don't care to talk about it."

"If you change your mind, I'm always here," she said.

"Thanks, Grandma."

The old woman couldn't have been as gullible as she pretended to be. "Grandma, what if something happens to Grandpa?" Linda asked.

"I'm his wife, dear. Everything comes to me." Grandma quickly changed the conversation. "For dinner, I'm making egg tagliatelle pasta."

She didn't measure the flour, just dumped a mound into a large bowl, made a hole in the center, added a dozen eggs, and a spill of olive oil. She worked the dough with her hands until it became firm. "We're also having beef and broccoli, skewed aubergine satay, dried tomato rolls, and broad bean and artichoke soup. For dessert we're having deep-fried amaretti cakes."

Grandma touched Linda's nose with a floured finger. "You're making the dessert from my recipe all by yourself."

Jenny came downstairs wearing a robe, hair mussed, eyes red. "Hello, Linda," she said as she kissed Grandma. "Is there any coffee left?"

Aunt Christina reentered the kitchen, tying apron strings behind her back. "I'll make another pot."

"No need, Mom." Linda's cousin loaded the espresso machine and added water.

"You must've had fun last night, Jenny," Linda said.

At thirty-five, Jenny partied like a teenager. "Life's nothing but—"

"Do you work?" Linda asked.

Grandma chuckled. "Work?"

"No." Jenny brushed her hair back and boasted, "I have a rich daddy who gives me a generous allowance." She placed a cup under the spout and hit the brew button.

Linda's voice carried over the hum of the machine. "You ever consider attending college?"

Jenny rolled her eyes. "What for?"

"To better yourself educationally, find a good job," Linda said.

The espresso machine sputtered to a stop. Jenny took her cup and headed back upstairs.

Linda yelled at her back, "Will you be joining us for dinner?"

"Yes," her cousin said. "You promised to party with me Saturday. No excuses this time."

Grandma frowned. "She does nothing around here."

Linda chuckled and threw a dishtowel over her shoulder. "Looks like someone spoiled her."

"It certainly wasn't me." Grandma spoke as if Aunt Christina weren't there. "Her parents went ballistic when I pushed them to discipline her."

Linda placed a bowl on the counter next to the sun-dried tomatoes. "Aunt Christina, why doesn't Jenny live with you and Uncle Ralph?"

Grandma looked at Linda and shook her head.

Her aunt placed beef cubes into a hot saucepan of olive oil to sear. "I don't want to talk about it."

Grandma waved a spatula in the air. "Know why Jenny can't find a husband? Because she's a whore."

Aunt Christina turned on Grandma, eyes wild and furious. "That's my daughter you're degrading. She just likes to party." She stomped out of the room.

Grandma warned Linda, "Be careful going out with Jenny."

"I want to know what she does at these places," Linda said. "I can always walk out."

Grandma peeked over her shoulder. "Tell me everything she does, you hear?"

"Sure, Grandma."

Linda knew the dirty laundry would eventually air, but not so soon. She turned her back to Grandma and smiled. The Mudici family was more dysfunctional than Linda had imagined. She clasped her hands together. "I think I'll start on dessert."

Grandma released her frustration by pounding the dough. She ran it through the pasta machine several times. It didn't take her long to finish the job.

Aunt Christina returned to the kitchen and stood over a pot of boiling water next to Linda. "Add the pasta a little at a time, dear. We don't want them to stick together."

Linda slowly dropped a handful of noodles into the hot water. "Why don't you just buy pasta? You two spend all day working in the kitchen."

Her aunt washed her hands. "Only on Sundays. If we used store-bought pasta, our husbands would divorce us. They want everything made from scratch, even at the restaurant."

Linda laughed. "Huh, bet they wouldn't know the difference."

"Oh yes they would," her aunt insisted.

"Grandma, do you know the type of work Grandpa does?" Linda asked.

"He and Ralph own a restaurant. You know that. They do very well," the old woman said.

Linda poured off the extra olive oil from the saucepan, added a heaping portion of water onto the seared beef, and threw some broccoli into the pot. She finished preparing the amaretti cakes and set them aside for deep-frying just before serving.

"You're becoming quite a cook," Aunt Christina complimented Linda. "You need a husband."

"This is the twenty-first century. Women don't slave all day in the kitchen just to feed men," Linda said.

Aunt Christina's cell phone rang, and she left the kitchen again.

Grandma looked over her shoulder and stepped closer to Linda. "They spoiled Jenny rotten. Ralph didn't realize how bad until she was fifteen. Public and private schools expelled her. She never graduated. Jenny and Ralph got into a huge fight, and Ralph kicked her out. We only allowed her to live here if she supported herself." The old woman's face wrinkled. "So what does Ralph do? He gives her a generous allowance. Does that make sense? Let her flip burgers for a living."

Linda whispered, "Grandma, you know she's on drugs, right?"

The old woman shrugged. "Of course. We all do."

***

Grandpa headed the table. Grandma took her usual position at the opposite end. Small talk dominated the setting, never business.

Linda looked around the dinner table, smiling. Over

the last two months that she'd known her family, her bond with Grandma had gotten strong.

Grandpa cleared his throat. "Linda, Ian asked about you today."

Why is he talking to Ian? she wondered. "He's a nice guy," Linda commented. "We have fun together. He reminds me of Beaulin."

The conversation took a nasty turn as Grandpa bellowed, "I don't see how you can like that Coombs guy, a man with no morals, a man who won't take care of his own son."

"Grandpa, I don't like Coombs. In fact, the more I know him, the less I like him."

"You said all you wanted was information from him," Grandpa said.

"That's right. He still feeds me his department's status concerning Beaulin's murder case. That's my only interest in Coombs."

"The mother of Coombs's child ended up in a mental institution," Teddy continued. "Her sister has the baby, takes care of her sick parents, and works two jobs. Your Coombs mentally abused the kid's mother to the point of suicide." His weathered eyes studied her expression. "Keep your distance from him."

Resisting the urge to yell, she raised her voice instead. "What part of 'I don't like Coombs' don't you understand? We're not even on a first-name basis."

Grandpa gazed at her, his bushy eyebrows dancing

when he frowned. "Coombs never knew his own father, so how can he let his kid grow up as he did?"

"He said his father was killed in a train wreck," Linda said.

"What train? Coombs's own mother doesn't know who fathered him," Grandpa said. "In her younger days, she spent most of her time trying to find a husband. She abused him as a kid. He grew up in foster homes."

"He asked to escort me to my New Year's Eve party, as a friend. I didn't accept," Linda reminded Grandpa. "How do you know so much about him?"

"The woman who had Coombs's baby used to cut my hair and helped your grandma take care of the house sometimes. We help her family out. You know, send the baby things. They're poor but good people. Her sister doesn't accept money from me, but her father does. Keeps him in booze. We have a box of things for the baby. I want you to take them over there. They're usually home Sunday nights."

"Why me?" she asked.

"You're not working the emergency room tonight. Do you have a date?" Grandpa had drunk more than usual. Even so, he took another sip of whiskey. "A man ended up dead in an alley when Coombs was in uniform. Bullets from Coombs's gun killed him. The true-blue wall protected him." He picked up the bottle, replenished his glass, and pounded his fists on his chest like a gorilla. "He tried to get information from two of my guys—promised them the world if they testified against the family. When they refused, he set them up—planted incriminating evidence, more than once. I have loyal people in the police departments who keep me informed."

The room became quiet too quiet. Except for Swift, everyone stopped eating, eyeing their plates as if in deep concentration. The old man had said too much.

Linda decided to let out a skeleton of her own. "Swift, three people were gunned down at the library last night. The composite sketch looks a lot like you in disguise. Was it you?"

Grandma and Grandpa lowered their heads. Everyone gasped. Swift abruptly climbed to his feet, dropping his napkin in the process. He yelled words in Italian at Linda, hatred rolling off his tongue. Grandpa spoke to him in their native language, and then Swift fled the room.

"What does Swift do for a living?" Linda asked.

Jenny giggled. "He's in real estate, sells six-feet plots."

Grandma rolled her eyes at Jenny, so did Aunt Christina.

Moments later, everyone started eating again, their silverware clinking on dinner plates. For the remainder of dinner, no one said a word.

After they were all finished eating, Jenny left the table and headed back upstairs.

Linda helped clear the table, then she walked up to Jenny's room and knocked on her door.

Linda heard Jenny's weak, "Come in."

Jenny lay in bed with her head under the covers. A commercial played on the TV, and the volume was muted.

Linda sat on the bed next to her. "Jenny, why don't you have your own place?"

Her cousin threw back the covers. "Do you know what a sweet deal I've got here? I pay my grandparents two hundred a month, and that includes my food, rent, and cell phone."

Linda asked, "Why do Grandma and Grandpa interfere in my life? Do they do that to you?"

Jenny propped her head on a hand. "No way. It's your fault, you know, going along with them."

"Every Sunday after dinner, the men go into the back office, and women aren't allowed," Linda said. "Why?"

Jenny sat up in bed. "They talk business in private, or at least they think they do."

Linda placed a hand on the bed, leaning in. "What do you mean?"

Her cousin fell back, hair spilling over her pillow. She giggled. "I have a hidden video recording system in the office that tapes everything. You wouldn't believe some of the stuff they say."

Linda chuckled, a phony facade. "What if they catch you?"

Jenny walked to her closet, retrieved a small, locked metal box, removed a key taped under her desk, and opened the box. She shoved a 64 GB Micro SD memory card into her laptop and powered it on.

Linda stared at the loot before her—a treasure trove. "No, Jenny. I don't want to watch it now. How long have you been recording them?"

Jenny bounced back on her bed. "Over five years. Each camera is voice-activated. Their meetings last about forty minutes to an hour, so the memory cards capture a lot of video footage."

Linda didn't want her to know how much she wanted to view the footage. She pretended to be nonchalant. "You have more than one camera?"

"Yeah. One downstairs in Grandpa's office, another at the restaurant. Those will really blow your mind."

"Why do something like this?"

"Hey, I'm a member of this family. I have a right to know what's going on, just like the men do. I do dirty work too. They sent me into your apartment first, before they retrieved the drugs."

Jenny told Linda she would keep the memory cards, perhaps as an advantage one day.

"Maybe you should keep them in a safe deposit box … just as a precaution," Linda suggested.

"They never come up here. Besides, I keep the box locked. If you ever change your mind, you know where the key is. Take some home and watch them."

With the video still on mute, Linda saw Grandpa sitting behind his desk, having a discussion with Uncle Ralph, Swift, and Billy. "How do you know I won't tell Grandpa?"

"You're afraid of him. You don't like him either. You won't tell," Jenny said confidently.

***

After dinner, Grandpa escorted Linda into his private office. She glanced at the clock that contained Jenny's video surveillance. "Nice clock."

"Yeah," Grandpa said. "Jenny gave it to me. There's one identical to it in my private room at the restaurant." He took the chair behind his mahogany desk. "I know you've been seeing this detective, Rick Coombs. He has a slick tongue, can talk a bird from the sky. Women fall for him easily. I don't know why. He's a cad."

Linda took the chair nearest him. "Grandpa, you have no right to spy on me."

He interlaced his fingers and gazed at her. "I take care of my own. You had a terrible childhood, and I don't want to see you hurt again."

She leaned over his desk and spat her words at him. "At least he doesn't deal drugs or murder people."

The hard slap across her face reminded her whom she'd sassed. She caressed her burning cheek and scooted her chair away from his desk. "Adler never hit me."

"No. He just paid someone to kill you," the old man said through clenched teeth. "You'll show me respect as long as you're under my roof. What I did, I did for you. Selva would have killed you."

"You said he wouldn't come after me. With him dead, you got to keep the drugs. Did you do it for me—or yourself?"

"Both. What's left of Selva's family is seeking revenge. Few people know we're related. Let's keep it that way."

She scooted her chair back another foot. "Didn't Swift kill them all?" she asked under her breath.

"What did you say?" he asked.

"Just talking to myself, Grandpa," she said abruptly.

He tossed a sealed envelope across the table to her with a handwritten address on the front. "Take this envelope and the box in the living room to this address. The box contains things for Coombs's baby. I'll let them know you're coming."

"He says his department doesn't consider me a suspect anymore. I've broken off all contact with him," she said.

He smiled. "That's my granddaughter."

When Linda left the Mudicis' house, she stopped at a pay phone, called the local authorities, and anonymously spilled all she knew about Swift's illegal activities.

CHAPTER 13

CONFRONTATION

Linda arrived at her combination hospitals' New Year's Eve party and charity ball at Manhattan's sophisticated Greenwich Village Country Club without a date, as usual. Each place setting at the tables included a party hat, colorful metallic foil horns, a tube of glitter, and two balloons.

Three other people shared the table with her—a single nurse and an elderly couple.

A crowd of hospital staff and donors of various ages filled every table.

After dinner, patrons slow-danced to the tune of "Sittin' on the Dock of the Bay." Men held women close, their cheeks caressing. Occasions such as these made Linda feel lonely. She'd never found the right man and didn't think she could ever trust one enough to give her heart away.

When the man at the microphone started counting

down the seconds until midnight, the audience cheered and threw their party hats into the air while the band played "Auld Lang Syne," ending another lonely occasion for Linda.

"This reminds me of prom night," the elderly woman at the table said.

Linda felt left out, crushed. She'd never been to a prom.

The elderly man said, "Let's go. Party's over."

Linda drove home, flowing along with the slow-moving traffic, parked in her garage, and took the elevator up to her apartment. She armed the security system and raided the refrigerator. She'd just cut up snacks on the counter when the doorbell rang. Checking her security TV screen, she recognized Coombs leaning on the other side of the door, wearing a black tuxedo.

She opened the door and placed her right hand on the frame. "What're you doing here?"

"Why did you refuse to let me escort you to your New Year's Eve party?" he said, slurring each word.

"You're not interested in a platonic relationship, which means we can't be friends," Linda said.

"Hey, don't I get to come in? I need to use your bathroom."

She attempted to close the door. "There's one in the lobby. It's late. Goodnight."

Coombs pushed the door open farther, dashed past her, and entered the open door just inside the living room. Behind the closed bathroom door, Linda heard him urinating, the toilet flushing, and then water running in the sink.

Coombs returned to the living room, removed his jacket, and tossed it across the back of her sofa. He eyed the cheese and cold cuts on the kitchen counter. "I'm hungry. What do you have to eat?"

Linda left the door open. The dread of dealing with him touched her spine like icy fingers. "You can't just barge into my place and demand food."

"Do you have any beer or wine?" he asked as he staggered into the kitchen.

She followed him, stopping at the counter. "I don't think you need any more to drink unless you're taking a taxi."

Coombs wrapped his arms around her waist and tried to kiss her neck, restricting her freedom of movement. She didn't want him touching her. "Get out."

He gently turned her around, tried to kiss her lips. "I'm in love with you."

She shoved him back, appalled by his audacity. "Is that what you tell all your women?"

Leaning against the counter at Linda's side, he posed as if for a photo shoot.

His words came softly as he flickered a ghost of a smile. "You're so beautiful."

"I'm not interested, Coombs."

Rick rolled his tongue over his lips. "I am." He moved the plate from the counter to the table and took a seat. "We've been seeing each other for weeks."

Coombs hadn't been to Linda's apartment since Beaulin's murder, and she had never been to his. They'd had lunch three times. He'd never put the moves on her until now. Maybe the booze was to blame for his actions.

She placed her hands on her hips. "Not on a date. You know how I feel about getting close to men."

He greedily consumed a piece of cheese and shoved cold cuts into his mouth. "You know everything about me. There's no one else." He smacked his lips.

She gave him a stern, acidic look. "Coombs, you don't get the prize."

His mouth dropped. "What?"

"I'm not going to bed with you. Ever. Now, get out of here before I call security."

His face reddened as he glared at her. "I thought we had something."

Linda remained calm. "You thought wrong. I'm not interested in anyone who thinks he's a ladies' man. I see the way you gawk at other women. Do you think I'm blind? What about the other Linda you're dating? Is that what you told the mother of the baby you don't have— the woman who committed suicide over you? Do you know your own kid's name?"

He stood up straight, eyes wild, furious. "You've been spying on me?"

She decided not to be gentle. He didn't deserve it. "I've met your son, his aunt, and his grandparents. Your son has red hair and green eyes, just like you. How can you have a kid and discard him like trash? He didn't ask to be born. You're a womanizing scumbag."

Coombs scooted his chair away from the table. Fury roared from his voice. "I didn't want a baby. When I refused to marry her, she deliberately got pregnant to trap me. Dammit. I had no control over the situation."

"But you did. Do you want your son to grow up without a father, as you did? Every time you open your mouth, a lie comes out."

He slapped the table. "I tried to get her to have an abortion. I offered to pay for it, but she refused."

"You don't care about anyone but yourself, do you? Have you ever seen your son? He's so cute."

The vicious fire in his eyes grew. "So, that makes me a bad guy? Lots of men have babies they don't want."

Linda eased her way to the cutting block on the counter and closer to the knife. "When I first met you, I assumed you were different, better. But you're only after one thing, and you're not gonna get it here."

His face twisted. Veins in his neck swelled. "What else do you know?"

She turned to face him, gripping the butcher knife in a hand behind her back. "Know why they don't have to put the baby up for adoption now? I let them live in a house near a daycare center, for free. That means you have to pay child support, Mr. Deadbeat Dad."

"You. You had no right, sticking your nose into my business," he shouted.

"You're on probation at work for flirting and having affairs with female victims and suspects. I noticed something strange about you the first time we met—the way you touched me. Cops don't behave like that."

Coombs stood, threw his hands into the air, took a few steps away from the table, and then stopped. Abruptly, he turned on his heels. "Well, at least I don't hang out with mobsters. Your visits to the Mudici house haven't gone unnoticed by the police department. I believed you were innocent of Bartell's murder. Well not anymore. The feds are checking on your assets, Miss Holier Than Thou." Coombs growled and took giant steps toward her, his fists clenched. His bloodshot eyes narrowed in on her like a fox after a rat.

Linda held the knife firmly in front of her now. Dark memories rushed through her mind as she went into defense mode. "Attack me, and you won't live to regret it."

He huffed, "You'll do it too, you psychotic, murdering bitch. You probably enjoyed that lesbian affair you had with your doctor when you were a kid. You didn't kill her for alleged sexual abuse. You probably prefer to have a woman up your legs."

His words hit her nerves like a live wire. She'd confided in him, and now he was using it to humiliate her. Linda threw the plate of food at him. The dish hit the opposite wall, shattering into jagged pieces. "You pervert." She rushed to the door and opened it wider with such force that it banged against the magnetic doorstop like a gunshot. "Get out, you pig."

As Coombs stomped out, Linda ran to the sofa, grabbed his jacket, stabbed the knife through the back, ripped it almost in two, and then threw it into the hallway behind him. "Don't forget your jacket." She slammed the door shut and pressed her back against it, panting, as her hands shook.

Five minutes later, her doorbell rang. She threw open the door, gripping the knife, ready to scream at Coombs.

The building's security guard backed up and reached for his weapon. Since Beaulin's murder, security had doubled in force, and the guards now carried guns. Linda had met Frank shortly after he came aboard. He stood about five-ten and was thin, with graying hair. "Dr. Harrison, is everything all right here?"

She threw her hands out at her sides. "Yes. I'm fine."

He focused on the knife and nodded. "You mind putting that thing down? We've received complaints from your neighbors about shouting coming from this apartment."

"Oh." Linda lowered the knife she'd been holding waist-high, aimed right at him. She concealed it behind her back. "I'm sorry about that. I had a verbal confrontation with a man. He just left."

Frank peeked into her apartment. "May I come in? Just to make sure you're all right?"

She stepped aside.

Frank cautiously entered and checked the left and right sides of her door. He moved into the living room, turned, and surveyed the place.

Linda tossed the knife onto the sofa as if it burned her hand. It bounced off and landed on the floor. "There's no one else here."

"I just need to make sure," Frank said. "New rules, you know. I just saw a detective I recognized putting on a torn jacket. Your handiwork?"

Linda took the opportunity to get back at her hostile intruder. "Detective Rick Coombs. He worked on the Bartell murder case. I was only interested in friendship, but he wanted a relationship. That's what sparked the argument."

"I'll make sure it doesn't happen again. I'm a retired police officer. Coombs's boss is going to hear about this. Due to the department's code of ethics, he's not allowed to socialize with you." He walked out the door. "Goodnight. Don't forget to lock up."

CHAPTER 14

COUSIN JENNY

Saturday morning, Linda tagged along with Jenny to a few luxury department stores in New York City. Her cousin promised to help her pick out party clothes. She didn't know what Jenny did at clubs, but she couldn't wait to find out. She could always walk out if she didn't like the place or the people.

Jenny wore six-inch heels and a miniskirt. "Come on, buy something sexy."

Linda couldn't imagine dressing like Jenny. "Aren't you cold?" she asked.

"No, are you?" Jenny pulled a blouse from one of the racks and held it up to Linda. "I know lots of places you can wear this. We're going to have so much fun tonight."

Linda didn't want to break her promise, but her instincts had kicked in. "Jenny, you party every night. I'm on call this weekend at the emergency room."

Jenny checked her makeup in a nearby mirror. "Don't

answer your cell phone. What a boring job. You never have any fun. I couldn't live like you."

At least I work. "I like my job."

Her cousin held another blouse up to Linda. "This is perfect. Hey, I gave an acquaintance your number. We skied together at the Poconos. Get to know her and come with us sometime."

"You gave my number to a stranger?"

Jenny shrugged. "Father introduced me to her. You and Megan will get along fine. She's sort of like you. Boring."

Linda placed clothes back on the rack as fast as Jenny picked them out. "I don't dress like this."

Jenny threw back her head. "Well, excuse me, Dr. Conservative. That's why you don't have a man."

Jenny dated a lot but didn't have a steady boyfriend. "You don't have one either," Linda said.

Jenny pouted. "I can have any man I want."

"Maybe I shouldn't go out tonight."

Jenny gave her a dismissive wave. "Oh, come on."

Curiosity had gotten the better of Linda. "Well … I did promise."

Her cousin squealed like a teenager. "Are you ready to party?"

Linda leaned on a wardrobe rack. "Are you sure this place is safe?"

Jenny chuckled. "Staying away from us deadbeats, huh?"

Linda shifted her stance. "I just don't think I'd fit in. I don't know how to dance."

"Didn't you party during college?"

"No, I spent my time studying."

Jenny shook her butt and jiggled her boobs. "Hey, have a few drinks, get on the dance floor, and do whatever. I can't believe you're not buying anything. Don't doctors make lots of money?"

"It's not the money but the clothes."

Jenny struggled with half of her loot, and Linda carried the other half.

Her cousin piled bags into the trunk of her car. "I heard that you're seeing this Ian guy. Is there romance in the air?" she asked, a smile in her voice. "Did Cupid's little arrow hit you?"

"Grandpa introduced me to Ian. We've dined together a few times. Nothing special, just friends. I sometimes volunteer at his free clinic. What time should I pick you up?"

"Ten. It'll take us an hour to get there," Jenny said.

Linda was usually sound asleep by then. "That late?"

Jenny opened her door and jumped into the driver's seat. "Hey, the party doesn't start until then."

Linda slid into the passenger seat and fastened her seatbelt. "Okay, I'll pick you up at ten."

***

That evening, Linda drove to her grandparents' house and rang the doorbell.

Jenny opened the door wearing six-inch stiletto heels, a miniskirt, and a low-cut blouse. She sported her favorite ten-carat marquise diamond earrings with a matching necklace. "Hey, what's this?" Jenny slipped into a suede coat and turned up her nose. "You're not wearing that."

Linda checked herself in the mirror. "It's a nice suit."

"We're not going to a business meeting. Show some cleavage and thighs."

"This is the best I can do," Linda said.

Jenny tossed her hair. "You're supposed to dress in something that says, 'Come on over, guys.'"

"Where's Grandma?" Linda asked.

"At her age, there's only one place she can be ... in bed."

Linda's cousin talked a lot as they drove to the club. Outside of partying, she didn't seem to have much of a life.

Linda pulled into the parking lot of the White Castle, a two-story structure that looked more like a municipal building than a nightclub. She could have passed the place a thousand times and never noticed it was there. People waited in line outside the entrance, but Jenny led her straight in like VIPs and checked their coats. She heard techno music pounding as they entered the double doors. When Linda turned around, Jenny had disappeared.

A person of questionable gender approached Linda. He or she had a small frame and a thin mustache and was dressed all in men's clothes except for what looked to be a size C bra. "Wanna dance?"

Linda diverted her eyes, searching for her cousin. "No thanks."

A swaggering man, who smelled like a Kentucky still, threw both arms around her neck. "Let me buy you a drink, honey."

She pushed him away and stepped back. "I don't think you can stand."

Men continued asking her to dance as she maneuvered through the club. Linda hated when guys nagged her, and she had become irritated, angry even, because she couldn't find Jenny. The more men asked her to dance, the more abrupt she became with her unwanted guests.

A man dressed in bright blue extended his hand to her. She shook her head. "No."

Another man grabbed her arm and jerked her toward the dance floor. Digging her heels into the carpet, she tried to break his grip. When that didn't work, she clawed the back of his hand, breaking the epidermis. He drew back his other hand to strike her.

Unconsciously, she went into the shuto-uke defense stance. "I have a black belt. Don't even think about it."

The man's hand stopped in midair, and his eyes became furious as he caressed his bleeding hand. "You rabid vampire. You probably have AIDS."

The crowd outside rushed in as if it were Black Friday. Linda had made a lateral leap into The Twilight Zone. She stood as straight as a board with her back pressed against the wall, as her eyes searched for Jenny.

Finally, she forced her way through the mob and made it back to the entrance. She gave the attendant her ticket. A few minutes later, he returned.

"That's my cousin's coat, not mine."

"You need to bring me her ticket," the man said. "Somehow they must have gotten mixed up."

Pushing her way toward the dance floor once again, Linda frantically searched for Jenny, excusing herself a thousand times. Bodies vibrated in Technicolor, camouflaged under strobe lights. Colors ran like confetti melting in the rain. Perfumes and colognes left the place stuffy, and she found breathing difficult. Linda wandered alone among weird people, and it was her fault for having trusted her drug-addict cousin. The music hurt her eardrums, but she continued toward the loud source. Through the vivid crowd, she spotted Jenny with a tall, muscular, bearded man who was all over her.

When the music stopped, Linda rushed to the edge of the floor and yelled, "Jenny, you have my check ticket, and I have yours."

Jenny shouted before the music started again, "Why do you need your coat?"

Linda yelled, "I'm going home. I don't like this place."

Jenny rolled her eyes and left the dance floor with

her friend. Linda stayed on Jenny's heels before the void filled in behind her. Her cousin's partner took a seat at a table with two other men. Jenny sat next to him.

Jenny seemed perky. "Hey, guys. I'm Jenny. This is my cousin, Linda."

Linda remained standing.

Now, seeing him close up, Linda realized that Jenny's dance partner didn't have a beard. Black and blue Egyptian-looking tattoos covered the lower half of his face. Although he wore long sleeves, his hands and fingers revealed tattoos as well. Linda couldn't help gawking.

Jenny placed a hand on her partner's shoulder. "Have a seat, Linda. This is Bear. He's from Chicago."

Linda sat opposite Jenny and her date, next to a man who put his arm around her chair as soon as she took a seat. He flashed a mouth full of gold. "I'm Clint." He poked a finger at the man next to him. "This is Manley. We call him Man."

Man was the smallest of the three. He flashed a whimsical smile and waved at her. His eyes were glassy and red, his head bobbing to the beat of the music.

Linda leaned forward, turned, and looked at Clint. "Please remove your arm from around my chair."

"Sorry." He obeyed, leaning across the table toward her cousin, he asked, "What's your name again?"

"Jenny. I come here a lot."

Clint jerked his head toward Linda. "Who's your stuck-up friend?"

"She's my cousin. This is her first time at a club."

Clint looked at Linda as if she had a disease. "Are you a nun?" He eyed her from head to toe. "You're dressed like one."

"No." Jenny yelled. "She just got out of prison for killing two men. They didn't have clubs there."

When the music started again, Jenny jumped to her feet. "I love this tune. Hey, Bear, let's hit the floor again." She threw her small shoulder bag into Linda's lap. "Hold this for me."

Linda shouted, "Jenny, I'm leaving."

Jenny didn't acknowledge her. She and her friend disappeared into the crowd.

Man threw his head back and wailed like a walrus.

Linda jumped.

Man started rocking and weaving in his chair, head bobbing, arms swinging, feet thumping the floor. He didn't grab a partner but lurched to his feet and hit the dance floor. He went into a liquid frenzy, moving like a flag in a windstorm. He bounced, jumped, bent, twisted, and twirled in every direction. Other people on the floor gave him space as he concentrated on a dance competition with his shadow on the wall.

"Can I buy you a drink?" Clint asked.

Linda cringed at the idea of drinking anything there. "No thanks. I'm not thirsty."

"Would you like to dance?"

"Sorry, we didn't have dance lessons in prison," Linda said.

She sighted him in her peripheral vision as he gazed at her. She kept her eyes fixed on the crowded dance floor.

"You don't look like a killer."

"We usually don't," she said.

Clint sneezed. Linda jumped again.

"Why are you so spooked? Someone after you?" he asked.

Linda didn't respond.

Most of the patrons had settled at tables. A few groups hugged the walls—mainly men and women, hooking up. Then she realized Clint had left. What a relief.

She glanced at two black men standing near her table, gawking at her, and then looked away. The tall and slender one had a light complexion. The darker one was the same height but more muscular. Did they stare because of the way she was dressed or because she refused to dance?

Linda's armpits were soaked. She wiped sweat from her face with a tissue. Thirst had taken its toll, but she didn't dare leave the security of the table.

When the music stopped, the heavier of the two men asked, "Have you ever seen the dark side of the moon?"

College physics danced through her mind. "We can't see that side of the moon from Earth."

He dropped his pants, mooned her, then pulled up his jeans, slapped palms with his friend, and walked away. Both laughed hysterically, and so did the people at nearby tables.

Linda sat rigidly, tapped her heels, and waited for Jenny to return.

A few moments later, a man walked up to her, grabbed a fistful of her hair, and yanked her to her feet. When she elbowed him in his side, he let go. Turning, she punched him in the nose with two quick, powerful blows, then rushed to the opposite side of the table, putting distance between them. An invisible fist squeezed her heart, then released it to pound in a furious rhythm. The man stood four inches taller than Linda, and his eyes were distant. He staggered, clenching and unclenching his fists. He wiped the blood from his nose with a closed fist as he advanced toward her. Then, like rival animals, they moved in circular paths around the table, each sizing up the other before going into battle.

In a fluid motion, a bouncer approached her, his biceps bulging like melons and arms swinging like a gorilla. He had a thin waist and a broad chest that filled his black T-shirt, which read "SECURITY" in bold white letters. "Sorry, ma'am. A customer saw what happened. Don't go outside unless one of us escorts you to your vehicle."

"Thank you," she said. "As soon as I find my cousin, I'm leaving."

Linda saw the check stub in the side pocket of Jenny's purse and exchanged it. Then she waited impatiently for thirty minutes before Jenny and Bear returned.

Linda shouted, "Where've you been? Some crazy man

pulled my hair. You left me holding your purse when you knew I wanted to leave."

"Are you all right?" Bear asked.

"Yes, I gave the clown a bloody nose."

Bear laughed and slapped Linda on her back. "Good for you."

"Linda has a black belt," Jenny said. "She can fend for herself."

Linda snapped at her cousin, "You said this place was safe."

"Hey, chill. You're too uptight." Jenny's breath smelled like booze. "Come upstairs with me."

Linda shivered. "What's up there?"

A man guarded a roped barricade at the landing. In front of him, a sign read: "PRIVATE PARTY."

Jenny tugged on her arm. "Grandpa's stuff." She gently punched Bear on his shoulder. "You stay put. We'll be back in a few."

Linda's mind went into alert mode. Nonetheless, she followed Jenny, eager to know the secret behind the closed door. "You know I don't do drugs."

Jenny led the way. "Come on. Let's have some fun."

The muscleman behind the rope looked to be about thirty-five. He was clean-shaven and wore a black, tailored suit. "Hey, Jenny. Who's your friend?"

"My cousin. She's cool," Jenny said.

Linda climbed the stairs behind her and entered a plush room with thick green carpet and matching drapes.

Six patrons sat at a bar with drinks in their hands. A sign posted behind the bartender read: "NO SMOKING." The place smelled of the sweet fragrance of the fresh flowers that Linda saw neatly arranged in vases on each table.

Jenny dropped into one of several available lounge chairs. A small table stood between her and a second chair. Linda remained standing.

A short man with a mustache milled around. Linda watched as a customer dropped some bills into his palm in exchange for a bottle of pills. The customer concealed them in his pocket and left.

So, this is the underworld. Linda studied the scene, absorbing it all.

A few people snorted white powder, no doubt purchased from Mustache, who placed a small tray on the table in front of Jenny. It contained two bags of white powder, small straws, and wax paper.

Her cousin cleared the tray, placed bills on it, and passed it back to the man.

Soft laughter emanated from nearby tables. A few patrons seemed distant, detached from reality. Another customer leaned back in his chair, both arms high in the air with his index fingers circling toward the ceiling. He looked familiar—he was a physician assistant from the hospice ward where Linda worked.

"Have a seat," Mustache said to Linda.

Jenny dumped her powder on the smooth paper,

snorted it through a short straw, and then looked up at her.

"Do you know what that stuff is doing to your body?" Linda asked.

Jenny snickered. "My own personal doctor. What do you prescribe for my symptoms?"

Something hit Linda like a thunderbolt. Were these the drugs Grandpa had taken from her place? Was this why Beaulin and Selva were murdered?

A wave of anger swept through her. "What part of 'I don't do drugs' don't you understand?"

"Come on," Jenny said. "It'll loosen you up. Everyone our age uses."

Mustache overheard their conversation. "Jenny, you can't bring non-customers up here."

Linda's stomach lurched. Did he think she'd go to the police?

Jenny pushed the drugs closer to her. "Come on. It's paid for."

Linda turned to leave, but Mustache blocked her path.

Linda had to get out of there before the physician assistant recognized her or the police raided the place. She took a step forward, eyed Mustache. "Step aside, or I'm calling my grandpa, Teddy Mudici."

The man's forehead wrinkled. "Mr. Mudici's your grandfather?"

"Yeah," Jenny said. "She's my geek cousin. Let her go."

Mustache stepped aside. Jenny bounced down the stairs behind Linda.

After Linda got her coat, she asked the bouncer to walk her outside. Jenny trailed behind them.

Linda's nightmare had ended. The night air refreshed her. It felt good to be back in the normal world.

Her cousin zoomed far out and floated high. Her eyes shimmered under the streetlamp. She danced around, threw back her head, and ran the fingers of both hands through her hair. "I'm going home with Bear."

"Jenny, you don't know those guys. Are you out of your mind? You're putting your life in danger. Do you pick up a stranger every night?"

Jenny shrugged. "All the time. Hey, it's cold out here. Later, cuz." She rushed back inside.

Linda continued to the parking lot with the bouncer.

"That man who pulled my hair is sitting there with his engine running," she said, pointing.

The bouncer walked to the man's SUV, opened the door, and dragged him outside. "Hurry. Leave now so he can't follow you."

Linda thanked the bouncer, stuffed a hundred-dollar bill into his back pocket, jumped in her car, and sped out of the parking lot. She considered going back for Jenny, but her cousin had a mind of her own. The drug-addict tramp knows her way home.

Before Linda reached her apartment, her cell phone rang.

"The guys said you were rude, snotty." Jenny's high-pitched voice flowed fast. The drugs must have really kicked in. "You embarrassed me. You don't walk into a place and then act as if you're better than everybody else. Do you know what could happen to you?"

Linda wondered where Jenny had found a quiet place to talk. She put her on speakerphone. "I'm a doctor. I only hope none of my patients saw me there. I don't have a rich daddy to support me. You're thirty-five and have never had a job."

"Don't need to work."

"Well, I do."

"Sorry if I don't meet your standards."

"I'll attend the family Sunday meals, but no more partying or shopping with you." Linda hung up.

Fifteen minutes later, Jenny called again, acting as if the nightclub scene had never happened. "Megan and I are going to the Poconos next weekend. You're welcome to come."

Linda rolled her eyes. "No thanks."

"We usually rent a townhouse."

"No," Linda said.

"No drugs," Jenny said. "I promise."

A taxi cut Linda off. She hit her brakes, almost rear-ending the car. "I'm not going."

Linda pulled into a parking space under her apartment building and killed the engine.

Jenny's words came faster, more persistent. "All you

need is a warm ski outfit. I can help you with that. We rent the equipment."

"I'm not going."

"Megan will call you tomorrow. Meet her for coffee or something. She's really a nice person."

Linda unbuckled her seatbelt but remained in her vehicle. "You're not listening."

Jenny's voice took on a sharp, annoying tone. "Look, we're blood relatives. I'm trying to bond with you."

Linda didn't care if she hurt Jenny's feelings. "After tonight, I'll never go anywhere with you again. We don't have the same interests, and we're definitely not on the same maturity level."

Linda hung up again.

CHAPTER 15

WHERE IS JENNY?

When Linda arrived for the Mudici Sunday dinner, a cloud of gloom covered the house like a fog.

Aunt Christina pushed her plate back from the table, crossed her arms, and lowered her head. She exhaled her words. "Linda, have you heard from Jenny today?"

All eyes focused on Linda. "No. Is something wrong?"

Grandma took a sip of wine. "We're worried. She called after you left her at the nightclub last night. No one has heard from her since."

"I didn't like her friends, so I left," Linda said. "She was dancing with some guy, seemed to be having fun."

"It's not unusual for her to stay out all night," Grandma said. "But we should have heard from her by now. She's not answering her cell phone."

Aunt Christina wiggled an accusing finger at Linda. "How could you just drive off and leave her there alone?"

"I tried to get her to come with me." Linda shrugged.

"She refused. The guys she hooked up with looked like gangsters."

Grandma gripped her glass with a shaking hand. "We're really worried."

Grandpa poured a glass of whiskey. "Maybe the Selva family has her. Last week, I told you to make yourself scarce, Linda."

"Grandpa?"

"Do what I tell you," he scolded. "I just hope that Selva's family doesn't know we're related."

***

When Linda drove into the parking lot of the hospital clinic the next morning, Grandma called. She spoke between sobs. "My grandbaby is still missing. We've turned in a missing person report."

Linda popped the trunk and retrieved a gift for a nurse's baby shower. "It hasn't been two days yet, Grandma. Maybe she'll show up."

Her grandmother wailed. "I have an ominous feeling about her disappearance."

Linda slammed the trunk and locked her doors. "Hope for the best."

"We don't want anything to happen to you too." Grandma sniffed. "Who's this man you're seeing? He could be a psychopathic killer."

"It's Ian Worthing. We're not dating."

Grandma blurted out, "Oh, Dr. Worthing?"

"I'm not a kid, Grandma. I can take care of myself."

"Like Jenny? We don't know if she's dead or alive. Someone could be torturing her at this very moment."

Linda walked into the clinic. "Don't get yourself worked up, Grandma. Do you want me to drop in after work?"

Grandma sniffed. "No, honey. Teddy said you should stay away from us for a while."

"I'm coming anyway. See you about seven."

***

Linda had follow-up examinations and pre-surgery patients. Things slowed in the afternoon when two patients had made last-minute cancellations, so she'd decided to take a long lunch break in the hospital's cafeteria.

She paid the cashier for a salad and a bottle of water and saw a colleague sitting alone, drinking coffee. Linda was walking over to him when her cell phone rang. It was Grandpa. He never called her.

"Grandpa, any news about Jenny?" She placed her plate on her colleague's table and whispered, "May I join you?"

The doctor smiled and motioned Linda to the empty chair.

"A few hours ago, the police found Jenny's mutilated body."

The old man always got to the point.

Linda's heart raced, her legs grew weak. She cringed, dropping into the nearest chair. "Jenny's dead."

Grandpa's voice revealed no stress or anxiety. "It was brutal. No one does that to my granddaughter and gets away with it. The police need to take your statement at the Twenty-Seventh Precinct. A Lieutenant Rosenberg is expecting you. We'll meet you there."

"Where did they find her? How was she killed?" Linda asked.

The call ended.

Grandpa probably had more access to information than the police did.

"Someone you know?" the doctor asked.

"Yes, we weren't that close. But other than her killer, I might have been the last person to see her alive. I need to go." Linda dashed from the table without another word, rushed back to her office, and asked other doctors to see her last patients.

Taking the subway across the city got her to the police station faster than driving. The waiting area was larger than the last one she'd visited and filled to its capacity.

Linda approached an elderly uniformed cop who occupied the front desk.

"May I help you, ma'am?" he asked.

Linda dug into her purse and pulled out her wallet. "I'm here to see Detective Rosenberg." She placed her license on the counter.

"Is he expecting you?" the officer asked.

"Yes, it's about my cousin's murder."

He jotted down her license and visitor's badge number, then slid both across the desk to her.

Familiar with the routine, she clipped the badge onto her collar.

"Jones," the man called to one of two younger cops occupying desks behind him, "Escort Dr. Harrison to Detective Rosenberg."

Jones stood and walked around his desk. "This way."

Linda followed Jones up the stairs to the second floor and through secured double doors. She entered a large room with multiple desks. Most were empty, with the exception of two.

They passed a woman who seemed mesmerized by her computer screen. The only other person in the room was an African American man with a shaved head and a chinstrap beard.

Jones said, "Detective Rosenberg, this is Dr. Harrison."

The big man's chair squeaked in relief as he stood. He extended a large hand. "Hello, Dr. Harrison. Sorry for your loss. I understand that you're Mr. Mudici's granddaughter?"

Linda pumped his hand a couple of times. "I prefer to be a little discreet about that."

He nodded. "I understand."

Rosenberg escorted her a few doors down to an interrogation room, closing the door behind them.

The expansive room was nothing like the one Jansen and LaFee had used to interview her. A large two-way mirror extended almost the entire length of the front wall, and a surveillance camera focused on them.

They both took seats.

"What time did you and your cousin get to the club?" Rosenberg asked.

"About eleven o'clock. Jenny said the party didn't start until then."

"Was that your first time at the ..." He checked his notes. "White Castle?"

"Yes. Jenny and I don't—didn't have much in common, but she kept pestering me to go with her."

"What happened when you got there?"

"Jenny walked us to the front of the line. We checked our coats. She was gone before I even turned around. When I saw her again, she was dancing with a guy who had the lower half of his face tattooed."

"How long were you there?"

"About an hour. I didn't like the place or the people, so I left," Linda said.

"Why did you stay that long?" Rosenberg asked.

"When we checked our coats, the attendant mixed up our tickets. I beckoned Jenny from the dance floor and asked for mine. I followed her and her dance partner to a table occupied by two other men."

"Was that the first time either of you had met these guys?" he asked.

"Yes. Jenny introduced her partner, Bear. Said he was from Chicago. The man with top and bottom gold incisors called himself Clint. They called the shorter one Man. Rather than give me my ticket, Jenny tossed her purse in my lap and headed back to the dance floor with Bear. She left me sitting there with two strangers."

Rosenberg locked eyes with Linda. "Were drugs involved?"

"I didn't see any," she lied.

His eyebrows raised in question. "Didn't Jenny do drugs?"

"I'm not sure."

"Did she have anything to drink?"

"When Jenny returned, I detected alcohol on her breath."

"Did she slur her words or seem off balance?"

"No. She appeared cheerful."

"Did you eat or drink anything there?"

"No. I just wanted to go home. I retrieved my coat, and Jenny walked me outside—said she planned to spend the night with Bear. I tried to get her to leave. Those were some shady-looking characters."

"We have the video footage, but it's a little grainy," the detective said. "I don't know why companies refuse to invest in better equipment. She did leave with three men. One's face was tattooed, as you described."

Linda shivered. What if she had stayed? Would she be in the morgue with Jenny? "How was she killed?"

"I'm not allowed to disclose that information." He leaned back in his chair and interlaced his fingers. "We thought we knew the entire Mudici family."

"I only learned three months ago that Teddy Mudici was my grandfather."

"Where did you grow up?"

"Florida, then Louisiana. Foster care," she said.

"Did you dislike your cousin or have a personal vendetta against her?"

"I hardly knew her."

"Did she mention any conflicts with anyone? Enemies?"

"No."

The detective interrogated Linda for over an hour. Finally, he got to his last question. "If I take you to a sketch artist, can you help her with the composites?"

"I can do better than that." She smiled. "I can draw them."

"Let's do it with the assistance of a professional." He stood. "She's just down the hall."

Linda fell behind Rosenberg, walking fast to keep up with his long strides. He looked back and slowed his pace.

He escorted her through an open door. "Hello, Sally. This is Dr. Harrison. She's here to help with the sketches of the suspects concerning the Mudici murder case."

Sally occupied an extra-wide chair, smacking a mouthful of gum. The orange-haired woman had a triple chin. Round-rimmed bifocals perched on her long nose like windows. She didn't stand but shook Linda's hand from her seat.

"I hate to meet people under such unfortunate circumstances," Sally said.

"Dr. Harrison knows how to sketch. Call me when you two finish," Rosenberg said to them as he strolled out.

Sally popped her gum. "Have a seat, honey. I've completed sketches from what I saw on the surveillance video. Not the best quality of cameras. You can help me fill in the details."

Linda sat next to Sally, eyes fixed on a large computer screen with black swivel lamps on either side. Stubby fingers hit a few keys, and a resemblance of Bear's face became enlarged on the screen.

"How about this for the taller man? I do sketches, mostly with computer technology. I do rather well with help from citizens like you. He looked about six feet to me."

"His height is about right," Linda said. "The sketch is a good match. His eyes were closer together, cheeks fuller."

Sally made the changes Linda suggested on her screen. "How about this?"

"Rounder chin, shorter nose," Linda said.

"Eye color?"

Linda leaned in, scrutinizing the photo. "Light brown. His forehead was less concave."

Sally popped her gum again. "How does that look, honey?"

"Excellent."

Sally rolled her chair back, picked up a trashcan, and spat her gum into it. "Sorry about that. I forget I make noise when I chew." The woman placed tracing paper on the side of her desk. "Can you sketch those facial tattoos? Remember what they looked like?"

"I can come close, even the ones on his hands and fingers," Linda said.

"It's hard to hide tattoos like that unless they're the type that wash off. Any other details before we move on?" Sally asked.

"He wore diamond stud earrings in both ears. They all did."

"What about his ears?" Sally asked.

"They look fine."

Linda and Sally completed composites of the other two men. Then Sally phoned Rosenberg, giving him the good news.

When Linda returned to Rosenberg's desk, two other detectives were there. Jenny's parents, Grandma, and Grandpa had arrived.

Aunt Christina sat next to Ralph and wailed uncontrollably with her head buried in his chest. She sucked in air as if fighting for her last breath. "Oh no. Not my child. My baby is gone," she sobbed.

Uncle Ralph held his wife in his arms, stroking her back.

Aunt Christina turned her rage and grief on Linda.

"If you hadn't left her there alone, she'd still be alive," she hissed. The words from her tongue were venomous. Her accusing finger pointed at Linda like a talon. Linda imagined blood dripping from it after a kill.

At a loss for words, her mouth fell open. "I'm sorry that Jenny is dead, but you can't blame this on me." Linda's voice trembled. "If I had stayed, I'd be dead too. I don't go to nightclubs. Jenny did all the time."

Uncle Ralph held his wife tighter, but she was inconsolable.

Linda's eyes darted around at the other family members. "Are you all blaming me for Jenny's death?"

Grandma wiped tears from her cheeks with a tissue. Her shoulders sank and her face remained frozen in sadness. "No, honey."

Grandpa stood with his back to them, gazing out the window. Then he turned on his heel, as if an idea had just popped into his head. He approached Rosenberg and whispered into his ear. They disappeared down the hallway. When they returned moments later, Grandpa carried a manila folder.

***

That night, only mourning occurred in the Mudicis' house. Grandpa locked himself in his office, talking on the phone. Grandma didn't talk much. Aunt Christina refused to speak to Linda at all. Uncle Ralph remained stoic, as always.

Linda walked up the stairs and entered Jenny's bedroom. The place stood empty, cold. She quickly retrieved the key taped under the desk, unlocked the metal box, dumped all of the memory cards into a shopping bag, and covered them with two sweaters. She hesitated just for a moment. What if Grandpa checks the bag?

When Linda bounced downstairs, Aunt Christina stood at the bottom, her hands on her hips. Anger roared in her voice as she bellowed, "What are you taking?"

Linda's stomach churned with anxiety. "A few things I lent Jenny."

Aunt Christina's voice went up a full octave. "They just found her body and already you're picking like a vulture."

Grandma walked Aunt Christina to the sofa. "Calm down, dear. I'll get you a drink."

As Linda walked toward the front door, Grandma rushed to her and hugged her goodbye. "Honey, you're shaking."

"I just can't believe Jenny's gone, Grandma."

"I know. Your aunt's in pain. She didn't mean what she said."

Aunt Christina yelled, "Yes, I did."

Linda left with her treasure.

***

Two weeks passed without any leads concerning

Jenny's murder or persons of interest.

Not wanting to repeat their last encounter, Linda avoided Aunt Christina whenever possible.

For a high school dropout and a drug addict, Jenny was smarter than Linda had given her credit for. Each memory card displayed the times, dates, and length of the recording. Unlike Jenny, Linda stashed most of them in a safe deposit box, keeping two in her apartment to view. She watched Grandpa implicating himself in Beaulin's murder. He'd orchestrated a hit on Al Selva. A hit carried out by Swift at the Blue Parrot Lounge and another in at a library. Grandpa had also aided and solicited other murders—along with drugs, and money laundering.

The evidence didn't surprise her. Grandpa was a mob boss. That was what he did for a living.

CHAPTER 16

ILLEGAL SURGERY

Linda's cell phone woke her from a sound sleep. The luminous clock dial on her nightstand read 2:07 a.m. She didn't check the number. "Hello?"

"Come to the clinic. I need your help," Ian's voice rang on the other end of the phone.

"Ian, why are you there at this hour?"

"Just get down here," he said. "We have an emergency." He sounded breathless, as if he had been jogging. Linda had never heard him so frantic.

"Are you ill or hurt?" she asked.

"I have two patients in need of serious medical attention."

"Dial 9-1-1," she suggested. "A clinic is not a hospital." She hung up.

Seconds later, her phone rang again. She recognized the number. "Grandpa, do you know what time it is?"

"Linda, get down here now. Don't take a taxi. Park in

the back of the clinic. I'll meet you at the back door." His voice didn't have a nervous edge like Ian's had, but his orders were clearly not a request.

Her skin crawled. "What's wrong?"

"Don't ask questions. Hurry," he demanded. "Do I make myself clear?"

"Okay, I'm coming."

Linda threw back her covers and jumped out of bed. She had a bad feeling about the situation. Something to do with Jenny's murder? Ideas ran through her mind like a computer program. If someone is sick or hurt, why not take them to the emergency room?

She slid into a pair of jeans and a T-shirt, then rushed downstairs, jumped into her car, and sped off. She waited impatiently at red lights. Where are people going at this hour? She took a shortcut through a high-crime, graffiti-filled neighborhood. Groups of men stood on sidewalks, smoking and drinking. When she stopped at a red light, two thugs started toward her car. Glancing in both directions, she hit the gas and sped through the intersection.

When she arrived at the clinic, Linda saw five cars parked in the back. Two of them belonged to Ian and her grandfather, but she didn't recognize the other three.

Grandpa stood in the shadows at the back door. He wasn't wearing his usual suit and tie but dark-colored jogging clothes.

Jumping from her car, she ran to his side. "What's wrong?"

"Get inside." He ushered her in. "We need your help."

She followed him—and a trail of blood—to a dusty, cramped back room that contained extra furniture and medical supplies.

Concentrating on the trail of blood, she followed it into the center of the room. There, two men lay side by side on examination tables, leaving just enough room for someone to stand between them. With the exception of their shirts, both wore street clothes. Ian had IVs running in each patient's arm—surgery was underway. Ian had opened the chest of Grandpa's bodyguard. The man's exposed heart pumped like a machine. A third man lay on the floor in a pool of blood to the left side of the doorway.

Linda stood frozen, baffled and confused. Her stomach fluttered, her heart pounded wildly, and her adrenaline pumped out of control. She'd entered a doctor's nightmare. Eyeing the man on the floor again, she held her breath.

Ian glanced up at her. "That one's dead," he said with a jerk of his head. "A bullet nicked this guy's coronary artery. There's another one in his right lung. I left you the easy one."

Swift lay on the opposite table, a bullet in his shoulder. He moved his head as much as his condition allowed. "Pain," he moaned.

His voice jerked Linda from her reverie. "What's going on here?" she asked, looking into Swift's pale face.

He extended a hand toward her, his face contorted, his shrunken eyes pleading for help—for life. His voice was weak and raspy. "Linda, help me."

The psychopath pleaded for his life. She examined Swift, assessing his wound. "Get these patients to a hospital."

Grandpa placed a restraining hand on her shoulder. "We can't. You're a doctor, get to work."

Linda turned to him, voice shrill. "Are you out of your mind? This is illegal. I can't work on patients under these conditions. I need proper surgical equipment, nurses, and an anesthesiologist."

She pulled her cell phone from her purse. "I'm calling for an ambulance."

Grandpa grabbed her phone and smashed it against the wall, shattering it into pieces.

She had the urge to smack him. "I'm not getting involved in this."

Grandpa stood nose to nose with her, teeth clenched tighter than a cell door. "They can't go to the hospital, and no cops. If you don't do something, Swift is going to bleed to death."

Linda headed toward the door. "I'm not performing surgery here. I could lose my medical license."

Grandpa caught up with her, turned her around, and slapped her face.

Anger exploded within her, like the bloody mess in her surroundings. She slapped him back, and he fell against the wall, almost losing his balance. "That's the last time you'll strike me, old man."

His deep-set eyes locked on hers, cold and cruel. "My father died in prison because of Helena. If you call the cops, granddaughter or not, you won't live to testify against me." He pushed her toward Swift. "Now move it. Help him before he dies."

Linda shuddered. First her adoptive parents had wanted her dead, and now Grandpa was threatening her life. She couldn't walk out. Linda had sworn to the Hippocratic Oath. She had to try to save Swift's life.

Ian had all the surgical instruments laid out.

Linda's mind raced. Her past had made her stronger than most. She could adjust to any situation. She had to suck it up and deal with the reality of what was happening.

"His X-rays are on the wall," Ian said, concentrating on his work. "Anesthetic's in that blue cylinder."

With trembling hands, Linda studied two images. The bullet had passed through Swift's shoulder and lodged itself near his back. Linda placed the small cylinder on the bed next to him, picked up the mask, and straightened it out in her hands. "Ian, I don't know how much to give him."

Ian screwed up his red face into a frown. "Cover his face with the mask, turn on the gas, and remove it when he's under."

Swift groaned. His face twisted in pain, his mouth open.

Linda attached the mask around Swift's mouth and nose, held his head up, and secured the elastic band around the back. "Are you sure this stuff's going to knock him out? I can't have a patient coming around in the middle of surgery."

"Turn on the gas until he falls asleep," Ian repeated.

"It's in PSIs," Linda said. "How much should I give him?"

Ian said, "Guess."

"I need sponge sticks or artery clamps, monofilament permanent sutures ..."

"We don't have any. Use what you've got and hope for the best," Ian said.

Two men rushed in, wrapped the dead man in black plastic, and carried him away. A third man soaked up the pool of blood with rags.

Linda hadn't put a patient under since medical school, and she had always injected the anesthetic directly into the patient's IV. Taking a few deep breaths to calm her nerves, Linda followed Ian's instructions, and Swift went out like a light. Her scalpel didn't cut deeply, but wide. She used a hemostat to control the bleeding. "Grandpa, I need you to suction the blood away so I can see, and then hold this while I suture the artery."

The old man held the instrument with steady hands and suctioned the blood as fast as it appeared.

Linda concentrated on stitching up the artery with fine sutures, glued the incision, and bandaged the gash.

"What about the bullet?" Grandpa asked.

"I need to go through the back to retrieve it. It's about two inches from the surface."

Grandpa helped her use the bedsheet to turn Swift over. She made a shallow incision in the infraspinatus, removed the bullet with forceps, and tossed it onto the bed.

Grandpa grabbed it and threw it into a trash bag.

Linda then stitched up the incision and changed her gloves. Grandpa helped her turn Swift back over, and she covered him with a blanket under which his chest rose and fell in short, delayed intervals.

Linda had been in a cold sweat since she entered the place, but she didn't pause. She moved to the right side of Ian's patient, squeezing into the space between the beds.

"What can I do here?"

Ian huffed. "I don't know if he'll make it."

"I'm a lung expert. You continue with the artery."

"I'm glad you volunteered for the job," Ian said. "I have the least experience in that area."

Warm blood oozed from a tube Ian had inserted into the man's right lung and dripped onto her pants and shoes.

Linda didn't concentrate on anything except saving her patient. She studied his X-rays. "The bullet broke the rib. Fortunately, the bone slowed it down. This fracture can cause internal damage each time he moves." She made an incision above the fourth true rib, dug out the bullet, and discarded it on the sheet. "Got it."

"What about damage?" Ian asked.

She wiped her forehead with a sleeve. "It just nicked the lung. It'll repair itself with time. Remove the tube when the bleeding stops. The rib is broken. There's nothing I can do about that."

Sweat dripped from Ian's chin and onto his patient's chest. "Use an intramedullary splint."

She gasped, "You don't have decent surgical equipment, but you have technologically advanced parts? How did you get those?"

Ian pointed a finger to a top shelf. "They're in the gray plastic container, Teddy."

Grandpa brought the box to Linda's side and set it on the bed next to the patient. He scooped out a handful of various titanium plates sealed in clear plastic. "Which one do you need?"

"The five-millimeter radius looks right. It's the one near your left thumb." She glanced around the area. "Ian, do you have a drill?"

"The upper cabinet near the sink."

Grandpa went in search of it.

With the surgery almost over, Linda relaxed a little, although she was still wired. "What about the man they took away?"

"He got two in the head," Ian said.

"I know that. I meant what's going to happen to his body?"

"He'll be taken care of," Grandpa said, handing her a small battery-operated drill.

She accepted the drill with bloody gloves. "Any of these things sterilized?"

"Nope," Ian said.

Linda scraped back the flesh and placed the plate on the section of broken ribs. "Ouch. I hope this guy doesn't have any infectious diseases."

"You didn't cut your finger?" Ian asked.

"Yes. I've never done that before."

"You're under stress," Ian said. "Try to relax."

Linda looked at him. "Are you relaxed?"

"No, but I've done plenty of surgeries with much less. At least we have anesthetic."

She donned a clean pair of gloves that Grandpa provided. He was performing as well as some nurses.

Ian started wiring up his patient's chest. "I'm closing here."

Grandpa washed his hands in the nearby sink, walked out of earshot, and made a phone call. Shortly afterward, two men stormed in, strapped Swift onto a stretcher, and hauled him outside with the IV still in his arm. Linda assumed they were taking him home for recovery.

The last man started cleaning the remaining blood from the operating table with gloved hands. He mopped the floor with rags soaked in cleaner, throwing everything into black trash bags.

Ian removed his gloves and dropped them into a bag.

He placed both hands on his hips and swayed back. "We need to remove these bloody clothes. All we have are scrubs." He opened a cabinet, tossed a bottom and a top to her.

Grandpa said to Linda, "Throw your dirty clothes in these plastic bags. We'll take care of them."

Linda stripped in the ladies' room, then slipped into a pair of extra-large green scrubs. When she returned to the room, Teddy's bodyguard was gone, and a man was waiting for her clothes.

Grandpa had left.

Ian started wiping down his table and cleaned the medical equipment. "You're done here, Linda. Thanks. Go home. Get some rest."

After stepping into a pair of oversized hospital slippers, Linda walked to her car, opened the door, slid into the driver's seat, and hit the door lock. She sat still, for the first time realizing that her neck and upper back ached. What had she just done? She could lose her license because of Grandpa. And she hated him for it.

After arriving home, Linda showered and threw everything into the trash, grabbed a bottle of white wine from the fridge, threw back the covers on her bed, and got in. Grandpa had used her—taken advantage of her, just as everyone else close to her had.

The alcohol caused instant, peaceful sleep.

***

Linda stood behind cobweb-covered bars. Long white hair draped over her shoulders. Her wrinkled, liver-spotted hands gripped a bone. The cell lock was rusted. No one else was in sight. And with the exception of a dim glow through a dirty window above her head, she saw only darkness.

Drenched in sweat, Linda awoke that Sunday morning with a migraine, not sure if the wine or the night's illegal activities had caused it. Her digital clock read 10:14 a.m. She lumbered into the kitchen, made coffee, and ate a cup of yogurt. Returning to her bed with a cup of coffee, she resumed the footage she'd been watching from one of Grandpa's secret meetings. The camera had captured the entire area but focused on him sitting at the head of the table in his private room at his restaurant. Uncle Ralph, Billy, and Swift attended. Three strangers implicated themselves in illegal activities with the family.

Grandpa said, "After taking out Al Selva, we didn't expect his family to retaliate."

"Word is, they're planning to hit us," Swift warned.

Grandpa rubbed his fingers under his chin. "His family is unorganized without that twerp, Selva. I didn't think they'd have the balls to come after us."

Linda froze the TV screen and called Ian. He had spent the night at the clinic. She drove down there to discuss the previous night's unlawful surgeries.

When she entered the employee lunchroom, Ian sat at the table reading The New York Times. The morning news aired on the TV in front of him. He hit the mute button.

He didn't make eye contact with her. "I made a pot of coffee. Looks like Teddy's security guard is going to make it."

Disappointment left a hard lump in her stomach. "Grandpa hasn't called to ask me how I'm doing or to apologize for threatening to kill me."

"Teddy Mudici is a very cold, cruel, and calculating man."

She remained standing. "I can't erase what happened last night from my mind. How did you get mixed up in this?"

He looked up from his paper, yawned. "It's a long story."

She pulled back a chair and took a seat. "I have time."

He hesitated, his eyes focused into the distance. "Your grandpa has done personal favors for me. Big jobs. Things money can't buy. I'm indebted to him for life."

Linda moved to the counter and poured a cup of coffee. "Ian, stay away from him."

For the first time, he looked her in the eyes. "And go where? I can't get out any more than you can. Last night you crossed the line. There's no going back now."

His words pierced her heart like a stake. Had she officially become a part of the family?

Doubt stirred in her mind. "I can break off all ties with them."

"Doesn't matter. They won't let you go." Ian chuckled. "I can't believe you slapped Teddy's face last night and got away with it." He paused, holding his cup in midair, his eyes now cold and distant. "Before you got there last night, I told Teddy I wanted out. He said I wouldn't like my retirement plan. I'm afraid he might have me taken out in the near future."

She said, "You still haven't told me how you got involved."

He took a sip of coffee. "I can't. I just made some stupid mistakes."

Linda took a sip of strong coffee. She frowned and dumped it into the sink. "You should've never told him you wanted out. Just left, disappeared."

"Yes," he admitted. "That was a stupid mistake." He frowned. "What's wrong with the coffee?"

The bitter taste still lingered in Linda's mouth. "It's far from gourmet. How many of these surgeries have you done?"

He took a deep breath and then exhaled. "Seven. Most were the results of drug-related fights. Two minor gunshots, a few knifings, but nothing like last night."

She sat at the table. "Check the flights to Heathrow."

He pushed the newspaper aside, opened his laptop, and logged on. "This may take a while. You think I should leave this week?"

"No. Today. Now. You've talked about returning to Africa," she said. "With your parents' help, you can go to England—South America. Change your name. Get a new identity."

"I need to wrap up things here, give notice to the clinic," he said.

Linda's muscles tightened. She pounded a fist on the table. "Does your life mean anything to you? Leave on the next flight."

He stroked keys on his key pad. "In order to know my movements, Teddy must have someone watching my every move."

"If you have something on Grandpa, I'm sure he does."

Ian concentrated on the screen. "Why don't I leave in a couple of days?"

She leaned over the table. "You're a dead man. I can take care of whatever business you have. Every second counts."

He closed his eyes. "I don't have money for a plane ticket."

"Is that why you're hesitant? Money?"

"I can't ask—"

Her phone rang. "Just a minute, Ian. It's Grandma."

"Are you dining with us today?" the old woman asked without preamble.

"No. I can't, Grandma."

"The cops still don't have any leads on the men Jenny left the nightclub with. Teddy is trying to find them also."

They'd better hope the cops find them before Grandpa does. "The men at the club with Jenny claimed to have been from Chicago. Maybe they live right here in the city."

"Teddy considered that too," Grandma said. "It's hard to hide a tattooed face like that one. They must have been washable tattoos."

"I really tried to get Jenny to leave that club, Grandma."

"I don't blame you. The way she partied, well … hey, I'm cleaning out her old room Saturday. Come over and help me pack her things. You might find something you'd like. She had some nice evening dresses."

"I don't think Aunt Christina would like that, Grandma."

"Christina wants you to help me pack. She can't stand to do it."

"All right, Grandma. Bye."

As Linda pulled her concentration from the call, she noticed that the midday news was in the middle of announcing another murder. It wasn't unusual for New York City—except that the photo was of the dead man from the clinic last night. Ian activated the sound with the remote control.

"*A parking attendant found Danny Catolano's body in a parking garage with two gunshots to the head. Police officials believe it might have been a mob-related killing.*"

She locked eyes with Ian.

"The next British Airways flight to London leaves at 7:45 this evening," he said.

"I'll help you. Pack, then go to the airport and wait in the secured area until your flight leaves."

***

Linda jumped into her car and followed Ian to a run-down apartment complex about twenty blocks from the clinic. Various colors of graffiti covered the lower walls. Numerous potholes littered the parking lot, which contained a few older model cars.

Ian led her up a metal staircase to the second floor and unlocked two deadbolts, flipped on the light switch, and entered. "Come in."

Loud music blasted from the apartment below, its noise competing with a shouting match occurring between a man and a woman next door. Linda didn't trust the old, tattered sofa in the living area, so she took a seat at the table. All of Ian's furniture looked as if it had survived the fifties ...barely. The dirty yellow walls were bare, dotted with uneven white plaster to cover up holes. Linda didn't see a TV. Now she understood why he carried his laptop everywhere he went. Half a dozen pizza boxes sat on the floor next to an overflowing trashcan. A small cardboard box and two stuffed garbage bags lined one wall.

Ian opened the refrigerator and peered in. "How about a soda?"

"Water," Linda said.

He placed a bottle of water on the table, grabbed a can of soda for himself, and took the chair across from her.

The fight next door had escalated from verbal to what now sounded physical. Linda looked at Ian for a reaction. Nothing. Then, something smashed against the wall. Linda jumped.

A woman screamed, "You hit me again, and I'll kill you."

"Bitch, you bit me," the man yelled. "Get your shit and hit the road. I can find something better than you."

"Should I dial 9-1-1?" Linda asked.

Ian popped the tab on his soda can and guzzled down half its contents. "That goes on almost every day."

"Get a move on. Pack your things," she said.

He drained the remainder of his soda and stood. "I need to shower first."

While he got ready in his bedroom, Linda purchased his airline ticket online.

When he reentered the living room, he sported slacks, a tie, and shiny new shoes. He rolled a large bag behind him with a carry-on bag hanging from his shoulder and a computer case in his hand. "I'll take a cab."

Linda stood. "No, I'll drive you."

He checked his pockets. "Let's see. I have my passport, wallet, and cell phone." After removing two keys from a chain, he slid them across the table. "These are my apartment keys. Let my manager know I won't be returning. He's on the first floor around the corner. Just follow the sign to his office." He then gave her two additional keys. "These are the keys to the clinic."

She nodded at the stuff stacked against the wall. "What about those?"

"Donate them to charity."

Linda raked the keys off the table and dropped them into her jeans pocket as she stood. "You sure you got everything? Personal things like papers?"

"Yeah," he said. "I wanted to leave this place anyway."

Linda followed him back downstairs, then placed his carry-on bag in the backseat of her car.

He placed the larger piece of luggage in the trunk, walked to an old, faded, four-door Dodge Shadow, and searched through the glove box. He pulled out a fistful of mail and stuffed it into his computer bag. Fast food boxes and wrappers littered the car's back seat and floor.

"What about my car?" he asked.

"It's a piece of junk. Forget it."

Ian passed her his car key. "I don't know how I can ever repay you."

She dropped the key into her pocket. "Just make a safe trip to London. Don't ever contact me again, or Grandpa might find you."

They headed to the airport just after four o'clock. Neither of them talked much during the drive.

Linda wanted answers, but Ian refused to provide them. Whatever he had on Grandpa, he would carry it with him.

"Leave your cell phone here. You won't need it in England," she said. "It can be traced."

He placed it on the console between the seats. "I'd like to pay back the money you spent on my airline ticket."

She hit her brakes, swerving to miss a bicyclist. "Don't contact me again. I don't need the money."

It took Linda almost an hour to reach the airport. She pulled up to the loading zone, popped the trunk, and retrieved Ian's carry-on bag while he unloaded his larger baggage.

Ian placed his luggage on the curb, hugged her goodbye, and thanked her again.

"Good luck, Ian. Remain in the secured area until your flight leaves." A weight lifted from her conscience when he entered the building. In less than two hours, he'd be safely out of the country—away from her family.

Before Linda arrived home, she noticed that Ian's cell phone was missing. He'd taken it after all. She called him numerous times, but she only got his voicemail. Perhaps paranoia had gotten the better of her, but an eerie feeling loomed over her like a dark shadow.

Grandma called her again. Linda no longer cared to associate with the family, so she made a lame excuse for missing Sunday dinner. She lounged around her apartment for the remainder of the day, watching more surveillance footage of Grandpa's business dealings.

At about midnight, her doorbell rang. Jumping from

her bed, Linda donned her robe and checked the security TV in the living room.

Detective LaFee held a folded paper in her hand. Jansen stood at her side. They were the last two people she wanted to see.

She slightly opened the door. "What do you two want at this time of night?"

LaFee's hair had grown longer since the last time Linda had seen her, and the blonde highlights were gone. "We need to come in."

"Can't this wait until morning?" Linda asked.

LaFee pushed the door wider, stepped inside. "No, it can't." She fanned the paper in Linda's face. "We have a search warrant."

Jansen entered, closing the door behind him.

Linda accepted the paper and studied it. "What are you looking for?"

Jansen's eyes narrowed in on her. "Why did you call Dr. Ian Worthing eleven times in a row?"

Linda looked from one detective to the other. "I wanted to make sure he made his flight. Is something wrong?"

"Dr. Worthing's body was discovered in a bathroom stall outside the secured area at the airport."

Linda clasped both hands over her mouth, closed her eyes, and let out a wail. She asked between labored sobs, "How did he die?"

"Murdered. That's all we can say," Jansen said.

Linda tasted bile. She rushed to the kitchen's trashcan

and threw up. She spat and clutched her stomach, waiting for another eruption. Grandpa had Ian killed. She hated him, couldn't deal with him anymore. She threw up again and breathed out the word, "When?"

"About 6:30," Jansen said.

Too bad New York didn't have the death penalty. Grandpa deserved the electric chair.

LaFee walked into the kitchen with Jansen in tow. "Dr. Harrison, men just aren't safe around you, are they?"

Linda had the urge to slap LaFee's face, but the last time she smacked a cop she'd ended up in jail, with a hefty fine to boot.

Jansen's words were malicious. "You got Coombs fired."

"Ian is dead, and you're holding a grudge? Coombs did that to himself. The security guard at my apartment building turned him in, not me."

Linda sat on the sofa and read the warrant while the detectives searched the guest room.

A few minutes later, they walked back into the living room.

"How long did Dr. Worthing live here?" LaFee asked.

"He never lived here. He only used my address to receive some of him mail here. Someone kept breaking his mailbox at his apartment."

LaFee asked, "Were you two romantically involved?"

Linda's words came out abruptly. "Platonic. Friends."

Jansen walked to her bedroom and opened the door.

Linda sprang from the sofa like a cat, ran in front of him, and nudged him out of her room. "You can't go in there." She shook the paper in his face. "This warrant is for the guest room and common living areas."

"What's playing on the TV?" he asked. "That looked like Teddy Mudici."

She had left her screen frozen on Grandpa and the six men. "A movie. Get out of my room."

Jansen leaned against the doorframe. "Where did you meet Dr. Worthing?"

She closed her door. "At the free clinic. I volunteer there sometimes."

"Did he have any enemies?" he asked.

"Not that I'm aware of. I've only known him for three months."

They grilled her for almost an hour before leaving her to mourn Ian's death.

What did Ian have on Grandpa that cost him his life?

CHAPTER 17

MOB EVIDENCE

The next Saturday morning, Linda showed up early at the Mudicis' house. The bodyguard reluctantly let her in, rousing Grandma.

Still groggy, the old woman ambled into the living room, yawned, and rubbed her eyes. "Why are you here so early, dear? We haven't had breakfast yet."

A bundle of cardboard boxes was stacked against the living room wall. Linda dropped her purse on the sofa. "I need to get started, because I have something planned this afternoon."

"Everything's going to charity," Grandma said. "Take whatever you'd like. I'll be up later."

When Grandma went back into her bedroom, Linda ducked into Grandpa's office and removed the last memory card and small recording device from the side compartment of the clock. It was exactly where Jenny had said it would be. She stuffed it under her sweatshirt and dashed through the living room. If Grandpa caught her with this evidence, he'd have her killed.

She ascended the stairs, hands shaking as if they were freezing. More boxes leaned against the hallway wall outside Jenny's door. Stepping into the room, she switched on the light. Everything looked the same, except for the dolly with large wheels sitting next to the bed. Rolls of packaging tape, scissors, a pen, and a small notepad lay on the dresser.

Linda opened the drapes. Jenny had always kept them closed. The early morning sunlight beamed brightly through a spotless window as she folded new boxes and taped up the bottoms. Removing underwear and sweaters, she went through Jenny's dresser drawers in haste. She wanted to get out of there as soon as possible.

Hearing noises coming from the kitchen, Linda stuck her head out the door and yelled, "Grandma, you want these boxes labeled?"

"Yes," the old woman shouted back. "And make an itemized list."

Nine boxes, stacked three high, lined the hallway when Grandma came up. The old woman still wore her robe. "Linda, you're sweating, and your face is so pale. Why are you working so fast?"

Linda shivered. "It's eerie, just being in this room." Actually, the recording device tucked in a bag terrified her.

"Go downstairs and get a cold drink," Grandma said.

Linda pointed to a bag in the corner. "I found a few sweaters and three evening gowns I'd like to keep."

Grandma pushed her toward the door. "Go get something to drink."

Bouncing downstairs, Linda found Grandpa sitting on the sofa, sipping coffee, and watching the morning news. He never made eye contact or acknowledged her.

She slowed her pace. "Grandpa, did you hear about Ian's murder?"

The old man kept his eyes on the television screen. Nonchalantly, he said, "I heard something about it."

Grandma had set Linda up on a date with Ian, yet she hadn't mentioned his death either.

Linda placed both hands on the sofa at grandpa's side. "Who would kill Ian? Why?" she asked, leaning over.

The old man didn't respond. He continued to stare straight ahead. "Why do you carry a gun in your purse?"

Her jaw dropped, and her eyes focused on her purse, which was near him. "You went through my bag."

What if she had put the recorder and memory card in her purse?

"Everything in it," he answered. "You have a black belt, so why the gun?"

She'd had her fill of Grandpa. "Karate doesn't stop a bullet. I only carry it when I come here. Since I've been associating with this family, I probably need an AK-47."

The old man turned and faced her, eyes menacing. "If

you ever strike me again, I'll make you regret the day you were born."

He still seethed resentment because she'd slapped him at the clinic.

Continuing to the kitchen, Linda opened the fridge, grabbed a cold bottle of water, and ran back upstairs. She looked forward to cutting ties with this family.

Grandma ran a roll of tape across the top of a box, sealing it. "I want this room empty and cleaned today."

Linda opened the bottle, downed half of its contents, and placed it on the dresser. "Don't you want to keep something of hers?"

"Christina took Jenny's photos and jewelry. I have a few keepsakes and her favorite teddy bear."

"I'm going shopping with one of Jenny's acquaintances for a ski outfit. We met for lunch the other day. She's a CPA, smart and nice."

"You're going skiing? That's great," Grandma said.

Linda opened the bottle and took another sip of water. "I'm glad Jenny gave her my number. Megan turned out to be a nice person, someone I'd like to have as a friend. I'm pretty excited about trying something new, especially after Jenny's death."

Grandma's voice became deep, low. "Does she use drugs?"

As if she'd associate with another drug addict. "Of course not. We've discussed that."

Grandma smiled. "I'm glad you're getting out more. You need to have a little fun."

Linda looked around. "We're almost finished here. It didn't take as long as I expected. Why don't you rest? I can handle it from here."

"This place looks empty without Jenny's personal things," Grandma said before disappearing down the stairs.

With the aid of the dolly, Linda moved boxes into the garage. She polished the furniture and vacuumed. Then, bouncing down the stairs, she stood in front of Grandma, who sat on the sofa. "I worked hard today."

Grandpa stood with his back to them, staring out the window. Like an eagle, he turned and zoomed in on the bag in Linda's hand. "What are you taking?"

"Some of Jenny's things. Grandma gave them to me."

He moved closer to her. "Dump them onto the sofa."

She froze in her tracks, gripping the handles of the bag, her fingernails digging into her palm.

Grandma came to her rescue. "Teddy, I gave her a few of Jenny's things. Leave her alone."

"Then why can't I see them?" he demanded.

Linda pulled out a sweater from the top of the pile and held it up to herself. "Want me to try on each item before I leave, just to make sure they fit?"

"You're picking on her, Teddy," Grandma said.

The old woman took Linda's arm, walked her to the front door, and threw it open.

Linda still held the sweater in her left hand. She hugged Grandma on her way out. "Bye."

"Thanks for helping me pack, dear."

Even the big, bad mobster had a boss.

***

The following Saturday morning, Linda sat in the passenger seat of an SUV with Megan, heading north.

Her Uncle Ralph had one exactly like it, and a sweetness similar to his pipe tobacco lingered inside.

Linda sipped on a cup of coffee as Megan bragged about having a sugar daddy who gave her everything, including a house in the suburbs. Even with the heavy traffic, they made it to the Poconos in less than two hours, arriving shortly past nine.

Megan pulled into the lot of a large complex and backed in, parking close to the stairs of the condominium. She said the place belonged to a friend.

Linda lugged her two bags up to the third floor of the building that would be her home for the next week. She'd had very few close friends in the past, and she liked Megan.

Like an eager kid, Linda quickly unpacked and donned a hot-pink ski outfit. Megan wore a black ski bib with matching gloves and jacket and a bright blue scarf. From the living room window, Linda saw skiers getting on and off a lift.

"We need to rent skis at the lodge," Megan said. "And you need ski lessons."

Linda shoved cash, a credit card, and her ID into one of several pockets and zipped it up. "You said we could ski together."

"Not until you learn how to get on and off the lift." Megan laughed. "You'll start on the bunny hill with the little kids. You ready?"

"Let's go," she said. "I can't wait."

Linda shivered as her rubber boots sank about six inches into the snow during the short walk to the lodge. Crunch. Crunch. Crunch. "I'm going to freeze up here."

Megan said, "Once you start skiing, you'll warm up."

Hundreds of skis protruded vertically from the snow in front of the ski lodge—most looked identical. The entrance had been cleared of snow, and salt crunched underneath her shoes. Early morning sunrays hit the crystals, causing them to sparkle like small diamonds.

When Linda entered the warm, crowded lodge, she saw patrons sitting around sipping coffee in front of a giant, blazing fireplace. Others ate breakfast, and a few sipped mugs of beer. The walls were smooth, polished oak with antique skis and old photographs plastered to them.

Linda kept in step with Megan's stride. They walked to the bar and grill, bought cappuccinos, and headed straight to the rental store. When they entered, two men stood behind the counter next to each other, helping other customers. Linda shifted from foot to foot in front of Megan. When she reached the counter, she said to a guy who looked about sixteen, "I'm a beginner."

Megan stepped to the next available assistant and requested her boot size and the type of skis she wanted.

The kid sat Linda in a chair and fitted her with a pair of boots and skis.

"Do you have an instructor?" he asked.

She stood, her feet restricted. "No. Can you recommend one?"

He handed her the rental equipment. "Lessons are next door. I suggest private ones with Mike."

Megan leaned on her skis. "Want me to tag along?"

Linda waved a hand. "No. You have fun. I'll be all right."

"Let's meet here at noon," Megan said. "You'll find me near the fireplace."

Loaded down with her gear, Linda entered the neighboring office and stood in line behind a couple with preschool-aged twins.

"Take them to the bunny hill," the man behind the counter said to the parents. "The area is surrounded by red flags. You can't miss it. They'll be in a group with six others." He smiled. "Have fun, kids."

When they left, Linda stepped to the counter. "Is Mike available?"

A guy about forty approached her from the rear. "Hello, I'm Mike."

She turned and accepted his soft, warm hand. "Nice to meet you. I'm Linda."

"What level are you?" he asked.

"Ah ... beginner."

"Complete this form." He was medium height, good-looking, and didn't wear a wedding ring. He probably has this job so he can meet women, Linda presumed.

Linda spent the next hour with Mike. She couldn't control her skis and fell repeatedly. Little kids skied better, and they snickered at her. Humiliated, cold, and exhausted, Linda left the bunny hill at eleven o'clock. At the lodge, she stuck the ends of her skis into the snow, flagged them with her scarf, and lumbered inside, wearing the uncomfortable plastic boots. Her leg muscles were aching, and her butt was sore. Finding an available table was impossible, so she milled around the crowded area waiting for a vacancy. A while later, giving up, she leaned against the wall near the fireplace with a cup of hot chocolate in hand, trying to thaw out.

At exactly noon, Megan entered the lodge, stomping snow from her boots. Linda waved her over.

Megan removed her gloves and rubbed her hands together. "How long have you been here?"

Linda narrowed in on Megan's red face. "About an hour. Couldn't find a table."

Megan led the way. "Just sit with someone else."

Linda fell into step behind her. "It's freezing up there.

I couldn't stay on my feet. At least I learned how to snowplow."

Megan patted her on the back. "It takes time."

"How long did it take you?"

Megan chuckled. "I've been skiing since I was four. How about some energy food—a burger and fries?"

Megan stopped at a table with four chairs occupied by two older men who were finishing up. "Anyone sitting here?"

"No, have a seat," one of the men said.

Linda sat across from her. "I'm giving up for today."

"Not me," Megan said. "I've just started."

Linda sighed, then leaned forward and rubbed her butt. "I couldn't stay on my feet."

The guys drained the last of their beers and stood. "Ladies, have a wonderful day."

Megan left for the restaurant and returned with two tall glasses of beer. "Food will be ready in a jiffy. Bet you're famished." Her cell phone rang. "Hello, Sweet Bear. We're having a wonderful time … Linda's not going out again today. She's exhausted. Yeah. Yeah. Love you too." This was the third conversation she'd had with her sugar daddy since they'd left the city, and interestingly she'd spoken as if he knew Linda.

Linda took a sip of beer. "Sweet Bear?"

"He's a great guy," Megan said. "Doesn't like being away from me for long periods of time."

**

By Friday, Linda's skiing had improved—turning was no problem. Stopping was a different story though.

Megan flew down the bunny hill like a pro. "Hi, Linda."

"Hey," a ski patrol officer yelled at Megan. "If I catch you speeding in this area again, you're off the slopes. Got it?"

"Sorry," Megan said. She never slowed down but skied up to the lodge and then abruptly stopped.

Linda remained on the slopes until about four, then turned in her skis. When she entered their condominium, it was empty.

Returning to the lodge, she ate dinner and had a couple of beers with her instructor. Before she realized it, she was engaged in conversation, laughing, and having a good time at a crowded table.

Proud of the progress she'd made over the past few days, Linda decided to ski every chance she got. If she couldn't ski with Megan, she'd go alone. She had lived in darkness all her life. A whole world of activities awaited her. Suddenly she had the urge to try them all—scuba diving, river rafting, and traveling the world. She would join singles groups. At thirty-two, she now wanted to live an exciting life.

Shortly after nine, Linda returned to the condominium. Megan's jacket lay on the sofa, and her half-packed suitcase sat on the living room floor. Linda knocked on her bedroom door.

"Megan, are you there?"

No response.

The door squeaked as Linda pushed it open. When she flipped on the light, she saw a lump lying in bed and covered up. An open bottle of whiskey and a glass stood on the nightstand. Next to it was a mirror with white powder and a straw.

Linda sucked in a deep breath and exhaled, "Oh no," Her hands went to her throat. She bent over, grabbed Megan's shoulders, and firmly shook her. "Get up."

A moan escaped from under the comforter, and a hand blindly groped for the glass.

Linda snatched back the bedspread and checked her roommate's eyes. Megan's pupils were dilated and her pulse was slower than normal.

Megan's eyes fluttered open and focused on the ceiling. "Turn off the light."

Linda had to say the words, not just think them. "Megan, you promised you didn't do drugs."

Megan forced Linda's hands away. "I'm not one of your freaking patients." She closed her eyes. "I don't do it all the time … like Jenny did. I've had a great week. This is my treat. Hey, don't tell your Uncle Ralph. He'll cut off my money if he finds out."

It all made sense now. "Uncle Ralph. He's Sweet Bear?"

"Oops … slipped out," Megan said.

Linda's mind went to Aunt Christina. "Did Jenny know about you and her father?"

Megan turned on her side, facing Linda. "Of course not."

Standing straight up, Linda looked down at Megan's haggard face. "We came here to ski. I trusted you."

"I've been flying high all afternoon."

Linda rested her fists on her hips. "I'm driving. Even after eight hours of sleep, you won't be able to operate a vehicle." Her voice was firm.

Megan sat up in bed. "Ralph trusts me with his SUV, not you. I drove up, and I'm driving back."

"I'm not getting into a vehicle with you behind the wheel."

Megan chuckled. "Then I guess you'll just have to find your own way home."

Linda turned off the light and went back to her room. In bed, all of the terrible things from her past flashed through her mind.

**

Linda's eyes fluttered open to the eight o'clock alarm on her cell phone. She showered and knocked on Megan's door. No answer. She entered the room and shook her awake. "It's time to go. We need to be out of here by ten."

Megan's condition hadn't improved. Linda's nostrils flared as she emptied her roommate's drawers and closet. She didn't fold the clothes, just stuffed them into Megan's luggage. Megan reached for the same clothes she'd worn the previous day.

"You're putting on the ski outfit you wore yesterday,

Megan." Linda helped her find a pair of jeans and a sweater.

Megan shook an electronic key on a ring in Linda's face, then dropped it into her bra.

"You're not driving," Linda said. "If you do, I'm dialing 9-1-1."

The more Megan moved around, the more coherent she became. She rolled her bags downstairs and managed to get them into the vehicle. When she removed the key from her bra to unlock the doors, Linda grabbed for it, knocking it from her hand. It landed in the snow some three feet away. Both groped around for it. Megan found it first. She shoved Linda to the ground, unlocked the vehicle, slid into the driver's seat, and locked the doors. The engine zoomed to life. The driver's window went down a couple of inches. "You coming?"

Linda sat beside her luggage in the snow, reflecting on the situation. "Not unless I drive." She climbed to her feet, glaring at Megan. "Don't do this. You're not thinking straight."

"Not going to happen." Megan didn't buckle up. She just hit the gas and sped off.

Linda jumped aside, avoiding the spinning tires. She dialed 9-1-1 to report the incident to the authorities, then thought better of the idea and hung up. She bit her bottom lip. What if the cops get Aunt Christina on the phone instead of Uncle Ralph?

She called her uncle. He picked up the phone on the third ring.

"Megan is high on drugs and alcohol, Sweet Bear. She's in no condition to operate a motor vehicle. She refused to let me drive, and now she's heading back to the city."

Silence.

"Are you there, Sweet Bear? What if Megan has an accident and kills someone? I forgot to take down your license plate number."

Silence.

"Uncle Ralph, are you there?"

"Yes," he blurted out. "I'll take care of it. How are you getting home?"

"I called my ski instructor. He's giving me a ride to a car rental agency. I should be back in two hours, depending on the traffic."

"I'll call you back when I find out what's going on," he said.

"Hurry. Get Megan off the road."

***

Linda checked out a rental car and headed home. The congested traffic inched along, bumper to bumper. She turned to a local news station and discovered that a vehicle had jumped the divider and crashed into oncoming traffic. She hoped it wasn't Megan. She used the GPS to take an alternate route—so did other motorists.

About forty minutes later, Uncle Ralph returned her call. "Linda, here's the story … I loaned you my SUV. Megan took the key without your permission. You had to rent a car to get home. Got it?" he asked. "We need to go to the local precinct and file a vehicle theft report. I've already contacted my insurance company."

Is the entire Mudici family nuts?

"She didn't steal your vehicle. You trusted her with it, not me."

"Christina can't know about this." His voice grew stronger, more demanding. "You do exactly what I say."

"Did the police find her?"

"All I know is my SUV was involved in an accident, probably totaled."

With her frustration mounting from the traffic jam, Linda said, "That's your problem, not mine. I'm not sending her to prison for your mistake, Sweet Bear." She could never face him again without picturing Megan and him in bed.

"If you call me that again, I'll ring your neck," he yelled. "You'll do exactly what I told you or suffer dire consequences. Come to Teddy's house as soon as you get back."

She raised her voice. "I'd expect something like this from Grandpa, not you."

The meek, soft-spoken man had turned into a vicious barracuda.

***

It was after lunch when Linda entered the Mudicis' home. Aunt Christina met her at the door, ranting. She threw her arms about frantically, her fingers dancing like blowing leaves on a tree. "What's wrong with you? For a doctor, you're pretty irresponsible."

Grandma stood behind Aunt Christina. She turned away to avoid eye contact.

Her aunt's words pierced Linda's heart like an arrow. "What're you talking about?"

Aunt Christina's gaze could stop a charging elephant. "First of all, why are you borrowing Ralph's SUV? Why not rent one?" She turned to her husband. "You lied to me. Said you loaned it to a friend."

Linda couldn't evade Aunt Christina's imperative questions. The stress between her and her aunt had already been palpable, now the dire situation was escalating beyond redemption.

Uncle Ralph sat next to a window, reading the newspaper. He dropped it at his side, staring into the distance.

Linda crossed her arms and zoomed in on Uncle Ralph. Her stomach curdled. She couldn't tell Aunt Christina that Megan was her husband's lover, that he'd let her drive his vehicle. "Megan said she didn't do drugs."

"A truck ripped our SUV apart." Aunt Christina stomped to Ralph's side, hands on her hips. "It's all Linda's fault. What the insurance doesn't cover is coming from her pocket."

"Megan was driving the vehicle that crashed into oncoming traffic. How is she?" Linda asked.

Aunt Christina stormed back to Linda. "She kissed a semi. How do you expect her to be? Dead."

Linda's heart pounded out of control. She glanced at Uncle Ralph, but his eyes remained distant.

Why hadn't he told her Megan died in the accident?

Her aunt pranced before Linda, venting. "How could you let some woman take Ralph's vehicle and wreck it? Couldn't you stop her? What kind of drug-addict friends do you hang out with?" She started sobbing violently. "First, you left Jenny at that awful place to be murdered, now this. You've caused nothing but grief in this family. I hate having ever met you."

Linda stood nose to nose with her aunt. "I won't let you blame me for Jenny's death. She went home with strange men almost every night, and you know it. It just makes you feel better to blame someone else, even me. You want to know why Jenny's dead? Look in the mirror."

Aunt Christina slapped Linda's face. Although tempted, Linda refused to return the honor. Instead, she stomped to the front door and threw it open.

Uncle Ralph yelled, "Linda, I need you to help me file that theft report."

Linda stormed out of the house, never looking back.

CHAPTER 18

LEAVENWORTH, KANSAS

Linda left her jacket and purse in the trunk of the rental and stuffed the key into her jeans pocket. She entered the visiting area in Leavenworth and perched herself on the circular bench at a round metal table. Sitting straight, her knees locked together and her mouth dry. She trembled, not knowing what to do with her hands. She'd checked herself in the mirror a hundred times before leaving the car. Still, she worried about how she looked.

What would she say?

A guard escorted a man wearing an orange uniform to her table. Tattoos covered his neck and arms. She shuddered. Is that him?

She slowly eased to her feet, and the prisoner and she studied each other for a moment.

"Linda?" the inmate asked.

Her heart pounded. "Tony?"

He looked nothing like the handsome young man in the photo she'd carried in her purse. Instead, a stocky, middle-aged man with graying hair and a five o'clock shadow stood before her. She hadn't expected him to look the same, but the man didn't resemble her father's picture at all.

"Have a seat," he said. "We have lots to talk about."

She slid back onto the bench. "Grandma didn't tell me much about you."

"Mother told me what happened to you when you were a kid. Don't let Father know she told me." He dropped onto the bench himself, covered his face with both hands, and wept for a long time. Through a flood of tears, he said, "I'm sorry I wasn't there for you." He wiped his eyes on his sleeves, sniffed a few times. "I never knew where you were, but I assumed you were safe with Helena. I've been a very poor father. Couldn't protect my only child."

Linda couldn't fight back the tears—tears not for her own past, but for the intensity of his remorse. The guilt had been eating away at him while he sat behind bars. He blamed himself for her past. She reached across the table and gently touched his arm. He was her real father, the man who'd given her life. When she moved to his side of the table, a guard walked closer.

She pressed her face into his shoulder, and they rocked each other for a while. "Let's not talk about the past. My attorney is reviewing your case. I asked him to look at Uncle Danny's too."

"Mark Brody. He contacted me. If Father couldn't get me out, no one can. I've come to terms with my situation. I'm going to die in here, like your great-grandpa. It didn't take long for him to waste away. Eight months and he died."

She shook her head. "Don't say that. We can contact the governor."

Grief covered her father's face like a haze. Pulling himself together, he leaned back on the bench and gazed at the floor, gravel in his voice now. "Don't waste your money. I've done some deep thinking during the past thirty or so years. I could have flipped burgers for a living. At least I would've been free."

"What if you get out of here? Will you go back to the family?"

"I don't think about that. I read a lot, write. I'm one hell of an oil painter. My cell is full of the junk. I gave some to Mother."

She smiled. "Grandma has them hanging all over her house. You're a professional."

He shrugged. "Well, I have nothing but time." He showed a hint of a smile. "I understand you're a well-known doctor with ties to Germany."

"I've done all right for myself."

His eyes were kind. Loving. "What do you do every day? When I read your letters, you mostly discuss work. Don't you do fun things?"

She lowered her head. "Not really. Don't really have friends. Seems everyone I get close to dies."

"Don't say that. You're a beautiful girl. Bet lots of men want to date you."

She couldn't tell him how men frightened her—how untrustworthy they were. "I'm not interested in dating." She let out a nervous laugh. "I read, write."

"Hey," he said, beaming, "if I mail you some of my work, will you read it? Tell me what you think?"

She cleaned her face, nodded. "Sure. I'd love to."

"There are some computers in the law library now, but we're not allowed access to the internet."

She flashed a warm smile. "What genre do you write?"

He laughed. "Mysteries. I've completed thirteen books. They were all handwritten until we got computers. Now I keep them on thumb drives. Know what I like about writing? Creating my characters with words, exploring their presents and pasts, and bringing them to life with language, emotions, actions." He caught her gawking at his arms. "Sorry about the tattoos. Inmates have to join a gang in order to survive in here."

They talked until their hour ended.

Before the guard escorted Tony away, he flashed a grin at the man. "Ed, this is my daughter. She's a doctor, a surgeon. I'm proud of her."

She waved. "See you tomorrow, Tony."

"Father. Call me Father," he said. "Come early again. That's the best time."

***

Before 8:00 a.m. that Sunday, Linda sat in the visitors' center, anxious for the first group of inmates to enter. Thinking about her father had kept her up most of the night. Finding it hard to sleep, she counted the hours until she'd see him again. Although he was a mobster, she hated Helena for sending him to prison.

Tony entered the visitors' area with a strut in his walk and a big smile on his clean-shaven face. His eagerness to see her again showed in the way he moved—in his eyes and in his voice. He hugged her and gave her a kiss on her cheek. "Thanks for being here. You don't know what this means to me."

Pleased to bring a glimmer of sunlight into his life, she threw her arms around his neck and squeezed. The guard kept his distance this time, giving them more privacy.

He smelled like toothpaste. "How was your night?" he asked.

"Not good. I spent most of it thinking about you— how to get you out of here."

He led her to a secluded bench and sat next to her. "Don't waste your time on me."

"I don't know," she whispered. "The governor's daughter is one of my cancer patients. With proper treatment, a good diet, and exercise, she has been in remission for five years. I may be able to pull a few strings if I have to."

His mouth gaped open. "You're the governor's daughter's physician?"

"That's between us. Okay?"

He glanced around the area. "I'm no idiot. I only pretend to have friends in here. Can't trust anyone in this joint."

"Would you go back to the family if I can get you out?" she asked again.

"I did lots of bad things for the family."

Maybe he'd been a hit man like Swift. "That didn't answer my question."

His eyes became distant, longing. "I'd move to Florida. Start a new life. Try to sell my paintings, my manuscripts. Do you know how many trades I've learned during my stay here? We don't just make license plates, you know." His face saddened. "You're not getting too involved with the family, are you?"

"At first. Now I'm keeping my distance. I do like Grandma."

"Mother is more involved than you think." He shook his head. "Don't trust her."

She touched his hand. "Father, I don't know you, but I love you. I'm going to make a weekend trip here every month."

He placed a hand on either side of her face, then withdrew, as if frustrated. "That's more than I see my parents. They visit once a year, a card, and an occasional letter. I gave my life to the family. They keep money in my account. Money is good. I can bribe inmates, but I prefer family visits. Promise me you won't stop coming."

Linda held his hand in hers. "I promise. I'll be here every month, unless something comes up. If I can't make it, I'll write. Do you have a phone card?"

"Lots of minutes, no one to call."

She asked the guard for paper and a pen, jotted down her number, and slid it across the table. "Call me. I'd love to talk to you as often as I can."

"Hey, I heard you met with Danny yesterday."

"Right after my visit with you."

"Why didn't you tell me you'd scheduled a meeting with Danny?"

She shrugged. "We only had an hour. I wanted to spend my time getting to know you."

"Danny and I don't see each other that much. They keep us apart in different pods, but we pass notes back and forth."

"Pods?" They were treating him like an animal.

"They're individual, self-contained housing units. They restrict and control movement of inmates, requiring minimal staff."

"Uncle Danny looks exactly like you, only about sixty pounds lighter."

"Danny spends most of his time exercising. I have pen pals too."

The guard ended their visit after an hour.

Her father had become a bright light in her life. "I'll see you next month, Father."

They hugged. "Goodbye."

CHAPTER 19

THE FORGOTTEN

Linda had a great day at work. Weeks had passed without a word from the Mudici family.

Good riddance.

Linda's nurse caught her between patients. "Dr. Harrison, congratulations. I heard you got another sabbatical."

"I'll be leaving in October. It's an exchange program this time. I met a nice doctor in Munich, and I hope to meet him again."

"Do I feel romance in the air?" The nurse snickered.

"Admiration. Not love," Linda said.

"Oh, by the way," the nurse said, "there's a young man waiting to see you."

"Does he have an appointment?" Linda asked.

"No, says he's a relative."

Not another Mudici family member. "I can't see him until lunch." The wall clock read 11:12. "Ask him to come back around one o'clock." Taking a late lunch caused her to miss most of the midday crowd.

When she entered the waiting room at 12:45, a young man jumped to his feet, his face pale, and his hands fidgeting with his backpack. The kid did look familiar, but Linda couldn't remember where she'd met him. "I'm Dr. Harrison, and you?"

Gray eyes locked on hers for a moment and then shifted to the floor. He stood tall, dressed in a college T-shirt, jeans, and athletic shoes. He had a smooth, clear complexion, and his dark brown hair was almost black. He stuttered in a whisper, "I'm ... Jim Walden ... a relative." His hands and voice trembled, and he behaved as if he were in the midst of some internal debate.

"Not from my father's side of the family."

Linda scribbled a prescription on her pad, ripped it off, and passed it to the attending nurse. "Give this to Mr. Davis. I'll be back at two o'clock."

"Your next patient is at 1:45," the nurse reminded her.

Linda opened the front door, stepped into the main entrance, and turned left. "I'm going to lunch. Care to join me?"

Jim threw the strap of his backpack over one shoulder. "I think we're related."

Linda didn't hear his footsteps behind her as she led the way, but she heard the wheels of his small suitcase thumping across the ceramic tiles. "So, exactly how do you think we're related?"

The boy cleared his throat and lowered his voice again. "It's an unusual story. I think … I think I'm your son."

Linda stopped dead in her tracks, and the kid bumped into her. Slowly turning, she eyed him from head to foot. She studied his nose, lips, chin, and forehead. He was a younger replica of the man who had raped her when she was thirteen. She suddenly felt violated all over again. Even his hair and eye color were identical. Everything came back, crushing her heart in a giant wave—the torture, her parents' deceit, and the fear of inevitable death. No matter how much air she sucked in, it wasn't enough. For years, she'd seen her attacker every night in her dreams—not his actual face, but a silhouette. Now he'd returned from the dead.

His eyes pleaded. "We can get a DNA test to make sure. I don't want to interfere with your life. I just want to know you."

Linda stood frozen, like a statue. He had just ripped her heart from her chest. Her legs weakened, and the room spun, leaving her on the verge of fainting. She didn't, and couldn't, utter a word. She'd never wanted to see the kid, ever.

"I've had a good life." Jim tossed back a lock of dark hair from his eyes. "I'm a second-year med student at Baylor University."

She struggled to a cluster of four empty chairs a short distance away, fell into the nearest one, and gripped the armrests to keep from tipping over.

He pulled his luggage to a chair between them but remained standing. "I guess I should've called first."

She continued gasping for air. Her heels involuntarily bounced up and down, tapping in a rhythm, as they usually did when she was under extreme pressure. Her calves became sore and her chest tightened, as if a car had parked on it.

"Do you need a doctor?"

When the boy received no reply, he ran down the hall and returned with a nurse.

"Dr. Harrison, do you need help?" the woman asked.

Linda shook, refusing to release her grip on the arms of the chair. "Yes, I ..."

The nurse checked her pulse. "Let's get you to the emergency room." She turned to Jim. "There are wheelchairs around the corner. Get one." The kid took off again and returned, wheeling a chair as if he were trying to win a race. With the aid of the nurse, he helped her into the wheelchair and took the shortcut across the parking lot to the emergency room.

Linda lay on an examination table in an open bay area separated by curtains, eyes closed, her memories assaulting her. Except for the C-section scar, she hardly remembered having a baby. The state of Louisiana immediately took it away. She had never seen it, never even known its sex.

A nurse checked her vitals while a doctor came to her rescue. "Dr. Harrison, do you have any pain?"

"Panic attack. My legs are weak, numb," she whispered. "Can't breathe. I need oxygen, water, and a strong sedative."

His cold stethoscope pressed against her chest. "Explain to me what happened. Get the oxygen mask," he said to the nurse. "Check her O_2 level."

Linda gasped, sucking in air. "I've just heard some shocking news."

He opened one of her eyes and then the other, shining a pencil-sized light into each. "Want to see a psychiatrist?"

"No," she said, "give me a sedative."

"Okay. You'll need someone to take you home," the doctor said.

She shivered and hugged herself. "I want to stay here."

"Sure. We can find you a bed," he said.

"Thanks. May I have a blanket? I'm cold."

***

When Linda awoke, the room was dark. Her calf muscles were still sore, but—with effort, she managed to move her legs. Sitting up in bed, she poured a glass of cold water from the bedside pitcher and guzzled it down. Lowering her feet, she gradually put weight on them. With difficulty, she managed to stand.

A nurse came into the room. "How do you feel, Doctor?"

"Better," Linda said.

The nurse held her arm, assisted her to a nearby chair, and checked her vital signs.

She gave Linda a paper cup containing two pills and poured water into a glass. "The doctor prescribed these muscle relaxers. There's some kid in the waiting room asking to see you."

Linda dumped the pills into her mouth and washed them down. "Tell him to leave."

The woman picked up the pitcher as she headed for the door. "Okay. If he gives us any trouble, we'll have security kick him out."

"Wait …" Linda knew she needed to face him. She'd always faced her problems. "I've changed my mind. Send him in."

"You sure?" the nurse asked.

"Yes. I'll talk to him."

Shortly after the nurse left, Jim entered her room, rolling his luggage behind him. He dropped his backpack into a chair against the wall and approached her as if she were so fragile that just his presence could cause her to break.

"I must admit, I never expected to see you." Linda's voice quivered. She had as much compassion for the kid as she had for a rock.

He shifted his weight from foot to foot. "I'm sorry for making you sick. Do you want me to leave?"

"The damage has been done."

His face wrinkled. "I don't mind spending the night in the waiting room."

"Don't you have a place to stay?"

Stepping closer, he said, "Not yet. If I can't stay here, I can sleep in the bus terminal or Grand Central Station."

Linda stood on weak legs and slowly moved around the room. "You're not allowed to sleep in those places, and they're not safe. There's a hotel a block away. I'll get you a room there."

Was he really her son, or a lookalike trying to extort money from her? "May I see your ID?"

Jim fished a wallet from his back pocket and showed her his driver's license, college photo, and adoptive parents' business cards. "I'll be here for a week, if that's okay with you." He hinted a smile. "Spring break."

Linda told the doctor she'd take a taxi home. She didn't think her legs would make the trip outside, but they did.

"Want to lean on me?" he asked.

She didn't want him touching her. "No, I can make it."

The more she walked, the stronger her legs became. She trudged to the hotel and checked him into a room for the week.

He walked outside with her. "Thanks for the room. When will I see you again?"

She hailed a cab. "Tomorrow, after work. We'll talk then."

Jim open the taxi door. "Good night, Dr. Harrison."

"Good night, Jim," she managed to say.

He closed her door and waved when the taxi drove off.

As the driver sped off, again her mind raced through the tragedies of her life.

Jim's mere existence brought back the worst of them.

***

The next morning, Linda stood at her patient's side wearing scrubs, a facemask, and surgical gloves. She stared down into her patient's pale face. "Hello, Betty. How do you feel?" she asked.

"Frightened," her patient said. "But my mom is here."

The statement sent a chill down Linda's spine. She realized that if she became ill, she would have no one to care for her, no one at her side.

Betty, a college senior, lay on an operating table with an IV drip in her arm and an anesthesiologist at her head. "It'll be over before you know it," Linda said. "Dr. Fieldhouser is your anesthesiologist. When he puts you under, you'll feel a slight burning sensation. He'll monitor your vital signs throughout the surgery."

Betty's eyes watered, and she sniffed. "Are you sure it's not cancer?"

Linda shook her head. "I doubt it, but we'll perform a biopsy to be sure."

"Count backward from a hundred," Dr. Fieldhouser said to Betty.

Linda's encounter with Jim lingered in her mind. Her legs were slightly stronger than they had been the day before but still weak. The overhead surgical lamps seared her eyes, and waves of pain pounded in her head. Blocking out this new entity in her life, Jim, was difficult. She'd worked under far more stressful conditions in the past, and today's surgery was a relatively easy one, removing a tumor from a young woman's breast. She didn't feel any better when her patient was under, but she had confidence in her ability to perform—not only as a surgeon but as an individual.

Concentrating on the target area, she said to the head nurse, "Hold the breast as far as you can to the right." She cut an incision into the left breast, approximately four inches above the rib cage, removed a lump about the size of an egg, and dropped it into a plastic container.

"That's a big one," the nurse said.

"I need suction here," Linda said, examining the surrounding tissue. "This area looks healthy too. More suction." She glued up the incision and secured it with a strip of tape. "I'm done here. Get this tumor to the lab. I'm sure it's benign, but a biopsy will give my patient some peace of mind."

She removed her surgical uniform, washed up, and headed back to the clinic to wrap things up for the day.

***

Linda dreaded another encounter with her nightmare, but the kid wasn't going away. She drove to his hotel and took the elevator to the fourth floor. Jim opened the door, shirtless. His hair was wet. The TV played a werewolf movie. Fast food wrappers covered a table, along with two empty soda bottles.

He turned off the TV and slid on a T-shirt. "Have a seat. I took a city tour today," he cheerfully said. "Spent a little of my money. I still have more than enough for a bus ticket back to Texas."

She sat in one of two chairs at a round table, with her purse strap hanging over her shoulder. She didn't know what to say to him. Why not just tell him to get lost?

He retrieved a large envelope from the bed, held it to his chest, then sat in the chair across from her. "Can I offer you a drink?"

Linda's headache was intensifying, and she feared she would succumb to the pain. "No thanks."

Silence stretched between them. She sat still, glaring at the black TV screen. Jim squirmed in his chair.

He removed photos from the envelope and shoved a stack across the table to her, tipping over one of the empty soda bottles. He balled up the wrappers from the table and tossed them into a trashcan, along with the empty containers. "Sorry about the mess. Mom says I'm a slob. She's an RN. My father's a chemical engineer. I have a brother and sister—twins." His words came fast, strained. "They're doing their internships."

Silence.

Jim continued. "I grew up in Minnesota. Got into med school at Baylor."

She didn't care to hear the explanation, but she asked, "How did you find me?"

"My parents helped." He sorted through more photos. "They didn't tell me I was adopted until last year. I brought these pictures, in case you want to keep them. They're from the time my parents adopted me at one month old."

"I'm glad you ended up in a nice home." She spoke to him as if he were a pet. Linda glanced at the photos on the table in front of her. "I'll look at them later. Let's take a DNA test tomorrow."

He stared straight into her eyes. "When will we get the results?"

"If we take it first thing in the morning, we should know in a few days." Her eyes welled up. "You look exactly like him—a younger version."

He focused on his bare feet. "Do you hate me?"

Not sure what to say or do, she placed her hands under the table and squeezed them between her knees. "I hate him."

His face was passive. "But I remind you of him. So you must hate me too."

"I don't hate you." She didn't love him either. "You didn't ask to be born."

"Why didn't you have an abortion?"

Her heart thumped, and pain shot through her stomach. "I was fourteen, a ward of the state in the South—Child Protective Services made my decisions."

His face brightened. "Do you remember how I looked when I was born?"

Her stay in the mental hospital was just a blur. "No, I don't."

Jim's eyes went to his feet again. "I'm sorry about what my—that man did to you. According to old newspaper reports, your parents disappeared before their warrants were issued."

"Yes, when the police visited our home they had already left. Gone."

"Where are they now?" he asked.

She didn't care to talk about them. "I don't know."

"You never got married? Had kids?"

His demanding eyes, his very presence, threatened her. "No. I spend my time concentrating on my job." Her voice sounded distant, unforgiving. "That keeps me busy."

"I found my biological father's relatives as well. They're not very nice people."

She sat ramrod-straight. "How did you find them?"

"His name's on my original birth certificate."

Appalled, Linda shook her head. "They listed him as the father?" She abruptly stood, picking up the envelope from the table. "I'll visit you again tomorrow after work."

"But you just got here." He reached for his running shoes. "At least let me see you home."

She just wanted to get out of there. "I drove. It's quite a distance."

He jumped in front of the door, blocking her path, his shoes in hand. "I know life must have been hard for you."

Linda straightened. "Yes. It was."

"Please don't go. Regardless of the situation, you're still my mother. I'd like to have a relationship with you." He blurted out his words. "If the feeling isn't mutual, let me know, and I'll move on."

"I'm not certain how I feel." At least his adoptive parents hadn't paid someone to kill him. "Ah …" She hesitated, and a hand went to her forehead. I can do this. "Have you had dinner?"

He beamed like a kid who'd just found his lost puppy. "I'm buying."

She let out an exasperated breath. Why had she promised to dine with him? As they walked the short distance, Jim talked about his life as a boy. His voice buzzed at her side while her mind drifted. She heard segments about high school years, sports, and prom night.

At the restaurant, she only ordered a glass of red wine. "Do you drink?"

Jim studied his menu. "Not really. I have a beer with the guys sometimes."

His father had emptied a few bottles of booze during the days he'd raped her.

Having Jim in her life would be a constant reminder of her ordeal.

"Order what you want. I'm buying."

"No," he said. "Dinner is on me."

She shouldn't have brought him to such an expensive restaurant. He was eager to please her at any price, just as she'd wanted to fit in with the Mudicis.

"I know you can't afford this place. How are you making it through school?"

"It's not easy, but I manage. I have a scholarship, loans, and grants. During pre-med, I worked part-time making pizzas." He stuck out his chest. "I can make any kind of pizza you'd like."

She gulped down her drink, ordered another, and relaxed a bit. "Before you leave, I'll let you make me a pizza."

He continued, "My undergraduate major was chemistry. I already have a summer job, working at a hospital."

He had entered her comfort zone. She asked, "Doing what?"

He had relaxed as well. "Patient medication studies."

The more they talked, the more comfortable both became. Linda ended the night by escorting Jim back to his hotel, where she'd parked her car. Why couldn't she tell him to go away, that she didn't want him in her life? He hadn't grown up alone in the world as she had, but he wanted a relationship with her, just like she wanted with her father. Was that why she tolerated his presence? She couldn't blame him for wanting to know her. She was his real mother, a blood relative.

Jim opened doors for her, pulled out her chairs. The kid was eerily nice. Too much of a gentleman for someone his age. Perhaps he was just trying to make her like and accept him.

***

The DNA test confirmed that Jim Walden was Linda's biological son. Her phone conversation with his adoptive parents was pleasant. They were good people, educated parents who loved Jim as their own. His upbringing scored better than that of the average child.

Linda took a few days off work to show him around New York City. She dined with him at nice restaurants, treating him to movies and theaters. Maybe the invisible motherly bond drove her, or her guilt over bringing an unwanted child into the world.

***

When the week ended, Linda was glad to see Jim go. "I'm buying you an airline ticket back to Houston. Spending two days on a bus must be painful."

He showed happiness, glad to be in her life. "It's not that bad. I spent my time studying."

She said goodbye to Jim at LaGuardia Airport, patting him on the back at the security checkpoint. They exchanged phone numbers and email addresses, promising to keep in touch. She then removed her checkbook from her purse, wrote a check, and stuffed it into his shirt pocket. "I'm helping with your medical school finances for the fall semester, plus giving you spending money, so you don't have to work."

He held up his hands, shook his head, and returned the check to her. "No. I'm not looking for anything from you. I just wanted to get to know you. I can make it on my own … like you did."

She shoved the check back into his pocket. "I insist. I can make your life easier. If this runs out, let me know. Don't deposit it until Wednesday."

He shook his head. "But I can't accept money from you."

She understood the longing in his heart. "You can and will. Look, I wasn't there when you were a child. I have money. Don't worry about it."

He didn't look at the amount. A wide grin spread across his face. "I'll be frugal, I promise."

Knowing what it meant to him, she hugged him goodbye.

Jim held on to her for a long time before letting go.

CHAPTER 20

MUNICH

Linda boarded a British Airways flight to Munich. She had one last hurdle—facing her adoptive parents, Helena and Adler Fluger. She needed the strength to confront them and her childhood again or there would always be a void in her life.

During her first sabbatical in Munich, she'd copied their address and phone number from Helena's hospital records. She'd informed the authorities in the States concerning their whereabouts, but nothing had appeared in the media regarding their arrests.

She took a taxi from the airport to a hotel, within walking distance of their apartment. She had no problem finding it. They occupied 224B, one of two apartments above Fluger's Fine Hats & Leather Goods.

The sign in the shop's window read: "Gesohlossen." Linda tried the door and found it unyielding, so she knocked.

A man on the other side yelled in German, "We're closed for lunch."

When she pounded harder, he threw open the door, his face in a gruesome frown. Studying his features didn't give Linda any hint to his identity. Was this man her uncle? More than nine years Adler's junior, he stood at average height and was lean with crooked teeth, short brown hair graying at the temples, and a receding hairline.

"Didn't you hear me? Come back after lunch." He slammed the door shut.

Linda knocked again and shouted in German, "Uncle Fluger, I need to speak with you." She couldn't remember his first name.

He hastily opened the door again. "Who are you?"

She forced her way past him and stopped to stare at his mother's portrait on the back wall.

"Who do you think you are?" He looked down at her and grabbed her arm, fingers gripping into her flesh. "Get out of here."

Helena and Adler hadn't recognized her when she saw them after all those years, so why would her uncle? Linda pressed her back against the door, refusing to move. "It's me, Linda."

He squinted and shook his head, his voice tense. "I don't know you."

She locked eyes with him. "I'm your brother's daughter. You and your family visited us in Florida when I was eleven. You were talking about starting your own business."

He blinked rapidly.

She motioned to the painting. "I heard that your mother passed away. I'm sorry I didn't get the chance to say goodbye to her."

He stared at her, mouth open. "Adler's only child was killed when a car ran over her while she was riding her bike. Is this some kind of a joke?"

"No, Uncle. Adler and Helena lied to you. What happened to me made the news in America, but not here in Germany. Let's go for a walk."

Doubt washed across his face. "If you're actually my niece ..."

"When your family visited us in Florida, you, your wife, your mother, and I took a bus to Disney World. Your wife bought me a stuffed koala bear I named Queenie. You caught your first catfish in my favorite pond. It finned you twice when you tried to unhook it, and you were allergic. Adler took you to the emergency room for a shot, because your hand swelled to twice its normal size. Adler attended your mother's funeral. He couldn't afford to pay for Helena and me to fly to Germany."

One of Uncle Fluger's eyebrows went up. He stood back and gawked at her. "You don't resemble either one of them."

"I know," she said.

He didn't remove his apron but donned his coat and locked up the shop. As they strolled down the street among the lunch foot traffic, she told him her entire childhood story. Old memories rose up and flew through her mind like a typhoon.

His face reddened as he patiently listened, but she didn't know if it was due to the cold fall air or hearing her life story.

He stopped, his keen eyes focused on hers. "But you must be mistaken. My brother would never have murdered his child for money."

"They're not my parents. Helena is my aunt, not my mother. Adler gave me to the man, told me to ride to school with him, and later denied it to the authorities. Ask him. They never visited me during my stay in the hospital."

The wind shifted, blowing the scent of leather from his clothes in her direction.

"I'm so sorry about what happened to you, but my brother couldn't have been responsible."

She removed the scarf from around her neck, wrapped it around her head, and folded the ends under her collar. "I'm the oncologist who performed surgery on Helena."

"You're a doctor?" He walked on. "Why didn't they recognize you at the hospital?"

"They haven't seen me since I was thirteen, and I've had plastic surgery."

"They couldn't find jobs, so I hired them." He sucked in air. "If they were responsible for what happened to you, they're fired." His words came out harshly.

"I didn't come here to cause trouble within your

family. The authorities will deal with them," Linda said. "I just need to confront them so I can move on with my life."

He stopped in his tracks. "Authorities? So that's why they moved to Germany."

"They didn't have money. I don't understand how they left the States so fast."

"Adler called me, frantic. Said that after you died, they couldn't live in America any longer. I purchased their tickets by credit card, and they took the next flight here."

Linda conversed with her uncle for over two hours. When they returned to the shop, her adoptive parents were there.

Her uncle opened the door. "Come in. Let's discuss this," Uncle Hager said.

Linda decided to let him break the news, because it would lessen the blow. "I prefer you tell them first."

She stopped at the door and said goodbye.

***

Linda walked back to her hotel room and later browsed local shops until five that evening. She had no appetite. The thought of food made her sick. Around closing time, she returned to Fluger's Fine Hats & Leather, and watched as Helena and Adler closed up. She followed them along a narrow side street, trembling and sweating under her coat.

Unaware of her presence, Adler and Helena walked side by side, holding hands and chatting.

Keeping her distance, Linda followed them into a small neighborhood café that had a dozen tables crammed inside. The place served coffee, sweets, and sandwiches. Adler and Helena exchanged words with the only waitress, as if they were regular customers. Linda slid out of her coat and took a seat three tables behind them, facing Adler. She ordered a cup of hot chocolate that tasted a lot like the cocoa Adler had made when she was a kid. She stared directly at him until she got his attention.

Adler's eyes bulged at the sight of her. His face froze for a moment, and he lowered his head and whispered something to Helena, who turned and gazed at Linda— her face as pale as a ghost.

Linda gripped the handle of her cup with one hand and fingered her napkin with the other. She pressed her knees together, and a rush of energy ran up her spine. Although she wanted to divert her eyes, she couldn't. Instead, she scrutinized Adler—the man who'd altered her life, forever. She hoped her glance haunted them, frightened them. They'd done the worst thing any adult could do to a child, to another human being. Neither acknowledged her again. Helena appeared healthier, more vibrant than the last time Linda had seen her. When their coffee arrived, Adler's cup shook so badly in his hands that his drink spilled on the table. The waitress came to his rescue and mopped it up with a rag.

Shortly afterward, he dropped some bills on the table. Both slithered into their coats, buttoned them, and headed for the door, walking past Linda with their heads down, eyes cast to the floor.

Linda's nails dug into her arms as she resisted the urge to confront them in a public place, like sticking out her foot and tripping them as they passed. She couldn't control the pain that riddled and ached her insides. They probably wanted her to go away, as she'd wanted Jim to disappear. But she had found the strength to face her son, and she could face them as well. Her adoptive mother would never endure the cruelty of repeated rape, the mental and physical torture Linda had suffered. Her father would never know the terror of being abandoned, and the intense drive to hold on to life at any cost. Neither would ever feel the agony of knowing no one cared. They couldn't have survived the ordeal she had endured as a child.

Linda was stronger. She followed them.

Adler and Helena left the same way they'd come, only walking faster. Adler turned, taking a few quick glances over his shoulder. They increased their pace, so did Linda. When they reached the shop, they hurried up the stairs, opened the door, and disappeared inside.

Linda lingered outside for a few minutes, then trudged up the stairs and rang the doorbell. The sound of footsteps approached from the other side of the door, but no one opened it. She leaned on the doorbell and then pounded on the metal door. No response.

"Helena. Adler. I know you're in there," Linda yelled.

Silence.

She knocked harder, more persistently. A man from the next apartment opened his door, studied her from head to toe, and then reluctantly closed his door.

Linda stared at 224B as if she had X-ray vision. She leaned on the doorbell again, then knocked harder, louder.

No response.

What more could she do? She gave up. Gripping the rails, she slowly descending the creaking stairs. She returned to her hotel and had a few drinks before settling into bed. All night she tossed and turned as her nightmares rose from the dark abyss, haunting her with each twilight hour.

***

Exhausted, Linda rolled out of bed the next morning with a pounding headache. She dressed and entered the restaurant downstairs, her stomach growling. After a few bites of breakfast, she couldn't eat any more. She walked to her uncle's shop, stood across the street, and watched the front door of 224B. She felt like a predator stalking prey. Helena peeked out the window of their apartment several times, then eventually went downstairs, opened the shop, and disappeared once more, ignoring Linda's presence. Linda gritted her teeth, her headache intensifying as she waited for the pedestrian light.

When the light finally turned green, she barreled across the street, only slowing when Adler came down the stairs to meet Uncle Hager, who had just arrived. They entered the shop together. Enraged, Linda pushed open the shop's door, stomped inside, and slammed the outside world behind her with a loud bang.

Uncle Hager jumped. Helena and Adler glanced at her, then diverted their attention.

Linda growled out her words, her eyes dancing between Helena and Adler. "I knocked on your door yesterday evening. You refused to answer, ignored me. You discarded me like trash when I was thirteen, but not today. You scumbags are not fit to be called humans."

She'd suffered all those years because of them, but she'd survived. She would not cry but remain resilient, like a rock.

Her uncle approached her, placed an arm around her shoulders, and led her into his shop, stopping near a desk. "Good morning, Linda."

Why was he so cheerful? "Uncle Hager."

He inhaled a giant breath and then exhaled slowly, as if enjoying the scent of a fresh meadow. "I forgot to ask, how long will you be here in Germany?"

What's going on here?

She'd prepared for a violent confrontation, but his nonchalant demeanor threatened to defuse her plan. "Six months."

Helena turned, dusted shelves, and rearranged hats. A customer entered, and Adler rushed to assist him.

Uncle Hager smiled. "Linda, why don't you have dinner with Anna and me tonight? You remember your Aunt Anna?"

Linda nodded, eyes on Helena. "Vaguely."

She'd rehearsed her speech, but would it come out as she'd planned?

After the customer left, Linda yelled at Helena's back. Like a famished beast, her heart thumping in her chest, Linda went for the jugular. "Why did you do it?" she snarled, shaking her head. "I knew you two never loved me, but I never imagined that you would have me tortured and raped for money. Did you hate me that much? There are still warrants pending for your arrests in the state of Florida, and I've given them your address."

Helena froze, still facing the wall. "We did nothing to you."

Linda's words rolled from her gut and bounced off her tongue like molten lava. Goose bumps prickled her skin. Her growl came deep and harsh. "You lying coward. Turn around. Face me." A shadow of gloom towered over her world as she again demanded, "Why did you do it? Do you know what that man did to me?"

Adler moved to his wife's side and held her hand. They faced Linda, their eyes cast to the floor. Linda attacked him as well. "You gave me to that man." She remained firm, in control, but her insides were crumbling.

Neither replied.

Uncle Hager intervened. "That's your daughter. Speak to her."

"I'm sorry." Adler swallowed hard. "We made a mistake."

Linda rushed to him and slapped his face twice, first with her right hand, then with her left, leaving her palms burning hot and heavy. "You made a mistake, all right. Your assassin didn't finish the job. I'll hate both of you for the rest of my life."

Her head became light, her vision blurred, but she fought against the weight pulling her to the floor. She exhaled, sucked in deep breaths. Her world calmed, vision cleared. "No one can sink as low as you two. After what you put me through, I still succeeded in life. I've never had anyone there for me."

Helena sobbed as she leaned on a shelf, and her head drooped further as she spoke. "We didn't know he was a pedophile."

Helena's words pierced Linda's heart deeper than a knife, and the pain almost brought her to her knees. Confronting them was only bringing back her nine days of torture. The ordeal ground and twisted her insides. She exploded from the agony, screamed, "So it was all right for him to kill me, but not to rape and torture me?"

Helena buried her face in her palms. "I'm so sorry." Her voice trembled.

Linda shouted, "You're sorry because your plan didn't work. You didn't care about me then or now."

They'd cheated her out of her confrontation, refusing to debate. Her disappointment flashed in waves. Linda clawed down the side of Helena's face with her finger-nails, leaving four deep, bleeding scratches.

Helena screamed out in pain and turned her head but didn't touch her wounds. She sniffed, shuddered, and backed into a corner.

Uncle Hager's face reddened. He clenched his fists and punched his brother in the face.

Adler's head snapped back from the blow. He then broke down and sobbed like a child, "I'm sorry, Hager." Blood gushed from his nose and mixed with tears as it spilled down onto his white shirt.

"You lied to me, Adler. Claimed you didn't do it." Uncle Hager shook his head in disbelief. "I don't know you at all." He rushed to the door and threw it open. "Get out. Both of you."

Like animals expelled from a pack, they staggered out the door with their shoulders drooped and their heads hung low, never retrieving their coats.

Uncle Hager slammed the door shut behind them, closing the world on Helena and Adler and the hollow feeling in Linda's heart. Her knees buckled. She clung to a shelf as she slid to the floor and cried out long and hard. The pain and emptiness rushed from her body like a swollen stream, then quickly diminished to a trickle.

Uncle Hager placed a firm hand on Linda's shoulder. "You—you stood up to them. I'm so proud of you. They told me an entirely different story yesterday."

Gripping Linda around the waist, he helped her to

her feet and led her to a chair. She melted into the chair, grasping her stomach. Her voice cracked as she heaved air. "After twenty-three years, I finally found the strength to face them. When I met them last year, I was so distraught I immediately returned to the States. I had to let them know who I really was. Uncle Hager—"

"Shh. It's all right," he said, patting her on the back. "Let it all out."

When her tears subsided, Linda wiped her face and blew her nose, composing herself. "I'm all right, Uncle Hager."

"Come home with me tonight, visit Anna. She'd love to see you again. We'll take you to our favorite restaurant."

Linda climbed to her feet. "I'm not hungry, and I won't be good company right now. I prefer to be alone."

He placed a hand on her shoulder. "You've just suffered a very traumatic experience. Anna and I can find something pleasant to talk about, keep your mind off your troubles. You shouldn't be alone at a time like this."

Linda remained in the shop with Uncle Hager for the remainder of the day, helping him with customers. She didn't know if Uncle Hager had fired Helena and Adler, and she didn't much care.

***

Linda didn't talk much as Uncle Hager's car crept through the heavy traffic. The confrontation with Adler and Helena was still raging inside her head like a relentless, turbulent storm. Her uncle pulled into the driveway of a small house covered with English ivy at the end of a cul-de-sac. The garage door opened, and he drove inside and closed it with a remote.

He unlocked the side door and led Linda into a modest home. She followed, admiring him for still referring to her as his niece.

"Have a seat," he said. Then he yelled, "Anna, we're here."

Linda would rather have gone to her room to mourn the fight she'd had with her adoptive parents that morning, but she realized Uncle Hager was right. Their company was better than being alone. Taking a glance around the house, she noticed that the chairs and kitchen cabinets were all bright white. Two-tone white drapes flowed from ceiling to floor, and the rug displayed a striking similarity to the curtains.

A pretty woman entered the living room wearing a long black dress, putting on earrings. She looked to be in her forties, but Linda knew she was at least fifty. She was tall and curvy with short blonde hair and green eyes. Her feet were rather large. Or was it just the pink fuzzy house shoes?

"Linda, this is your Aunt Anna. Do you remember her?"

Unlike Uncle Hager, her aunt still looked much the same. "When I first met Aunt Anna, I wanted to be as pretty as she is."

Anna hugged her. "Hello, Linda. Nice to see you again."

"Hello, Aunt Anna," Linda said, embracing her.

Anna gave her a long, tight hug, then let go, stood back, and stared at her. "Let me take a good look at you. The last time I saw you, you were a skinny little girl with hair down to your waist. Now, you're a beautiful young woman. Hager says you're a surgeon—an oncologist."

Linda tried to force a smile but failed. "Yes. I work for a prominent hospital back in New York City."

"Have a seat," Anna said. "Hager mentioned you'll be here for six months. Why don't you live here with us? We have more than enough room, and your company would be nice."

Linda sat on a white sofa, and Aunt Anna joined her. Uncle Hager took the matching loveseat opposite them.

"I already have my own place. I'll be moving in next week," Linda said.

"You speak perfect German." Anna's eyes sparkled under the chandelier. "Where did you learn?"

"My—Adler taught me when I was a child."

"How about a glass of wine?" Anna asked.

She needed a drink. "Yes, thanks."

"I could use one too. How about you, Hager?" Anna asked.

"Sure," he said.

Anna disappeared into the kitchen and soon returned with a tray containing a bottle of chilled Riesling and three glasses. She placed it on the coffee table between the two chairs.

Linda cajoled herself into the hint of a smile. "Your favorite?"

"Yes." Anna poured about two inches of wine into each glass.

Uncle Hager picked up his glass and raised it above his head with his hairy paw. "To our niece."

Her aunt did the same. "To Linda."

Linda blushed. "Thank you both for inviting me to dinner, for caring about my well-being."

They all took a sip of wine.

Anna's eyes met Linda's. "It must have been difficult for you to go to medical school all on your own."

Uncle Hager cleared his throat to get his wife's attention, then shook his head, discouraging her questioning.

"Oh … well, I …" Anna batted her eyelashes.

"That's all right, Uncle. Now that it's over, I feel better."

Anna said, "The restaurant is about two blocks away. We usually walk."

Linda asked her uncle, "Is it the one we drove past?"

He stretched. "Yes. The best food in this area."

Linda drained her glass, she wanted a refill but didn't ask.

Aunt Anna emptied her glass and donned her coat. "What kind of food do you like, young lady?"

"I really don't have a favorite food. I usually eat light—low in fats and carbohydrates," Linda said, pumping cheer into her voice.

Her aunt laughed. "So, that's how you keep that little schoolgirl figure."

Linda's aunt and uncle told her about places she should visit during her trip to the Black Forest, as they escorted her to the small restaurant wedged between an antique shop and a bakery. They sat near the front door in the cozy restaurant, waiting for a table. Strong aromas of delicious food permeated the place but didn't whet Linda's appetite. About fifteen minutes later, a waitress led them to a table with four place settings. Customers chatted and laughed, bringing back memories of the first time she'd visited Grandpa's restaurant.

Linda ate light, choosing a small salad. She no longer heard her aunt and uncle but gazed into emptiness. The confrontation with her adoptive parents still consuming her thoughts.

"Linda?" Aunt Anna asked. "Are you with us?"

When she sprang back into reality, the couple gazed at her, concern in their eyes. "I'm sorry. Were you talking to me?"

"For the past fifteen minutes," Uncle Hager said.

Linda stared at her half-eaten salad. "Sorry, my mind keeps drifting to … them."

"We know Helena and Adler have had a great impact on your life. It'll be hard but try to forget them." Anna took Linda's hand. "Concentrate on positive things in your life. We'll always be here for you."

"Thanks," Linda said, squeezing her aunt's hand. "I appreciate your support."

Linda's experience with the Mudici family had intensified her paranoia. Her uncle and aunt appeared to be nice people, but she didn't know if she should trust them. Linda walked back to her aunt and uncle's house, had another glass of wine, and chatted for another two hours.

"It's getting late. I need to be up early tomorrow morning for my trip to the Black Forest."

Aunt Anna reached for her coat. "When do you start work?"

Linda cracked a smile. "Monday. Don't bother. I'll take a cab."

"No," Anna said. "We'll see you to your hotel."

Linda hit a speed dial number on her cell phone and requested a taxi. "You've done more than you can ever imagine. When I get to my room, I won't agonize as much."

Aunt Anna asked, "Why don't you have Sunday dinner with us? Meet your cousins and our grandchildren? We adopted. Our son's a dentist, and our daughter's a chemical engineer."

"Yes, dinner will be fine," Linda said. "I should be back about midafternoon."

Until her taxi arrived, they discussed highlights she should see during her three-day tour of the countryside. They then walked with her to the cab and hugged her goodnight.

Linda now had a family in Germany, people she could bond with and visit. Confronting Helena and Adler had closed a final void in her life that she never had to address again. She felt her future would be brighter. Now, she would complete her six-month sabbatical and tour Europe in the process.

***

Linda rented a car, opting to drive the three and a half hours to the Black Forest Hotel and Resort. Large trees surrounded the five-story complex. A walkway crossed the Danube River, leading to shops on the other side. The resort looked nothing like the ones in the States, but more like a gigantic bed and breakfast, tucked away in the forest.

Linda parked, stepped out of her vehicle, and welcomed the view. Snowcapped mountains loomed in the distance. Thick evergreens were plentiful, hiding buildings near and far. A few cars in the lot had cross-country skis and snowboard racks on top. A heaping pile of snow stood at the edge of a raging river. Rushing water drowned out most other sounds. Linda had requested a room near it. Falling into a deep, hypnotic sleep near such a natural wonder would be soothing.

Another car pulled up next to hers. The engine died. Two couples exited the vehicle—Americans. The tourists entered the hotel, but she remained in the parking lot. Fumbling with her camera, she managed to take a few photos before the wind stirred up the surrounding snow. She'd never envisioned anything so beautiful, so unspoiled. Crisp, clean air fogged her breath.

When she rolled her one-piece luggage into the lobby, a bellhop reached for it. "Good morning," he said in English. "May I help you with that?"

"No," she replied in German. "Thank you."

She apparently looked American. The man could tell by her clothes. She didn't like being stereotyped.

She continued to the front desk, checked in, and received an electronic key.

After taking the elevator to the third floor, she stepped off, bumped into a man about her age, and accidentally knocked the coffee cup from his hand, leaving a brown puddle on the light blue carpet.

"Ouch," he said.

Linda gasped and apologized to him in German. She looked up at his face and blinked in recognition. "Oh—Doctor—ah."

"Bauer. Eber Bauer. Glad I bumped into you," he said.

"Dr. Bauer, you're burned. Let me find some ice and get someone to clean this up."

"It wasn't that hot, Dr. Harrison."

"You remember my name," she said.

"Yes. Why did you leave Munich so abruptly last year?"

"I had an emergency back in the States. Sorry I didn't get a chance to say goodbye."

"Let's try to meet next Friday. This time, don't stand me up."

"Let me find some ice and get someone to clean this up." Her doctor instincts had kicked in. "Follow me. My room should be somewhere in this area. I'll buy you another cup of coffee … and lunch."

She found her room four doors down from the elevator and inserted her electronic key into the lock. The light flashed green, she opened the door, and he followed her inside. "There must be ice in here," she mumbled, more to herself than to her guest.

Rushing into the bathroom, she retrieved a towel and tossed it to him.

He caught it. "Thank you."

She opened the mini fridge and peeked inside. "No ice."

"That's not necessary," he said.

She notified the front desk about the coffee spill. When she got off the phone, the man stood in her bathroom, holding his hand under the cold tap. She tensed, realizing that she'd just invited him into her room, and the door had closed behind them. Concerned about him as a patient, she'd put her own safety in jeopardy.

She relaxed when he stepped back into the room, flashed a friendly grin, and extended his hand. "Good to see you again."

She pumped his soft, warm hand. "Good to see you again too."

"What brings you to Germany this time?"

"Another sabbatical."

Sex appeal emanated from him like heat from a fire. How can an average-looking man be so strikingly handsome? "Are you sure you're all right?"

Eber's lips curved into a perfect smile. "If you buy me another coffee, I'll forgive you."

She smiled. "All right."

They took the elevator down to the main floor. Ski season had started, and a small crowd filled the place. A waitress led them to a table next to a window. Like a gentleman, Eber pulled back her chair.

"What would you like to drink?" the waitress asked.

"A glass of wine for me." Linda looked at Eber. "What do you recommend?"

He opened his menu, studied it. "Cabernet Sauvignon from Napa Valley."

Linda laughed. "I came to Germany to drink wine from California?"

"Two glasses," Eber said to the waitress.

He turned his attention back to Linda. "How long is your sabbatical this time?"

"I'm in Munich for six months. And you?"

"Still a cardiologist, still in Munich."

She sneezed into her elbow. "I'm teaching classes and practicing at the Munich University Hospital. Are you here vacationing?"

His face brightened. "Yes, just for a few days. I grew up

in a small farming community, so whenever I can, I visit the countryside. I've been here twice. I'll show you all the neat places to visit, if you'd like."

"I'd like to stroll along the river. I'm eager to visit a cuckoo clock house—can't leave here without buying one. Do you know where I can get a good deal?"

He rubbed his chin with his forefinger. "If you want a good clock, you pay more. Cheap tourist clocks are about half the price."

"Did you drive or take the train?" Linda asked.

"The train," he said. "I hate driving the distance because the roads are too crowded."

Eber talked a lot about his parents and siblings, three brothers. He enjoyed music, watched sports, and traveled a lot. He was an extrovert, happy, and outgoing—her polar opposite and probably exactly what she needed in her life.

"My parents are dead." She closed her menu. "I grew up in foster care." He had the idyllic life she desired—a family with loving parents, a feel of belonging.

After lunch, they ordered a piece of Black Forest cake. Eber insisted on paying the check.

Because it was so windy and chilly, they toured the area in her car. She took pictures of houses, farms, unique shops, and landscapes. After a few hours, she felt as though she'd known Eber all her life.

He took her to a small restaurant for dinner. The warm, cozy place had only ten tables with menus tucked between the condiment racks.

A waitress placed a basket of hot bread and butter before them. "Do you two need time to study the menu?"

Eber looked at Linda. "Two draft beers?"

Linda laughed. "All right."

"You're not wearing a wedding ring. Are you dating anyone back in America?" he asked.

He was straightforward. "No, I don't have a boyfriend."

"You are so beautiful. I don't believe you."

She blushed. "I really don't."

His brown eyes sparkled. "I have always wanted to visit America. Now that I have a friend there ..."

Just the idea of him visiting New York made her heart thump. "I'd love to show you around my city."

He studied his menu. "Perhaps next year."

"Why don't you take a sabbatical in New York City?"

"I don't qualify, because my English is not good, and I don't want to be away from my son too long. He's six."

Linda's heart sank. But he wasn't wearing a ring either. "You're married?"

"Divorced, two years. I'm also not dating anyone at the moment," he admitted.

When their drinks arrived, Eber toasted his glass with hers. Their fingers touched, sending a surge of tension throughout Linda's body. He made her heart go wild—a feeling she'd never had for a man. His glance brought a trembling lightness to her head. He wasn't the tall, handsome man of her dreams, but he was undeniably charming. Was this love at first sight?

Spending time with a friend made her countryside visit more pleasant. She spent the next two days with him and gave him a lift back to the city. An innate bond made it hard for her to leave him. He had renewed her trust in people, made her life joyful. They exchanged email addresses and phone numbers, and she couldn't wait to see him again. She really liked him, and she knew the feeling was mutual.

***

More excited than exhausted from the drive from the countryside, Linda continued to her Sunday dinner engagement. When she arrived at her aunt and uncle's house, a boy—about eight—answered the door. He wore a Nike T-shirt and jeans. He glanced up at her with a blank expression on his face.

"Hello there. Is Anna Fluger home? You must be one of my nephews. What's your name?"

The boy didn't reply, just stared.

"Who is it?" Anna called.

Linda said, "It's me, Linda."

Anna came to the door. "Come in. You said you'd be late, but not this late."

Linda stepped inside and removed her coat. "Sorry about that. I met a nice man, a doctor, and I found it difficult to leave him. He works less than a kilometer from my hospital."

Aunt Anna took Linda's arm and led her into the dining area. "He sounds special. We'd like to meet him."

Linda blushed like a teenager. "Aunt Anna, I don't know him that well."

Anna beamed. "So that's why you're so cheerful. You seem to like him. After dinner, tell me all about your new friend."

The adults and one child occupied the main table, and two other children shared a smaller table in the corner.

"Hello, everyone," Linda said.

"Have a seat," Uncle Hager said. "We started without you."

Anna seated Linda at the table with the other adults and next to the boy she'd met at the door. "This is our son, Alexander, our daughter, Carla, and my three grandchildren. These are Carla's children—twins," Aunt Anna said with a wave of her hand. "Elsa and Derek. You've met Gary. He belongs to my son."

Linda waved at Alexander and Carla. "Nice to meet you. Cute children."

Alexander didn't resemble the Flugers at all. He was tall and overweight with red hair and brown eyes. He slouched in his chair and appeared bored.

Carla was a pretty blonde, much like Aunt Anna, energetic and talkative. Her children were six years old with brown hair and blue eyes.

Everyone wanted to hear about New York City—life in the Big Apple.

After dinner, Linda and Carla cleaned up the kitchen. They insisted Anna rest in the living room, where the men started a game of chess and the children played.

She noticed that neither of her cousins wore wedding bands.

***

Linda had gone to Germany in a fury and had fallen madly in love. She conversed with Eber daily, and she looked forward to hearing his voice. Due to their long working hours, they saw each other a few times a week, mostly on weekends. They had become inseparable. He made her pulse jump when he neared. She melted when he smiled at her, and her body heated to his touch, causing unfamiliar energy to stir within her. She'd met his son, ex-wife, parents, and siblings. After two months of dating, he wanted to get physical, but each time an invisible barrier went up. Stop. something within Linda would scream.

They were hugging on her sofa, watching TV, when the story aired about Adler and Helena Fluger. The news showed photos of Linda's adoptive parents being placed under arrest by the German authorities. They were awaiting extradition to America for outstanding warrants for attempted murder-for-hire.

Linda gripped her hands. Her heart thumped. Suddenly, something occurred to her. Since the man who'd raped her was dead, they might get away with what they'd done to her, or maybe she'd have to testify at their trial, and it would be her word versus theirs. She had no choice but to wait until the authorities contacted her with their decision.

"How awful," Eber said. "This story makes me believe in the death penalty. They lived right here in Munich for over twenty years."

As Eber held her in the safety and comfort of his arms, she knew he was the only man for her. A tingling sensation ran down her spine, and she felt his heart throbbing against her chest. He squeezed her breast.

She jumped back. "Stop." Her body tightened in response to his touch. Moving to the next level terrified her. His touch made her feel dirty, distant, and uncertain about his intent. Did he just want to use her, toss her aside like an old shoe when he was done with her?

"What's wrong?" he asked. "You give me the impression that you want to. Are you toying with me?"

She trembled and hugged herself, trying to shake away the feelings his hand had left on her breast. "I don't like it when you touch me that way. I can't."

"Can't … or won't?" he asked. "Every time I try to get closer, you back off."

She lurched to her feet and stalked around the room. "You just saw a couple being extradited back to America, because they'd paid someone to kill their daughter. I'm that little girl. A man raped and tortured me for nine days on their order."

Eber moved to her side and gave her a reassuring hug. "That's why you told me they were dead?"

"As far as I'm concerned, they are. I've never been with a man since my rape. I'm afraid, and I still have nightmares. I don't know if I can ever have sex with you. Maybe you should find someone else."

He held her tightly. "I don't want anyone else."

"In the past, each man I came close to hurt me in one way or another. It'll be very difficult for me to totally trust you."

"I won't hurt you, Linda. I love you," he said.

***

She cared enough for Eber to have a private detective perform a background check on him and his family. After Beaulin, the Mudicis, Helena, and Adler, she didn't need any more surprises in her life. According to the detective, Eber's family was a generation of farmers. Still, she had ambivalent feelings about their relationship. Getting close to him made her happy and frightened at the same time. She worried about losing him and feared a broken heart.

Eber wanted to know all about her life. He digested everything that had transpired since her childhood. She told him about how she'd escaped from her abductor, and about the Mudicis, Beaulin, Ian, and her uncle and aunt in Munich.

Without another word, he held her in his arms for a long time. Finally, he said, "You should remain here in Germany with me."

CHAPTER 21

FATHER AND SON

L inda kept in touch with her father and Uncle Danny in Leavenworth, Kansas, during her stay in Germany. Her father and Uncle Danny called her, and she often wrote them letters. Mark Brody worked on getting them clemency from the governor of New York. Meanwhile, she lost touch with Jim. Two months had passed without a word from him. Emails bounced, and his cell phone was disconnected.

For the second time, she contacted Jim's adoptive mother. "Hello, Mrs. Walden. This is Linda Harrison, Jim's biological mother."

"I'm glad you called." Mrs. Walden wept softly. "You haven't heard ... Jim's in jail."

"I've been here in Germany for two months. What happened?" Linda asked, startled by the news.

Mrs. Walden sighed. "He raped and murdered a

fifteen-year-old girl. The authorities say she's not his first victim. DNA, you know."

Linda collapsed on her bed, watching the ceiling. "Rape. Murder. No. Not Jim."

"We know what his father did to you." Mrs. Walden wept louder. "Jim had a problem with a girl in high school, and we assumed it was a misunderstanding. He wasn't charged."

Linda wiped saliva from the side of her mouth. She closed her eyes and denied the possibility. "What happened?"

"A girl claimed rape. This is a small town. She had a promiscuous reputation. My husband has lots of influence here. The district attorney dismissed Jim's case."

Linda broke into a cold sweat. "Any chance he's innocent?"

"No," Mrs. Walden said. "They caught him in the act this time. By the time the police arrived, the girl was dead, strangled. The authorities just closed seven open teenage girls' rape and murder cases, because Jim's DNA was a perfect match for each."

Linda's hands became numb, and the phone slid from her fingers. She immediately retrieved it. She had brought her rapist's monster child into the world, and the boy was just as destructive as his father had been. Guilt burned in her like a torch. If the state had aborted her baby, eight girls would still be alive. "I'm so sorry. He turned out exactly like his father."

"It really shocked us," Mrs. Walden said, her voice strained.

Linda regretted making the call. "Did he confess?"

"To the police—without the presence of an attorney."

The horrible things Jim had done clutched her heart. She shuddered. "Jim seemed so nice when he visited me, responsible, intelligent." Her body chilled as she exhaled her words. "Did ... he torture them?"

Mrs. Walden sniffled. "Yes, he did." Her voice trembled out of control. There was a brief, heartbreaking silence between the two women before they continued.

"It's been hard on my family, especially his father," Mrs. Walden choked out. "They were very close. I've never believed that bad genes could be inherited until now."

Linda couldn't keep her emotions from exploding. She wanted to cry but couldn't. "Was there anything else that might have indicated his illness besides the incident in high school?" she managed to get out.

"No. He was a sweet boy, well-mannered, smart, skipped grades in school. He looked forward to becoming a doctor."

"I had a strange feeling about him, but I couldn't determine why. He seemed too polite for such a young boy. I guess serial killers are usually nice until they get their victims alone. Does he have a good attorney?" Linda asked.

"A public defender. We can't afford an expensive lawyer. Our twins are in medical school as well."

"I'll get him a good attorney," Linda said, forcing herself to calm down.

"Jim doesn't want anyone spending money to defend him … said he prefers death rather than life in prison."

Relieved that she'd never gotten close to Jim, Linda asked, "Is the state of Texas seeking the death penalty?"

"Yes. One of the victims was a judge's daughter. It made national news. I've been calling you but didn't know you were out of the country."

Linda tried to think of the right words. "I—I don't know what to say. Those poor girls—their families."

Mrs. Walden broke down again. "Our community acts as if we're responsible. Most of our neighbors and friends avoid us. It's as if we're on trial. Reporters are still camped outside our house. They approach us each time we run for our cars."

"Are you going to his trial?"

The woman blew her nose. "Why, of course. We expect you to be there as well."

The thought of sitting through a trial, mentally reliving details of her own abduction, made her sick. "I don't want anyone to know he's my son. Hope you can understand."

Mrs. Walden hesitated and then said, "I do. Thanks for being in his life. It meant a lot to him. We love him and will always support him. When are you returning home?"

"In four months. Give me time to monitor the story

on the internet. I'll call you back later. I need time to process this. I'm too upset to talk anymore."

The woman began sobbing again. "I understand. Thanks for calling."

"Goodbye, Mrs. Walden. Take care."

Linda logged onto the internet. Her unsteady fingers kept hitting the wrong keys during her search for Jim Walden. Several websites popped onto the screen. She clicked on one with Jim's photograph, and a larger view of him filled the screen. Jim stood with a cop on either side of him, dressed in an orange prison uniform, trussed up in chains like a wild animal. Linda blinked away the tears as she read the story.

***

After a few months of dating, Eber invited Linda to his apartment for a candlelight dinner. He did all the cooking, refusing to let her in the kitchen. The scent of the fresh flowers he'd given her still engulfed the room when they finished their meal and moved to the sofa.

"I have a surprise for you," he said, displaying the proudest smile she'd ever seen.

"The flowers are magnificent. What now?" She beamed.

He got down on one knee, pulled a small black box from his pocket to reveal a sparkling diamond ring, and slipped it on her finger. "Will you be my wife?"

She squealed like a teenager. "Eber, it's so beautiful."

He flashed that crooked smile that always turned her heart to mush. "I want you to wear it for the rest of your life."

Holding her hand at a distance, she admired the diamond ring. Then, her smile faded. "I can't accept this. We don't know each other well enough."

He held her hands in his. "I love you. I want to marry you. I know the feeling is mutual."

"I love you too, but …"

"What? You're still afraid of a relationship?"

She lowered her head. "There's one thing I haven't told you."

Eber smiled. "After hearing your life story, nothing can shock me."

She held his hand to her lips and gently kissed it. "I had my rapist's baby at age fourteen. Other than the rape, the hardest thing was carrying a living being inside me for nine months. I tried to cut it out of my stomach. It was a boy."

"He's dead?"

"Not yet."

"Why do you say that? Where is he?"

She squeezed Eber's hand. "In jail. He raped and murdered eight teenage girls in Texas. He turned out to be just like his father. The district attorney is seeking the death penalty."

Still on his knees, Eber kissed her palm. "Did your son have a bad childhood?"

"No. I met Jim a few months prior to coming here. He seemed like such a nice young man, came from a good family, attended medical school, and earned excellent grades. Other than his adoptive parents and you, no one knows I have a child, and I want to keep it that way."

Eber's other knee went to the floor. He leaned in and hugged her. "A medical student. Have you heard his side of the story?"

"No. I don't care to," Linda said.

"Sorry to hear that." He rose to his feet and lifted her chin with his fingers. "You're not blaming yourself?"

"I had no control over the matter ... but I feel bad about it."

"You still haven't answered my question. Will you marry me?" he asked.

"I—I ..."

"We now know everything about each other," he said. "Let's set the date."

She snuggled into the safety of his arms. "Don't you think we're rushing things?"

He embraced her. "You're really looking for excuses."

"All right, let's set the date. How about after I settle everything in New York City?"

"We can have the wedding at my family's farm," he said.

She smiled. "We can have an outdoor wedding. Just a small gathering."

Eber held her in his arms. "We're so lucky. We have each other."

"Let's do something special," she added, smiling.

He took her arm and prepared to lead her toward his bedroom, but she slipped out of his grip.

"I was thinking about a night on the town."

***

The next night, Linda had just ended a phone conversation with Eber when she checked the New York City news on the internet. Pictures of the three men Jenny had left the nightclub with captured her attention.

Clicking on the subject, she read more: *Authorities found the bodies of three persons of interest related to the murder of Teddy Mudici's granddaughter, Jenny Mudici. Two teenagers stumbled upon the gruesome carnage of three men dangling by their feet from a tree in Cranch Park in Erie, Pennsylvania. The police found the victims' hands bound behind their backs. Their heads had been severed from their bodies by a chainsaw. These men were the last ones seen with Jenny Mudici prior to her murder. The police would not comment on whether or not the deaths were mob related.*

Linda leaned back in her chair. Grandpa had them killed. It felt great to have an ocean between her and the Mudici family. She would move to Germany, marry Eber, and never see them again.

CHAPTER 22

A.K.A. SWIFT

When Linda's sabbatical ended, she and Eber flew to New York City. She had left most of her personal things at his apartment, because they were to be married upon their return to Germany. Her future husband saw the Statue of Liberty from the plane, and said he wanted to visit it first.

Linda spent a week giving him a tour of the city. They dined at nice restaurants and took in a few shows. He attempted to have sex with her, but she still refused. He had been patient during the past six months. He respected her, allowing her to take her time. Linda knew he wanted to move to the next level, but she couldn't cross that invisible barrier—fear. She lay in bed, yearning for him—his sweet kisses, the warmth of his body, the smell of his scent. Her hormones raged every time she thought about him, and he slept just down the hall. The desire to go to his bed stretched within her. She didn't want to crave him but had no control.

A cold shower hadn't suppressed her sexual urges, so she left her room and eased down the hall, trying in vain to curb the desires coursing through her body. She didn't knock but quietly opened his door and stepped to the side of his bed. With the light of the open door, she watched his chest rise and fall. Standing there for a moment, she listened to the rhythm of heavy breathing. Passion shoved its way to the forefront of her consciousness.

Linda reached out to touch him, her hand stopping in midair. Longing exploded within her as she trembled. Then, holding her breath, she dropped her robe to the floor, eased back the covers, slid into bed beside him, and wrapped her arms around his neck. He groaned and hugged her back. She kissed his mouth. Their warm tongues caressed, their hands stroked, their passion rose. For the first time in her life, she willingly submitted to a man. They made passionate love for the remainder of the night.

***

The next evening, Linda and Eber snuggled on the sofa in front of a blue glow in the fireplace, watching a movie. Linda had now faced all of her fears and looked forward to a bright future with Eber. She had everything she wanted in life. Nothing stood in her way. Her cell phone rang. She retrieved it from the nearby lamp table, not looking at the number. "Hello."

"Linda, this is Swift. Come downstairs. I'm outside your building," he said.

She didn't like the tone of his voice. Oh no, the Mudicis are back. "Come on up," she said.

"I can't. Get down here, will you? I'm double-parked in a black limousine with tinted windows." The phone went dead—a trademark of the Mudici men.

"Who was it?" Eber asked.

"My cousin by marriage, the psychopathic gangster. He wants to meet me outside."

Eber rose from the sofa and stepped into his shoes. "I've never seen a mobster."

"You don't want to meet this one. Stay here," she said. "I'll find out what he wants."

"I'm coming," he insisted.

When they made it to the sidewalk, the driver opened the back door of the limousine. Rather than get inside, Linda hesitated, gawking at the unexpected scene before her. The dome light revealed a huge, shirtless man lying in the back seat on a shower curtain with three bullet holes in his hairy torso.

Swift eyed Eber from head to feet. "Who's he?"

Linda gasped, pointing to the man in the back seat. "Who's he?"

When Swift tried to push her into the vehicle, she spread her arms and legs far apart and gripped the doorframe to prevent him from forcing her inside. Eber jumped on Swift's back and tried to bring him down, but Swift shook Linda's fiancé off, punched him in the face, and sent him collapsing on the sidewalk like a ragdoll. The driver helped Swift fold Linda's arms and legs, then forced her into the blood-soaked back seat.

"No. Go hospital," Eber said in broken English.

Swift jerked Eber to his feet, pushed him into the front seat between him and the driver, and slammed the door shut as the car sped off.

The psychopath glanced back at Linda, his dark eyes cold and piercing. He gritted his teeth. "Get off your knees and do something for my man back there," he hissed.

Linda examined the stranger's wounds. He was barely holding on to life. She couldn't save him. "If you don't get this man to the emergency room, he's going to die," Linda yelled. "I don't have a magic wand."

Swift put his gun to Eber's head. "If you don't save him, I'm going to kill this jerk."

Linda had the opportunity to leap from the vehicle at red lights, but they had her future husband, and she knew Swift would shoot him if she attempted to escape.

The driver growled to Swift, "We made a big scene back there. People are probably calling the cops."

"Just drive," Swift said.

Eber looked back at Linda, his face as white as a sheet.

"Beruhigen, Eber," Linda said. How could she tell him to be calm?

Her cousin poked his gun into her fiancé's ribs so hard Eber grunted. "Stop looking back at her."

"We can't have a witness," the driver said.

Linda panicked. She had to save Eber's life. "He's a doctor. He can help. Please, don't hurt him."

"Slow down," Swift demanded. "We don't want to get pulled over."

The driver complied. When they pulled into the back-parking lot of the free clinic, it was just after eight. Two men came outside, helped Swift, and the driver carry the wounded man inside and placed him on an examination table in the cluttered storage area where Ian and she had performed surgery the last time.

"Can't you guys shoot each other during decent hours?" Linda asked.

One of the strangers asked, "Who's he?"

"Another doctor," the driver said.

Eber remained frozen just inside the doorway.

Linda laid out all the necessary surgical tools. "We need you guys to help us."

"You're the doctors," Swift said.

She opened a bottom cabinet and grabbed two boxes of rubber gloves. "We need one of you to assist as a nurse."

Eber's eyes still revealed panic.

Linda didn't know how to operate the X-ray machine the way Ian had. "A bullet has gone through this man's left lung. I need your help please," she said, addressing Eber.

The psychopath pressed his gun into Eber's back, forcing him forward. "Don't just stand there, dummy. Get to work."

Eber moved to the other side of the bed, stood at the patient's side, and resumed his frozen stance. His wide eyes cast down at the injured man's chest, but he didn't touch him.

So many fears rushed through Linda's head.

Would he forgive her for getting him involved in this? Did he regret asking her to marry him? Would he leave her if he survived? How could she stop Swift from killing him?

She spoke to Eber in German. "I'll attack the one with the gun. No, that won't work, they both have guns."

"Hey, speak English," Swift yelled.

"He doesn't understand English. I have to tell him what to do," she yelled back.

Suddenly, a dozen uniformed men in black stormed through the open door with drawn assault rifles. The two helpers rushed to Swift's side. The limousine driver gasped. Linda jumped backward. Helmets and body armor made the team look more like aliens than humans. Boxes piled from floor to ceiling in front of the side door came crashing down as a group of men forced their way through, stirring up a blanket of dust and causing the room to erupt like the sound of thunder.

A SWAT team had crowded them into the cramped room, standing between the equipment and spare examination tables.

"Police. Get your hands in the air," a hollow voice vibrated throughout the room.

Swift had been leaning against the opposite wall, a cigarette dangling from the corner of his mouth. Startled like everyone else, he hesitated, then pulled out his semi-automatic, spraying several rounds in the direction of the officers. One of the cops dropped to his knees, yelping in pain. The team immediately returned fire and riddled Swift with multiple bullets. His body jerked in spasms as he crumbled to the floor. Blood oozing from his wounds. Loud gunshots echoed throughout the room, deafening Linda. A burning pain penetrated her right shoulder. Her arm went numb—a stray bullet. She reeled and fell back onto the patient's chest. His warm blood matted her hair. The two accomplices who'd stood near Swift had been accidentally gunned down in the crossfire. They squirmed on the floor and yelled out in panicky screams, followed by hostile, foul language. Then, everything quieted.

"Move away from the bed. Everyone hit the floor," a voice demanded.

Like a movie, the cavalry had shown up at the last minute, saving everyone. If the patient got immediate medical treatment, he might live, and Linda no longer worried about Swift killing Eber. Looking down the barrels of the guns frightened her, but she wanted to drop to her knees and kiss the nearest cop's feet.

"Everybody hit the floor," another cop repeated.

"I'm a doctor. Help the man on the bed first," she pleaded. "He's in critical condition."

As soon as Linda had gained her balance, her knees buckled, and she slid down. The limousine driver dropped next to her. Eber remained frozen in his tracks.

The ringing in her ears continued as a shiver ran down her spine. "Holen sie sich, Eber."

When Eber didn't move, two officers grabbed his arms and body-slammed him to the floor. One placed a knee on his back while the other cuffed him.

Tears burned Linda's eyes, then ran down her face. "He doesn't speak English. Don't hurt him. Please."

Linda kept her head down and remained still. She didn't resist arrest, but two cops fell on top of her as if she were an alligator that was thrashing out of control.

"Frisk 'em," one of them ordered.

Two cops patted down the driver. "Gun." One cop removed the weapon while another cuffed him.

The cavalry showed no mercy concerning Linda's injury. They jerked her to her feet, handcuffed her, and shoved her out the door behind Eber. A dozen police cars waited outside. One of the officers attempted to place her into a squad car.

"Hey," another officer yelled. "I don't want her bleeding in my vehicle. Put her on the ground and wait for an ambulance."

Pigs.

Unbearable pain throbbed in her shoulder as blood dripped down the front of her T-shirt.

A police cruiser drove off with Eber in the back seat. He craned his neck, looking back at her. Was this farewell? A second patrol car carried the limousine driver away.

The first ambulance to arrive took the patient away, its siren blaring and red lights flashing. Other officers placed the limping cop into the back of a squad car, and it raced away too. A few minutes later, another emergency vehicle screeched to a stop. At the medic's request, the police removed Linda's handcuffs. The medical crew checked her vitals and placed her in the back of the vehicle, which sped away with blaring sirens. One of the EMTs sat in the back with her, monitoring her vitals.

The medic introduced himself, but his name didn't stick in her head. "What's your name?" he asked, attempting to get her mind off her injury.

"Dr. Harrison," she whispered.

"Are you an MD?"

"Oncologist." She could lose her medical license and then do what, become a nurse? Her accomplishments and her practice were ending. She hated the Mudici family and grew furious at herself for allowing them to sucker her into the Mob. They had haunted her past, now they threatened her future. Her desperate desire for love, attention, and belonging had changed the course of her life, her future, forever.

The EMT placed a bandage on her shoulder and applied pressure. "We don't get many doctors. Can you tell me your symptoms?"

"The bullet broke a spur. It's pressing against a nerve. The pain in my shoulder is sharp. My right arm is numb—paralysis."

"Think positive. It might not be permanent." He checked her blood pressure again. "Do you need pain medication?"

Linda did not like being a patient. "No." She could deal with the pain but not the humiliation of seeing her photograph plastered over every news station in the country.

She had never ridden in a vehicle on her back. Every pothole jarred her. She concentrated on the ceiling rather than the EMT. The light blinded her, so she closed her eyes. "I feel sick. I may throw up," she said over the deafening siren.

He placed a barf bag on her chest. "Just let me know when, and I'll assist you," he said as he continuously monitored her vital signs.

"Thanks for stopping the bleeding." Using her left hand, she placed her right across her chest. "Which hospital are you taking me to?"

"Presbyterian," he said. "How do you feel now?"

Linda's eyes fluttered open, and she shivered. "I don't want to go to Presbyterian. I can't be a patient there." Since Linda worked the emergency room at Presbyterian, she knew all the staff on a first-name basis. She'd had coffee or lunch with them all. They respected her, said she was the best doctor on their team. She could not suffer through the humiliation of being there when the police questioned her colleagues and staff. The hospital would no doubt fire her prior to her losing her medical license.

"We've already called ahead. A medical team is waiting for you. Sorry, we can't change hospitals. We're almost there," the EMT said.

When they rolled her inside, the staff met them at the door. Linda concentrated on the ceiling, avoiding eye contact.

"Why, Dr. Harrison, what happened to you?" the intake nurse asked. "Were you attacked?"

Everything looked blurry. "Innocent bystander," Linda said softly.

"But what happened?" the woman pushed.

The room spun. If she wasn't already lying down, she would have fainted. "Not now."

Dr. Adams, a coworker, examined her. "What happened, Dr. Harrison?"

She closed her eyes. "I need blood—AB negative. Dizzy."

"I need X-rays ASAP. Prep her for surgery," the doctor said to the nurse. "Get three units of AB negative."

In the operating room, Dr. Fieldhouser, the anesthesiologist, put her under. "Count backward from a hundred."

"One hundred, ninety-nine ..." she said groggily.

Linda didn't remember the ER taking X-rays. She closed her eyes and submitted to darkness.

Peace.

***

When she came to, the only light sources were the yellow glow from the open bathroom door and the green IV pump controls. She tried to move her left hand, but something constrained it. The police had handcuffed her to the bed railing with the call button in her palm. An officer opened the door and peered inside.

She was under arrest again. She needed Eber to hold her, kiss her, and tell her everything would be fine. Where is he? Since he wasn't at her bedside, he was probably in jail. Or maybe he'd taken the first flight back to Germany.

Two men wearing suits entered her room and flipped on the light switch. They introduced themselves as detectives.

Linda just wanted them to leave. "I'll speak to you only in the presence of my attorney. Goodnight, gentlemen."

Sunrise eased from the dark abyss and shone through her window shortly after the detective left.

Later that morning, Attorney Mark Brody came to her rescue. He placed a clear vase of yellow roses on her nightstand.

Face emotionless, he said, "Good morning, young lady. How do you feel?"

Tears rolled down Linda's cheeks. "Like I've been hit by a train and dragged ten miles." She raised her bed to a sitting position. "Thanks for the flowers."

He got right to the point. "Dr. Harrison, you're in serious trouble."

"Swift asked me to come downstairs, then forced us into a limousine. He threatened to kill Eber if I didn't cooperate," she blurted out.

Brody frowned. "Who are Swift and Eber?"

"Eber is my fiancé."

"The man from Germany?" he asked.

"Yes, this is his first time in the States. Must've been quite a shock to him. Swift is my cousin by marriage."

"We need to concentrate on getting you out on bail."

She shook her head but couldn't stop a flood of tears. When she attempted to move her right hand, pain shot from her shoulder down her arm. Her body jerked in response to the agony. "I realized the patient wouldn't make it without emergency room treatment. I never worked on the man, just examined him." She wiped her eyes on her pillow. "Eber doesn't understand much English."

"I've talked to the detectives on this case. The patient died, so you're being charged with manslaughter."

She broke down. "Where's Eber?"

"In jail ... charged as an accessory. They got him a translator. He told them everything—and I mean everything. Are you really Teddy Mudici's granddaughter?"

Linda concentrated on a painting on the wall. "Unfortunately, yes."

Brody pulled a chair next to her bed, took a seat, and removed a notepad from his laptop case. "I want you to tell me everything that happened."

***

After Brody left, Linda spent the remainder of the day watching the news. Her photo flashed on the screen of every station. She cringed from the publicity. *"Teddy Mudici's long-lost granddaughter, Dr. Linda Harrison, joined the family months ago. Dr. Harrison performed illegal surgery for the Mob, and the patient died."*

***

The authorities moved Linda from the hospital straight to a jail cell with her arm in a sling.

The next day, she stood in front of a judge with Brody, ready to argue her innocence. The judge looked about sixty, haggard with bags under her eyes, as if she lacked sleep. Her job seemed mundane, but her decision could alter Linda's life within a matter of seconds.

"How does the defendant plead?" the judge asked.

"Not guilty," Brody answered.

The district attorney voiced his legal opinion. "Your Honor, Dr. Harrison is Teddy Mudici's granddaughter. She performed illegal surgery on a patient who died because of her botched work. The state is requesting re-mand without bail. She's a flight risk with strong ties to Germany."

"Germany has an extradition treaty," the judge an-nounced. "Bail is set at a hundred thousand dollars. The defendant must surrender her passport prior to her release."

"But, Your Honor—" the prosecutor said.

The judge pounded her gavel. "Next case."

A female officer escorted Linda and her attorney into a secured room behind bars.

Brody pulled forms from his carrying case. "I brought these, just in case."

She read and signed a temporary power of attorney, permitting him to collect bail money from her account to pay the court, and allowing his paralegal to retrieve her passport from her apartment.

**

When the police department released Linda, she went directly to the criminal justice office.

The guilt of costing Eber his freedom gnawed at her insides like a piranha. Three women sat behind glass windows. Two were helping customers.

"I can help you here," said a stocky woman who looked thirtyish with a short ponytail dangling behind her head.

Linda stood before the woman. "How much is bail for Dr. Eber Bauer?"

The clerk hit a few keys. "Middle name?"

"No," Linda sniffed.

"Let's see. We have an Eber Bauer. Bail is set at $200,000," the clerk announced.

"But mine was only a hundred thousand," Linda protested.

The clerk didn't bother looking up at her. "Take it up with the court."

Linda stammered, "Where … is he?"

The woman still focused on her screen. "He's at Rikers Island."

The news hit her like a bolt of lightning. "What?"

The clerk made eye contact with her. "Make sure you're on his visitation list, or they won't let you see him. That's the law."

When she exited the courthouse, she frantically called Brody. "Eber is at Rikers Island. Will you represent him? We need to get him out of there before he's raped or murdered. Why did they send him to Rikers?"

"Calm down, Dr. Harrison," her attorney said. "All males are detained there. I can't represent both of you. I have a good attorney in mind for Eber."

Her voice quivered. "Why is his bail so high? $200,000?"

"He probably had a public defender. Are you willing to pay his bail?"

"Yes, I'll take care of it as soon as I can get to my bank," she said.

"If you settle his bail today, you can probably pick him up tomorrow. I'll contact the court concerning his release."

A chill swept throughout Linda's entire body as she trembled in fear. "I'll be at Rikers tomorrow afternoon."

"Dr. Harrison, don't worry. They won't put him in with the violent offenders," Brody said.

Linda pleaded, "Can we schedule an appointment with you and Eber's attorney tomorrow?"

"Let's make sure there are no problems getting him released. I can't see you until Monday. I'll call you tomorrow morning, let you know his status."

"Thanks, Mr. Brody. Goodbye."

Linda paid Eber's bail with a certified check, went home, and collapsed on the couch, sick with worry. She sat there, twisting her engagement ring around her finger in semicircles, tormenting herself with questions.

What if he refused to marry her now? Had she jeopardized her relationship with the only man she wanted to marry?

Linda retrieved Agent Jackson's card from her wallet and called him.

"Agent Jackson. This is Dr. Harrison. I need to talk to you. When can we meet?"

***

The next morning Linda sat in the FBI's New York field office with Agents Jackson and Truet. She placed a small cardboard box on Jackson's desk.

"The last time we spoke, I didn't tell you the truth about my family," she said.

"We know," Truet said. "What's in the box?"

"Memory cards with Teddy Mudici's secret meetings discussing illegal activities over a five-year period. I'd like to tell you all I know and allow you to watch the surveillance footage. I'll testify against my grandfather if my manslaughter charges are dropped, and I can keep my medical license."

"That depends on what you have to tell us, Dr. Harrison," Jackson said.

Linda took a deep breath and started talking.

***

Linda arrived at Rikers Island Thursday at 12:30 p.m. sharp. At the institution's checkpoint, she showed her driver's license to an officer and stated the reason for her visit. The guard presented her with a map and detailed instructions on how to get to the visitors' center, although she didn't need them. The directions were clearly marked. The parking lot seemed filled to its capacity, and she felt lucky to squeeze into a space next to a Hummer.

The huge complex housed over ten thousand of New York City's most violent offenders. Tall buildings dotted the island like a city. Jets took off and landed at nearby LaGuardia Airport. A gentle breeze chilled the smoggy April air. Linda shivered, not because of the cold, but because of her anxiety over facing Eber again.

She rushed into the fenced-in sidewalk, hesitated, and read a sign in bold letters: "VISITING HOURS 1:00 P.M. to 9:00 P.M. WEDNESDAY AND THURSDAY, 8:00 A.M. to 4:00 P.M. FRIDAY AND SATURDAY. NO VISITING HOURS MONDAY AND TUESDAY."

She stopped in her tracks when she read another sign: "HOME OF NEW YORK'S BOLDEST." Are they praising their inmates?

"Excuse me, lady," a female said.

Linda looked back, then stood aside as a teenager pushing a doublewide stroller with a toddler and a six-month-old passed her. "Sorry," Linda said. The girl should've been thinking about college, not diapers.

"Just follow the line," the young girl said.

Linda continued down the sidewalk that ended at the front door of an older building. She entered a large waiting room in the visitors' center. Cameras covered every angle of the place. On the other side of a glass wall, booths were set up for phone visitations. No one had visited her during her stay in juvenile detention. Straight ahead, a secured door stood in the middle of a gray tinted-glass wall. Visitors had created two lines in front of roped-off areas with IDs and forms in hand. She chose one of the lines that wrapped around the room. People talked, some coughed. Babies cried, and annoying kids ran about unsupervised.

An elderly black man, wearing a blue T-shirt that said: "NYC CORRECTION SSO" with white letters on it, walked through.

Linda said to him, "Excuse me. I'm here to pick up someone. Must I wait in line?"

He eyed her from head to feet. "Yes, ma'am, Miss Ann."

She frowned, recalling that she'd heard the term used by a black student in Louisiana when he addressed a white teacher in a derogatory manner.

She studied the crowd of mostly women and children. They were there to see a husband, a brother, a boyfriend, or a father. Many were similar to the crowds of people who had visited the free clinic. They remained in ruts from one generation to the next. If doctors hadn't influenced her in her teen years, she could have turned out just like them.

At exactly 1:00 p. m, two clerks came in, manned their desks, and logged on to their computers.

"Next," said one, then the other.

Linda shifted from side to side for almost an hour. Her cell phone rang. Brody.

"Good news. You can pick up Eber," he cheerfully said.

Linda's anxiety increased. "Fortunately, I arrived here early. The line is so long."

"I want you both in my office first thing Monday morning."

One of the clerks barked, "Hey, no cell phones."

She quickly ended the conversation. "Thanks. We'll be there. Bye."

Linda turned off her phone while the clerk gave her the evil eye. When she reached the next available desk, she said, "I'm here to pick up Eber Bauer."

The woman reached for Linda's form and ID, then typed something on her computer. "He'll be released as soon as an officer is available." The woman returned her license. "Take a seat."

Linda shouldn't have asked but did so anyway. "How long will this take?"

"Could be an hour. Could be four. Next," the woman yelled.

Linda sat in a hard plastic chair, put her phone on vibrate, and surfed the internet—mostly checking the news concerning Jim. She continuously glanced at the wall clock, fidgeting more by the minute. Each time the secured door opened, her head snapped up, and her heart fluttered. Guards escorted inmates in and out of the secured area where the men sat behind glass windows and conversed with guests over phones.

Linda had been waiting for two hours and forty-three minutes when the security door opened and Eber stepped out. She jumped to her feet, her stomach in a knot. He had a black eye and stitches on his forehead. Oh, no. What have they done to him?

She wanted to hug him but feared he'd push her away,

and she couldn't deal with that. Blinking back the tears, her voice choking, she asked in German, "How are you?"

He threw his arms around her neck, and she hugged him back, melting into his arms.

She gently touched his face, weeping. "What happened to you?"

"Linda, get me out of this place," he whispered. "These people are animals. The guards are inmates in uniform. They schedule fights and bet on them—just for the fun of it."

A young boy stared at them when he heard the foreign language. They walked outside holding hands.

"Eber, I'm so sorry … you're a good person. Do you hate me?"

He kissed her lips. "I could never hate you, Linda. I want to spend the rest of my life with you."

Relieved and melting with love, she asked, "What did you tell the authorities?"

"Everything except that we are engaged and about your son." He shook his head. "I shouldn't have?"

"You did fine. Always tell the truth."

He placed his hand on the small of her back. "How is your shoulder?"

"The bullet hit a spur that presses against a brachial plexus nerve. My arm will be numb for a while, but it should return to normal within a few months."

He pulled her closer to him. "I was so worried about you, didn't know how badly you were hurt. The things that occurred at the clinic that night were so surreal. I—I froze. I couldn't react."

She hugged him, holding on tightly for a long time. "I'm sorry about what I got you involved in at the clinic. I'm trying to get you back to Germany soon."

He kissed her again. "It wasn't your fault, but that wacky cousin of yours ..."

She sighed, trembling. "I have to testify against my family. The authorities don't need your testimony."

"American justice," he said. "Return to Munich with me."

"I can't. The FBI has taken charge of the case. They've interrogated me repeatedly."

"Linda, I knew your family was dangerous, but I never imagined ..."

She unlocked her car. "I told the authorities we were forced at gunpoint. The driver corroborates our story."

He closed his door. "When is the trial?"

"I don't know. I've given the feds the entire memory card collection containing Grandpa's mob meetings. If I play ball with them, they won't charge me with failure to report a death. After all, they're after the big fish— Grandpa—and they have him on a silver platter."

Eber looked back. "Linda, let's get out of this place."

She started the engine, backed up, and drove away. The farther they drove, the more relaxed Eber became.

He glanced out at the water as she drove across the

bridge. "You said you won't be charged for the patient's death, so why make a deal with the government?"

"During the first surgery I performed at the clinic, one of the men was already dead when I arrived. I didn't report the incident to the police," she said.

"It's too dangerous for you to testify against your family." He stared at her, his forehead wrinkled. "Your grandfather said he'd have you killed if you turned against him."

"I'll have to take that chance. Protective custody is my only option, maybe witness protection."

CHAPTER 23

PROTECTIVE CUSTODY

The FBI hid Linda in a Hilton Hotel in White Plains for over a month. She'd settled into a room on the top floor with two queen-size beds, a loveseat, and a mini fridge.

The feds said they'd release the memory cards as evidence, but she hadn't heard anything related to the Mudicis' arrests. No one knew her whereabouts, not even her attorney. She couldn't do anything except watch TV and read. The room wasn't large enough for exercising, but she did her best. The drapes remained closed at all times, and the agents refused to allow Linda to look out the window.

How much more of this could she take?

Two female agents remained in her room from 10:00 p.m. to 6:00 a.m. Agent Teberger, an African American, stood a stout six feet. Agent Paxton, a short Caucasian with a small frame, didn't appear as if she could defend herself against a gnat. They took turns sleeping in the second queen-size bed. One stood watch while the other slept. The women didn't bring overnight bags or toiletries but slept in their clothes—jackets off, guns exposed. There was no phone in the room. They allowed her to speak to Eber twice a week over a government phone. Her heart ached for him.

Would he wait for her, as he'd promised?

Linda was sitting with her back resting against the headboard, watching more of Jim's coverage on TV when Teberger's cell rang, followed by a knock on the door.

Shift change.

When Teberger opened the door, Jackson and Truet entered. They exchanged a few words with the two female agents who were on their way out the door.

On the TV screen, Jim's adoptive parents were pleading with the state of Texas to spare their son's life. They said he was a product of rape, claiming he'd inherited his father's genes.

"Morning, Dr. Harrison," Truet said. "Do you mind turning off the TV?" He dropped onto the loveseat and leaned back, making himself at home. As cold as the police officers who'd arrested her, he showed no compassion. He was just a hollow shell.

"Agent Jackson," she acknowledged, ignoring Truet.

Jackson carried a plastic bag, probably her breakfast. He was more personable. "Good morning, Doctor." He reminded her of an exhausted agent waiting for retirement.

"I brought you a gourmet breakfast, egg and cheese crepes. You haven't been eating well lately. We can't have you getting sick." He opened a bag and placed a white Styrofoam container and plasticware on the table, studying her reading material in the process. Retrieving two prescription bottles from his pocket, he tossed them onto the bed next to her. "Our psychiatrist prescribed these."

Linda picked up the bottles and read the labels. "I said I don't need medication." The prescriptions were Trazodone and Valium.

Jackson tugged at his belt. "Dr. Harrison, the US district attorney has thoroughly reviewed the evidence you've provided of the Mudici meetings. We have Teddy Mudici in a corner. He can't work his way out of this one. You didn't tell us everything.

Truet looked smug. He seemed the type who likes to make people squirm.

Linda had been suffering insomnia since being in protective custody, so she was too tired to care if she came across as a bit arrogant. "I've viewed everything on the video footage, just like you. Why bring it up now?" She bounced off the bed, stopped at the window, and snatched open the drapes, allowing the bright sunrays to warm her face for the first time in over a month.

Truet raced to the window, abruptly closed the curtains, and scolded her as if she'd behaved like a disobedient child.

"Don't ever do that again." Truet took a seat, violently

punched a pillow, and stuffed it behind his back. "There are other things you didn't tell us. Your cousin, Jim Pignataro, a.k.a. Swift, murdered six people. The local authorities plastered his sketch all over the news. Didn't you recognize him?"

Linda said, "I turned him in to the local authorities twice, no results. I wasn't a witness to his crimes, so I couldn't pick him out of a lineup." She had the urge to wring the little geek's neck. "I told you everything that was important. You have all the evidence."

The geek sneezed into his hands and rubbed his palms together. Gross.

She jerked her head in the opposite direction. The FBI held her future in its hands, and that frightened her. The feds had always kept her in the dark about everything— until now.

She stood, placed her hands behind her back, and stalked around the room like a caged animal. "I'm going crazy in this place. At least let me have my laptop."

"No," Jackson said. "We don't want you on the internet."

Linda turned to Jackson. "This is worse than jail. Eber has been back in Germany over a month, and I haven't seen anything on the news about the Mudici family even being arrested."

"We don't want it aired. Neither do the Mudicis," Jackson said. "Their lawyers had to review the evidence. They tried to get the surveillance evidence thrown out of court, claimed you illegally obtained them from your cousin, Jenny, after her death."

"They lost." Truet grinned, crossed an ankle over his knee, and leaned back. "You should see their arrests on today's news. We got Teddy, Ralph, and Billy Mudici, plus indictments for seventeen others with ties to the family. We don't expect them to make bail."

Edging toward insanity, Linda slumped in a chair at the table in front of Jackson. "When's the court date? In New York City, it could take years."

"It'll take no more than a couple of months in federal court." Jackson thumbed through a magazine. "I know it's hard to stay cooped up like this, but you'll survive."

She stuttered. "You mean I can't leave this room until … after the trial?"

Truet nodded. "Exactly."

Linda sighed. "I want to leave protective custody. Grandpa can't gain anything by having me killed as long as the FBI has the surveillance footage."

Jackson leaned back and tugged at his belt again, as if trying to relieve the pressure on his stomach. "We'll have a stronger case with your testimony, and you need to clear yourself. Remember, you're an accessory, Dr. Harrison."

She leaned forward in her chair. "You said I wouldn't be charged."

"If you testify," Jackson reminded her. "We have an agreement and expect your full cooperation."

"You guys are just like Grandpa. You don't care who you hurt as long as you get what you want," she shouted. "I demand to speak to my attorney, in person. I have rights."

Truet's nostrils flared.

Jackson reluctantly called Brody and scheduled an appointment. Linda spoke with him briefly over Jackson's phone.

The agents were silent for the remainder of the day. They watched TV and played with their phones or laptops.

Jackson entered the bathroom several times to make personal phone calls.

The midday news aired the Mudici family's arrest. Linda could not bear to watch it, so she switched to another channel. A reporter was interviewing her father and Uncle Danny at Leavenworth. They stood outside the prison, wearing street clothes.

A news reporter said, "I'm here with the Mudici twins, Tony and Danny. How does it feel to be free after over thirty years in prison? That's right, viewers, the governor gave the brothers clemency, provided they live west of the Mississippi and never participate in organized crime again, or they will serve the remainder of their life sentences."

The reporter held the microphone to her father's mouth. "I don't know what to say. At first, we didn't believe it. We owe it all to my daughter. She really came through for us."

Linda started hyperventilating, and a tremor went through her body. "They're out of prison."

"Thanks to you," Truet said. "Getting two Mudicis out and sending three in doesn't make sense."

"He's my father," she stammered and then squinted at him. "My real father."

The geek's cell phone rang. "Agent Truet. Yes ... yes." He put his phone back into his pocket.

When her father's interview ended, she switched to a movie. She had accomplished something great. She'd gotten her father and uncle out of prison.

Jackson dropped the magazine onto the table in front of him. "You know that Helena and Adler Fluger pled guilty to their crimes?"

"Yes." Linda hit the mute button. "They're waiting to be sentenced."

Jackson said, "They got four years. Will probably serve eighteen months."

Linda rolled over on the bed, facing the wall. She prepared for a deluge of tears, but they didn't come. After all they'd put her through—a lifetime of pain, suffering, nightmares, and now defeat—that was all they'd get. That scared Linda. Even with all the evidence mounted against Grandpa, would he walked too? Her hopes of nailing him were fading like a puff of smoke.

Paxton and Teberger returned at the next shift change.

Linda was glad to see the snotty-faced Truet leave. He was as irritating as a sore thumb and just as unpredictable as Swift.

***

Three days later, Jackson and Truet escorted Linda from her hotel to an SUV with tinted windows. They made the hour's drive to the city, took the Triboro Bridge from Manhattan to Queens, and made a right turn on Hazen Street. There was only one possible destination—Rikers Island.

The news reports announced that Jim Walden had gotten the death sentence. He wasn't going to appeal, because he preferred death over life in prison. Linda closed her eyes, letting the news sink in. She didn't mourn.

As they drove across the bridge, she shifted anxiously in the back seat. "Why are we going here?"

"This is where you're meeting your attorney," Jackson said, speaking over the morning news report on the radio.

The closer they got to the island, the more fidgety she became. She no longer believed the feds, no longer trusted them. Thoughts of opening the door and leaping from the vehicle when it slowed entered her mind, but she had no place to run.

Were they going to lock her up because she'd requested to leave protective custody? They could do anything they wished with her, and no one would know. Stay calm, she told herself. Her heels started tapping involuntarily.

It was Monday—no visiting hours—and the parking lot was almost empty.

The agents escorted Linda through the same fenced-in path she'd taken to pick up Eber. When they entered the visitors' center, she saw a guard leaning against the wall, as if waiting for them.

"I'm Agent Jackson, this is Agent Truet. I phoned Friday."

The guard walked them to a computer station and opened a logbook. "I need to see your IDs. Sign in here please."

The agents didn't introduce Linda, nor did the guard inquire about her. He unlocked the secured door and led them into the back.

Linda walked between Jackson and Truet. Jackson followed the guard down a wide, dimly lit hallway. They passed three doors, all closed—not another person in sight.

A short distance farther, a door stood open, and a light from the room shone into the hallway. The guard walked to the far side of the door. Jackson stopped on the near side, peeked in, and beckoned her with a wave of his hand.

Linda stepped into the doorway, her heart pounding. Her attorney sat in the small room, facing her, with his laptop open.

"Mr. Brody." Her eyes welled up as she stepped inside, closing the door behind her.

He smiled, stood, and extended his hand.

She ignored his outstretched hand, rushed forward, and hugged him like an old friend. "Thanks for coming."

He hugged her back. "You're looking well, thinner. The last time I saw you, your arm was in a sling."

"You've helped me so much. I really appreciate all your work."

"That's how I make my living," he said. "Have a seat."

Linda took the hard plastic chair opposite him.

Brody seated himself. "Why haven't I heard from you?"

"The FBI duped me. Said I couldn't contact anyone, including my attorney. Why are we meeting here?"

"They're taking precautions in case my office is being watched. I have clients at Rikers, so it's not unusual for me to drive here."

"What's happening? The feds didn't tell me much."

"The authorities made more arrests than they'd anticipated," Brody said. "The Mudici organization is like a beehive without a queen."

The idea of the family in chaos caused her to shiver. "Grandpa must be desperate. He'll do anything to save himself."

"Cooperate with the feds. They'll have a stronger case with your testimony. I'm sure Teddy Mudici is gunning for you. After the convictions of Teddy, Ralph, and Billy, you'll go into witness protection. The FBI won't need you for the other cases, because many of your family's business associates have made deals."

Linda slid to the edge of her chair and leaned in. "What about Eber?"

"He's no threat to the Mudicis."

"The agents said I could spend another month in protective custody" she said.

Brody closed his laptop. "Because of the publicity of this case, it could get into federal court earlier. A date hasn't been set."

"I want to move to Germany after the trial."

"I'm working on that," he said. "Witness protection only applies within the States. Don't worry. I'm not giving up. You'll end up in some menial job though—nothing in the medical field."

"No way," she gasped. "I'm a doctor. Medicine is my life."

"Witness protection is a whole new life. You know that."

She shook her head. "I can't give up my practice."

"You won't need a medical license. Think it through. Your grandpa might have Eber watched."

She lowered her head. "So we can't get married."

"Not unless he's willing to enter witness protection with you."

She shook her head. "I can't ask him to give up his career—his life."

Brody leaned back in his chair. "Teddy Mudici can find you through Eber."

Silence.

"Thanks for getting my father and uncle out of prison." A slight smile appeared briefly and then faded. "Now you're telling me I'll never see them again. Do they know I'm in protective custody?"

"Yes. Sorry about that," Brody said. "Your father and uncle might be able to protect you."

"Not as long as Grandpa's alive. The last time I spoke with Eber, he said we could live in another city in Germany or even move to the countryside."

"You're very much in love?" Brody asked.

She smiled. "Yes. I can't wait to see him again."

"Does Teddy Mudici know you're engaged?"

"Not from me or Eber. Maybe I won't need witness protection. After Grandpa is convicted, I don't think he'll come after me."

Brody's face became stern. "Are you willing to risk your life on that?"

She glanced at the floor. "He'll probably have me killed, just out of spite."

"The feds said you have enough funds to live on for the rest of your life without working."

"Yes, but I want to be a doctor. Just curious—will the government seize Grandpa's estate?"

"Until the IRS determines where his assets came from."

"Grandma and Aunt Christina will become penniless." Linda couldn't manage any sympathy for them.

He tucked his computer back into its case, removed papers from a side pocket, and shoved them across the table to her. "They might be able to retain the restaurant. My knowledge about mobsters suggests they hide money in a thousand different places and under just as many names."

Linda read and signed the documents, giving Brody total power of attorney over her estate. She had no choice but to trust him with all of her finances.

"The only thing the US attorney has on you is not reporting the drugs and the death of Mr. Catolano at the clinic. The FBI can clear you on those. The bail checks for you and Eber are probably sitting in your mailbox. I'll deposit them into your account. Thanks to the limousine driver, you both were cleared in the death of the last patient, Mr. Ramsey."

"Where's my passport?"

He retrieved it from his bag and gave it to her. "I picked it up at the police station. You must surrender it to the FBI."

"I want out of this country as soon as possible. If the feds refuse to give me a new identification in Germany, I'll leave protective custody, take my chances."

"You may not be any safer in Germany," Brody said. "Does your family have ties in Italy?"

"My cousin, Jenny, said the family in Italy is not mob

related. I'm not sure if they know what Grandpa does for a living."

Linda made a list of personal things she wanted from her apartment. "Look out for my apartment. Grandpa can't live forever."

He pulled a cell phone from his pocket and placed it on the table in front of her. "It's a burner phone. My private number is on the back. Call me anytime."

"Hope it has lots of minutes. I get pretty lonely sitting in a room for days on end."

Linda enjoyed her conversation with Brody, making it difficult for her to leave him. She spent over two hours with him, discussing her role in the upcoming trial. She also admitted how she had allowed the Mudicis to lure her into the family.

Jackson opened the door and peeked inside. "Let's wrap it up, Doctor."

She stood. "They want me to return to my dungeon. I don't want to go back there."

Brody rose from his chair. "You have to. I know you're suffering."

"You don't know how much," she said. "Goodbye. I don't know if we can meet again. Thanks."

"Good luck, Dr. Harrison."

He extended his hand, and she accepted it.

CHAPTER 24

THE TRIAL

Agent Teberger woke Linda before dawn. "Let's get ready for court."

Linda looked at the clock on the nightstand and yawned. "It's four o'clock. Court isn't until eight."

"We need to arrive early, so get your butt out of bed," Teberger urged.

The sleeping pills left Linda sluggish. She showered, then slipped into a black suit and a green blouse.

A cell phone went off, followed by a knock on the door. Jackson and Truet stepped inside. Truet pulled a bulletproof vest from a shopping bag and tossed it onto Linda's bed.

She blinked rapidly, took a step back, and held her breath. Is that for me? He can't be serious.

Jackson spread a sketch of a map on the table, and the other three agents hovered around it. "We're taking this route. There'll be a car in front of us and one in back.

This is the side entrance to the courthouse. Four US marshals will be waiting for us here. We have a sniper on buildings here, here, and here. Let's move."

Truet helped Linda into her vest. "Wear your coat over it. You ready?"

It was too hot for a coat. They were behaving as if she were the president.

Suddenly, reality hit her in the face like the wind from a hurricane, and a hand went to her throat. My life could end today. "No, I'm not," she said, shaking her head.

"We need to get going," Jackson snapped.

The two women opened the door and stepped out into the hallway. Jackson fell in behind Linda, nudging her out of the room with Truet holding up the rear. They rode the elevator down to the lobby and took a side door to a waiting SUV parked at the curb. Although Grandpa had threatened to kill Linda, there was a chance he'd never act on his promise. Many people blew hot air, making threats they didn't keep or mean. Did she really need a bulletproof vest, or were the agents overestimating the urgency of the situation? Jackson slid into the front seat with the driver, and Linda sat in the back with Truet. The two female agents entered another vehicle in front of them.

The closer they drove to the city, the heavier the traffic became. When they reached the courthouse, dawn had ended. Sunlight peeked over the buildings.

Their vehicle stopped at the courthouse side door.

Truet and Jackson exited. They opened the back door, grabbed Linda's arms, and rushed her outside as they hurried toward the door.

Four more men in suits approached them. Suddenly the one next to Linda whimpered in pain. He collapsed in his tracks, hands gripping his shoulder, as if the action could stem the flow of blood squirting from his wound.

Jackson drew his weapon, eyes searching above. "Get inside."

Something hit Linda in the back, and the impact knocked her face-first onto the sidewalk.

"He's up there," one of the men yelled. "Where are our building snipers?"

Someone jerked Linda to her feet as pain shot through her left arm. Gunshots echoed overhead, the sounds bouncing off the buildings.

Two people dragged Linda into the courthouse. The shooting stopped, and sirens sounded in the distance, followed by ringing cell phones.

"EMTs are on their way, Dr. Harrison." Truet's voice trembled. "We'll get you to a hospital." He gave her a handkerchief and led her into a vacant conference room, absent of windows. A mixture of a dozen plain-clothed and uniformed cops swarmed the hallway outside. Truet helped Linda out of her coat and the bulky vest. When he helped remove her suit jacket, his hands shook as much as hers.

She examined her injury. The bullet had gone through

just above her elbow, just missing the bone. "The EMTs can bandage it. There's no way I'm leaving this courthouse until I testify. I'll put Grandpa where he belongs, behind bars." She couldn't stop the flowing tears or the fear penetrating her like a knife.

For the first time, Truet showed compassion. He was human after all. "You sure you don't need a doctor?"

Blood dripped from her nose. "No," she said. "Nothing serious."

Two officers patted down the EMTs while another searched their equipment. The medical team entered the room, examined her wound, and checked her vitals.

"It's not so bad," one of them said. "Yeah, we can patch this up. Do you need anything for pain?"

"No, thank you. My doctor has already prescribed me Valium."

The other EMT cleaned her nose. "You have a nasty bruise here."

After the medics finished treating Linda, they left Truet and her alone in the room.

A female officer entered and gave Linda a makeup job, camouflaging her red nose. "We can't have a jury seeing you in this state without causing a mistrial."

Linda sat on the edge of her chair until 8:45. Then the door swung open. "You're up, Dr. Harrison," Jackson said.

Linda slowly rose to her feet, her legs stiff and achy. "I don't know if I can make it."

Jackson took her right arm. "Just put one foot in front of the other. You can do this."

Linda leaned on Jackson as he led her down the hallway, shielded by an army of police officers. She moved as fast as her condition would allow. The group protected her, as animals protect their young from predators.

News reporters were camped in the hallway, because the judicial system didn't allow cameras in the courtroom. They stormed toward her with cameras rolling as she approached.

"Clear the path," Jackson yelled. "Coming through."

The last time Linda had captured the headlines, she was a juvenile in the state's custody—protected from harassment. She couldn't dodge the cameras this time.

A reporter asked, "Dr. Harrison, can you—"

"No questions." Jackson ushered her down the crowded hallway.

Although the US district attorney had briefed her thoroughly, Linda wasn't ready to face her family, especially after the recent attempt on her life. Jackson led her into the courtroom, leaving his army outside. She got a side view of Teddy, Ralph, and Billy Mudici sitting at the defense table with two attorneys. Teddy and Ralph scowled. Billy showed no emotion. Linda's eyes fixated on them, but they didn't acknowledge her. In the audience, Grandma and Aunt Christina stared at her with indignation, their eyes piercing. The grandmother who had once showed her loved now showed vivid, outward hatred.

Jackson led her to the front bench, took his position in the back of the packed room, and leaned against the wall. Linda sat frozen like a statue, focusing on the flags, her heart pumping out of control. Her armpits had become soaked, and she still trembled.

One of the Mudicis' attorneys appeared to be just out of law school—a younger version of the older attorney. Both wore Gucci suits.

The judge sat behind a mahogany bench and wore a black robe. She looked about fifty and had reading glasses perched on the end of her nose. The plaque on her bench read "HON SALLY BETHEL." Brody had referred to her as the judge from hell.

"Is the court's first witness present?" Judge Bethel asked.

The bailiff roared, "Yes, Your Honor. Dr. Linda Harrison."

The judge said, "The court will take a short recess. I'd like to see the US district attorney, the defendants' attorneys, and the witness in my chambers please."

"Court's in recess," the bailiff said.

The judge stood, led them through the side door near her bench, and entered an office at the end of the hall. She took a chair behind a desk cluttered with stacks of paper. "Have a seat, Dr. Harrison."

There were three additional chairs, yet neither the district attorney or the Mudicis' attorney sat.

Judge Bethel removed her glasses and addressed the defendants' attorneys. "I understand there was an attempt on Dr. Harrison's life this morning, right outside this courtroom." She turned her attention to Linda. "Your bulletproof vest saved your life, Doctor."

The Mudicis' attorneys glanced at each other, as if unaware of the event.

"Dr. Harrison, do you feel competent enough to testify today?" the judge asked.

"Yes, Your Honor," Linda replied eagerly.

The judge relocated a stack of files on her desk. "You've been shot and injured. Are you all right? We can postpone this trial—"

"No," Linda said. "I've had worse things happen to me. I want to proceed while I'm still alive. I'd like to complete my testimony today, if the court permits."

"The court can't determine how long trials will last. Someone just tried to kill you," the judge reminded her. "You must be terrified."

"I'm afraid, not terrified. I'm a very determined, strong-willed woman—have been for years."

"You look terrified to me." Judge Bethel addressed the prosecutor. "How do you feel about this?"

The district attorney stood the same height as the older of the two defense attorneys. He looked to be in his mid-forties and wore a suit off the rack. He rounded his shoulders. "I trust her competency."

"I'd like to hear from the defense," the judge said.

The older of the defense attorneys nodded. "Let's proceed."

Linda snapped her chin up, gritting her teeth as she addressed the Mudicis' attorneys. "Tell Grandpa that Helena and Adler tried to have me killed. They failed. So did he. Even if it costs my life, I'll testify against the family. He doesn't frighten me."

Despite her words, Grandpa did frighten her, and she was terrified.

The judge pushed back her chair, then stood. "Okay, Doctor. Gentlemen, let's play ball."

The group filed back into the courtroom. The judge resumed her seat behind her bench.

The bailiff announced, "Court's back in session. The court calls Dr. Linda Harrison to the stand."

Linda approached the witness stand, her back as stiff as a board. Facing the courtroom audience petrified her. She took the oath, stated her name and occupation, and took a seat on the witness stand.

"Dr. Harrison," the prosecutor said. "Give the court the date and time, to your best knowledge, of when you first met with Mr. Teddy Mudici and the exact reason why."

Linda lasted on the witness stand for four agonizing hours. The prosecutor had briefed her well concerning the complexity of the trial. He said the court held all the cards, leaving the defense nothing to work with. Well poised, Linda felt she'd mesmerized the jury. Avoiding eye contact with her family gave her more confidence. Linda didn't want to focus on desperation, anger, fear, or whatever other emotions the Mudicis' expressions might reveal. Instead, she concentrated on the jury and the questions thrown at her by the prosecutor.

Before lunch, the prosecution rested with a request to redirect.

Linda didn't want lunch, but Truet almost spoon-fed her a cup of soup. "You need something in your stomach, especially since you're taking medication."

She washed down two more Valiums with a container of orange juice.

The prosecutor had warned Linda that Grandpa's attorneys would devour her like a pack of famished wolves over a fresh kill. He'd covered every possible question the defense could ask, and from every angle.

Mr. Arrigo, the family's lead attorney, approached the witness stand with hands behind his back. "Dr. Harrison please tell the court how you obtained the memory cards."

The prosecutor jumped to his feet. "Objection. That question is irrelevant and immaterial to this case."

The judge's face reddened. "Mr. Arrigo, the grand jury has determined that the audiovisuals are admissible in this court of law. Let's not go there."

Facing Grandpa's attorney wasn't as awful as Linda had expected. The remainder of her testimony consisted of objections from the prosecution. The surveillance footage never came into play, because by the end of the day, the Mudicis took the same plea bargain the prosecution had offered them during their pretrial hearing—life in prison without the possibility of parole.

Linda slumped into her chair and covered her face with her hands. The Mudicis' sentences hit her like the bullet that had knocked the wind out of her that morning. Court had ended, but the hot glow from Grandma's eyes still burned into her flesh.

Jackson appeared at her side, placed a hand on her shoulder, and gently shook her. "It's over. Let's go."

When she walked out of the courthouse, a warm, gentle breeze swept across Linda's face. The glare from the sun caused her to squint. She heard the sound of zooming engines from delivery trucks over other vehicle motors, honking horns, people talking, and birds chirping— things she hadn't noticed that morning. If Grandpa had her killed now, it would be out of revenge—because his future was sealed.

***

Linda entered a different vehicle with another driver along with Jackson and Truet. They didn't drive back to White Plains but instead proceeded to a sprawling, fenced-in, European-style estate in New Jersey. Mounted above the electronic gate was a security camera with a weather cover on top. The driver pushed a red button on the security pad. A man answered, "Who is it?"

"Summers. I have Jackson, Truet, and a guest."

When the gate slid open, they entered the complex of three homes, drove past the main house, and pulled into the driveway of the second largest home. It had the same architectural design as the other two homes but with a walkout basement and two tucked-under garages. The driver parked in the garage nearest the stairs and drove off in a vehicle that occupied the second space.

Truet said, "This is home for now, Elizabeth Ledbetter."

Linda stepped out of the vehicle. "I don't like that name."

Jackson stuck a key into the basement door's lock, turned it, and then did the same with the deadbolt. "You'd better get used to it, Elizabeth." He opened the door, stepped inside, and silenced the beeping burglar alarm.

Linda followed him into an expansive basement with a tile floor. It had a full gym with cardboard boxes stacked in one corner.

Truet closed the door and reactivated the alarm system.

"These boxes are yours, Elizabeth," Jackson said. "Your attorney said you wanted these things from your apartment."

They took the stairs up to the main floor, where Agents Paxton and Teberger waited. The living room had the same mauve carpet as the stairs, with matching custom drapes. The house looked like something out of a plush manor magazine.

Paxton approached the group, patting everybody on the backs. "This is a great day for the FBI."

"We brought champagne," Teberger yelled from the kitchen.

"We're on duty," Truet reminded her.

"We're having sparkling cranberry juice. The champagne is for Dr. Harrison."

"Elizabeth," Jackson corrected.

"Sorry, Elizabeth. Would you like some champagne?" Teberger entered the living room with five glasses and two bottles on a tray.

Linda laughed and nodded. "Yes, I would." She hadn't laughed in weeks, even when conversing with Eber. A wave of relief and conquest restored her confidence. She had left her fear and frustration in the courtroom. She had won, beaten Grandpa. He wouldn't get off with a light sentence, as Helena and Adler had.

"One more mob family bites the dust," Paxton said.

Truet did a geeky dance. "Two mob families. The Mudicis wiped out the Selvas and most of their associates."

Is this the real FBI? They are behaving like children.

"What would you like for dinner, Elizabeth?" Teberger asked.

Linda smiled. "Whatever you're having."

Teberger laughed. "Hamburgers and salad, coming up."

Jackson flashed a wide grin. "You did a great job in court, Elizabeth."

Truet raised his glass. "Thank you for doing your civic duty. May you be happy in the future, wherever you end up."

Everyone toasted her. Delighted, Linda held up her hands, palms outward. "When do I get out of this prison?"

"Let's see what tomorrow brings." Jackson couldn't stop smiling.

Truet drained his glass, then yelled into the kitchen, "We're leaving."

Linda chuckled. "See you guys in the morning."

Paxton escorted the men downstairs. Linda heard the alarm next to the upstairs door beep.

"The food smells good," Linda said. "Which bedroom is mine?"

Teberger shouted from the kitchen, "Upstairs, the one at the end of the hall. We put your things in it."

She entered the privacy of her own room and tumbled onto the bed.

Freedom.

She called Eber and left a voice message, telling him the good news.

***

When Linda awoke the next morning, her stomach was growling. She'd had her first good night's rest in weeks without the aid of medication. She yawned and arched her back with outstretched hands reaching toward the ceiling. During the night, she'd floated on the soft bedding as if on a cloud. Stepping onto the floor, she hummed the lyrics of "I Want You Near Me."

Her cell phone displayed 10:13 a.m. Eber hadn't returned her call. She showered, dressed, and bounced downstairs, where Jackson sat, watching the news.

Truet returned from a fifteen-minute perimeter check. "Morning. How's your arm?"

"This is a great morning." Linda's voice contained hopeful energy. She gently pumped her arm as she answered, "Still sore. I just changed the bandage."

Jackson adjusted his belt. "We have some bad news about your cousin Billy and his father, Ralph."

"What could be worse than them trying to take me out?"

"Two of Selva's loyal subjects killed Billy at Rikers Island after court yesterday. When your Uncle Ralph heard about his son's death, he committed suicide—hung himself with a bed sheet."

Linda didn't shed tears, mumble kind words of sorrow, or shrug her shoulders. "It wasn't on the news last night." She had no compassion for the Mudicis. She hated them all, even Grandma.

"Rikers didn't release the information until the facility completed an investigation. Elizabeth—"

"Dr. Harrison. I'm not going into witness protection." She twirled a lock of hair around her finger.

Truet stopped in his tracks. "You can't do that."

"The trial is over. The FBI doesn't need me anymore."

Jackson jerked his head askance. "Witness protection is for your safety."

Linda picked up the morning newspaper, took a seat

on the end of the sofa with Jackson, and leaned back. "I spent time thinking about my situation last night. I'll always be a doctor. My choice."

Truet took a seat across from them. "Are you forgetting the Mudicis tried to have you killed yesterday?"

"Prior to the trial," she said. Jim's face flashed on the screen. "Now ... Grandpa may or may not try to have me assassinated."

The two agents looked at each other, then back at her.

Her phone rang. Eber. Her heart quickened.

"Hello, love," he said.

Forcing her eyes from the TV, she headed back up the stairs. "Hello. When I didn't hear from you, I got worried."

"I miss you. Glad the trial's all over," Eber said.

"I just turned down witness protection. Once I take care of things here, I'm taking the next flight to Germany, maybe in two weeks."

"No," he objected. "Your family hired a killer. They might try it again."

"My cousin Billy is dead, so is his father. Grandpa might be too distraught to come after me."

"How did they die?"

"In Rikers. I'll tell you later," she said.

"They were murdered?"

"You could say that," she added.

"Linda, I want to be with you, but it's not safe for us."

She entered her room and closed the door. "Most of Grandpa's enforcers have been arrested."

"He had at least one loyal subject left, maybe more."

She dropped onto the bed and rolled over on her back. "Eber, I'm willing to take my chances."

His breathing became heavy. "But it's too easy to find you when you're using your real name and identification. We can't spend our lives looking over our shoulders."

"We would need to go into witness protection together. I can't ask you to give up your practice. Look. The old geezer isn't going to live forever. I love being a doctor. If it were you, what would you do?"

The shaky intake of his breath was loud on the other end of the line. His silence answered the question.

She closed her eyes and dreamed he was there. "I have a feeling that everything will be all right, and I'm going with it."

"Both of us could be killed," he stammered. "Let's take our time, think this through."

"Take all the time you'd like. Maybe we shouldn't get married right now. Grandpa has no reason to come after you. Why don't I move to Germany, wait six months, see what happens?"

"You're making this very difficult for me. If you move here, I wouldn't be able to maintain my distance from you." Eber sighed. "Okay. Let's try it."

"I'll call you back today after I return to my apartment," she said. "Bye."

When Linda entered the living room, both agents were on their phones. She went back upstairs and closed her door, giving them privacy. Then she called Brody and left him a message concerning her decision.

When she entered the living room half an hour later, both agents were staring at the TV screen. She passed them, entered the kitchen, and peered inside the refrigerator. Finding nothing appetizing, she entered the living room again and stood in front of the men.

"Are you guys giving me a lift home, or do I need to find my own transportation?" she asked.

Jackson closed his eyes, shook his head.

The geek gawked at her. "Are you out of your mind?"

She stared him down. "I'm not hiding or running from Grandpa anymore. Tonight, I'll sleep in my apartment, in my own bed."

Like zombies, both agents stared straight ahead.

She picked up the remote and turned off the TV. "Did you two hear me?"

Jackson grimaced.

Truet stood, facing her. "Why don't you consult with our psychiatrist first?"

Linda threw her hands into the air. "So now I'm crazy?"

"We've started the paperwork, processing you into witness protection," Jackson said. "It's the best option for you."

"Stop the paperwork before I'm erased," she demanded. "I have rights. My things are in this basement. Ship them to Eber's address. I'll foot the bill."

"I called Brody. He agrees with us," Jackson said.

"You talked to my attorney?" Just then, her phone rang. Brody. He did not greet her. As if he'd read her mind, he said, "Dr. Harrison, you must accept witness protection. You have no other choice. It's not safe any other way."

"I do have a choice." As Linda talked, she marched up to her bedroom and checked her purse. Her driver's license and passport were still there.

Brody's voice sounded distant. "Stop thinking with your heart."

She pranced around the room. "I can live like Helena did, no driver's license and no utilities or accounts in my name. I'll just stay under the radar for a while."

"Right, you can live most any place as long as you're not employed but associating with Eber could be a fatal mistake."

"This way, I won't lose my standing as a doctor. I'll start practicing again after Grandpa passes. He can't live forever."

"What about your father and uncle? They know about Eber and you," Brody said.

"Before I went into protective custody, both said they'd never told anyone," she said.

"Eber was in a state of shock after his arrest. He can't be sure what he said. You're willing to risk your life on this?"

"Fax your bill to my apartment," she said, sitting up on the bed.

"At least stay in protective custody until you leave the country," Brody pleaded.

"Where is my father?" she asked.

"He and your uncle are in Florida."

"Give me his phone number. I want to talk with him."

"Dr. Harrison, that's not a good idea."

"If you don't give it to me, I'll find it the hard way."

She jotted down the phone number that Brody provided and jumped to her feet. "I'm going home. Call you tomorrow. Goodbye."

She immediately called her father and told him everything that had transpired.

Linda collected her personal items, threw them into a tote bag, and trotted downstairs. "Are you guys ready?"

Jackson stood and picked up a ring of keys from the lamp table at the end of the sofa. He sighed. "If this is what you want. Have you discussed it with your fiancé?"

"Yes. Let's go before the interstate turns into a parking lot."

CHAPTER 25

THE WEDDING

Linda had lived in Germany for six months without incident. She'd even met with Eber on a regular basis. Both agreed to continue with their wedding plans.

On the most exciting day of Linda's life, she stood in a white wedding gown, shivering in eager anticipation. Eber sported a black tuxedo. The crisp, clean air outside had forced the wedding into her soon-to-be in-laws' farmhouse. It was a traditional wedding. A three-tier cake with scalloped buttercream and blush fondant cascading around it occupied a small table in the living room. Appetizers, paper plates, and plasticware covered two tables. She'd asked for a small wedding, but over fifty guests attended, mostly friends and family of Eber.

Through the windows, endless brown grass met the horizon as white clouds drifted into infinity. As certain as the clouds, she would drift through life with Eber at her side.

During the ceremony, Uncle Hager gave her away. Eber's youngest brother was his best man.

Linda stood, gripping her bouquet. She smiled, her toes curled up in her shoes. Goosebumps covered her body. A year ago, she could never have dreamed that this perfect moment would arrive.

Mrs. Bauer gave her a warm hug. "Call me 'Mother.' I insist. You're the daughter I've always wanted."

Aunt Anna wept and laughed at the same time. "Where are you spending your honeymoon?"

"Not in America," Eber said. "Berlin."

His mother frowned. "What's wrong with Paris?"

Linda laughed. "Berlin is fine with me. I'd love to see the city."

With Eber at her side, she'd travel anywhere.

***

Three weeks after the wedding, Linda received her boxes from New York City. The feds had held on to her items until she paid the shipping charges. Now, double-stacked in Eber's dark living room, the boxes didn't leave much space.

The couple was relaxing on the bed with the bedroom door open. Eber played on the internet, his back resting against the headboard.

Linda lay sprawled on the covers with her nose in a book. She heard a slight creaking noise coming from the living room, like the sound the front door made when it opened. Her head snapped up, ears alert to the sound. "Did you hear that?" she whispered.

"Hear what?" Eber asked, still typing on his keyboard. He had become more relaxed over the weeks, not as cautious as he was before their wedding.

Linda placed her opened book face down on the bed. As she stood, a man appeared from the darkness, holding a pistol with a silencer attached.

"Eber." She rushed the man, but not until two muzzle flashes exited the weapon, pumping two rounds into her husband.

A sharp, explosive pain shot through her stomach, almost bringing her to her knees. Adrenaline kicked in, overriding the throbbing inside her. It was up to her to save their lives. Quickly, she kicked the gun from the intruder's hand. When he brought back a fist to strike her, she ducked, driving a blow into his windpipe. He fell backward into the dark living room, and boxes crashed down around him.

As Linda dashed for the gun, the agony in her stomach became crippling. She lost her balance and fell on the weapon. Rolling over, she grabbed the gun from the floor and fired three rounds into the intruder as he charged. He fell back into the darkness with a thud—then silence.

Clutching her stomach, which was bleeding profusely, she staggered to Eber's side, falling onto the bed next to him. He was unconscious, but still breathing—lingering between life and death. His heart pounded slowly, pulse weak.

She dialed 1-1-2. Emergency vehicles were on their way. She held him in her arms until the emergency team arrived. Guilt lay heavy in her heart, a million times greater than the pain in her stomach. Would Eber make it?

He might die, and it would be all her fault.

**

When Linda awoke in a hospital, her mother-in-law was sitting at her bedside, holding her hand.

She fingered her sore, bandaged stomach. "Eber ..." she whispered. "How is ..."

"Eber is in intensive care," Mother said. "His father is with him."

"I caused this. You must hate me. I ..."

"Don't talk. The doctor says it's not good for your stomach. I don't hate you, dear. Eber discussed the situation with us prior to your marriage. The decision was his too. There's a policeman outside both your doors." She poured a glass of water and served it to Linda through a straw. "The doctor said you should drink plenty of liquids."

"Tell me ..."

"Shh," Mother said. "Eber is critical but stable. We'll know his condition within the next twenty-four hours.

By the way, the police identified the man you killed ... an American from New York City."

"I killed him?" She swallowed hard. His was the third life she'd taken.

"Fortunately for you and Eber, the assassin used a small caliber."

"How did they find us? Why ambush us now?" she asked.

"The authorities believe they followed your boxes from the States. That's not important now," Mother said.

Linda wasn't able to be at Eber's bedside when he awoke two days later, so they talked via cell phones. She spoke about divorce, but he wouldn't hear of it.

***

From her hospital bed, Linda called Agent Jackson in New York City, telling him what had happened and asking the feds to place Grandpa in solitary confinement. They agreed. Meanwhile, the FBI worked with the German authorities, trying to get her and Eber into witness protection.

A week after her release from the hospital, Linda took refuge in the countryside with a family who grew wheat, beets, and potatoes. The two-story house was nothing like her in-laws' place. Its occupants were a gentle couple with a son in his mid-twenties.

Linda's chores consisted of feeding the livestock,

collecting eggs, cooking, and cleaning. Becoming a farm-hand hadn't been in her plan, but the wide-open spaces, fresh air, and serenity reminded her of her childhood in the South.

Two weeks later, Eber joined her.

When they were alone, she fed him a cup of soup. "I'm so sorry, Eber. I thought we were safe. I really did."

"So did I. You never should have had your things delivered to my place."

Linda said, "I assumed the government would have been more careful, discreet. We have nothing to worry about now. Grandpa's in solitary confinement. He can't stand to stay cooped up in a cell without company for days on end. Leaving the general population will take a toll on him. He's an old man. I doubt if he'll last long."

"Everything will work out. We have each other," Eber said, holding her hand in his.

***

One day, after they had been at the farm for three months, Linda was sitting in the yard, peeling potatoes, when Eber came barreling through the back door. He ran up to her and gave her a tight hug, kissing both cheeks. "Linda. Linda. Your grandfather had a massive coronary: DOA at the hospital."

Linda sighed with relief, then grimaced. "Never show happiness over someone's death. Even if he's a mobster."

"He tried to have us killed."

"Yes, he did. He was a very heartless man." She smiled. "Okay, I'm also very relieved."

Eber threw his arms above his head as if reaching for the sky. "Do you know what this means? We don't have to hide out anymore."

He put his arm around his wife, and the couple slowly walked together toward the beckoning fields and beyond.

Made in the USA
Columbia, SC
29 June 2020